All Roads Lead Home

Jason H. Campbell

This is a work of fiction. All of the characters, names, incidents, organizations, and dialogue in this novel are either the products of the author's imagination or are used fictitiously.

Scripture taken from the King James Version of the Bible.

WestBow Press books may be ordered through booksellers or by contacting:

WestBow Press
A Division of Thomas Nelson & Zondervan
1663 Liberty Drive
Bloomington, IN 47403
www.westbowpress.com
1 (866) 928-1240

ISBN: 978-1-9736-2631-2 (sc)
ISBN: 978-1-9736-2630-5 (e)

Print information available on the last page.

WestBow Press rev. date: 08/08/2018

Chapter One

With a heavy heart Joseph turned the team of Belgians down the blacktop road toward the bus station. The horses' hooves made a lonesome sound, their metal shoes clicking on the highway as they pulled the wagon. Maybe the mares knew he was leaving his home, never to return this way again. He glanced back at his wife, Mary, sitting with their daughter, Rebecca, and their two twin sons, Caleb and Benjamin. Instead of looking downhearted, they all seemed excited except for Rebecca. He would be strong for their sakes.

"I guess this'll be our last hay ride." Rebecca shifted restlessly on a bale of hay.

"It's my pleasure to escort you today," Bishop Adam said, scooting over beside Joseph on the wagon seat. "I figured my buggy would be a little crowded with your luggage, so I brought my team of Belgian mares."

"I think Adam has given wagon rides to every child in our district." His wife, Grace, smiled as the wagon bounced her around.

Joseph glanced at Grace, realizing how much she had aged. She was a small, gray-headed woman who didn't look as though she could weigh a hundred pounds. Joseph felt small sitting next to the bishop, who was over six feet tall and very heavy. His snow-white beard hung down to his chest, and his hair was gray. Joseph was of a medium build himself, not so tall, but very muscular. His curly hair was dark brown, and his beard wasn't very long.

"Joseph, if you and your family ever need to come back here to live, you are always welcome," Bishop Adam said as Joseph brought the wagon to a stop.

"I appreciate it." He held back a tear. "But I think we are ready for a new beginning."

"Well, spring is a time for resurrection," Bishop Adam said.

"I think that's the Greyhound coming, Daed," Caleb gasped, pointing behind them.

"I can't wait to ride in one," Benjamin said, leaning over the side of the hay wagon to watch the vehicle. "It looks so big."

"You all take care." The bishop frowned as the bus stopped close by. "I will be praying for you, Joseph. Please keep in touch."

"I will." Joseph handed him the reins.

"Let me give you a hug before I break into tears." Grace gave Mary a hug.

"We will miss you all. You have been so gut to us." Mary kissed Grace on the cheek.

"The way everyone is staring at us out of the bus windows," Adam murmured aloud, "I don't think any of these people have ever seen a horse and buggy." Bishop Adam cried silently as the family said their goodbyes.

"Gather your luggage, children, and we will be on our way." Joseph helped Mary down from the wagon.

He led the way to the bus, his family following close behind. He looked back just once to the land that he had called home all of his life. His heart pounded hard in his chest, and the pain was almost more than he could bear. He had felt this way before when his parents had died. He didn't know that leaving his home behind would rip such a horrible hole in his spirit. He boarded the bus slowly, carrying his worn out suitcase.

"Are we traveling far today?" the driver asked, taking their tickets.

"We're heading to Ohio. My wife's grandfather willed us a farm." Joseph saw many eyes on him, and some people laughed when they saw him with his family. He was used to people laughing at the way his family dressed. No matter how people treated him, he had decided long ago that he wouldn't stoop to their level. He would try to be the better person.

"God does take care of His own," the driver said.

Joseph spotted some empty seats in the middle of the bus. "Follow me, children."

"We can put our bags overhead," Rebecca said, pointing to the overhead rack.

Joseph handed Rebecca his bag and knocked her kapp off in the process. Rebecca's face turned red and her dark brown eyes widened as she grabbed for her kapp. The kapp had fallen down in the middle of the aisle. For just a minute, her long black hair flowed wildly. Rebecca wasn't as tall as her mother yet, as she was only thirteen. She was, however, a striking beauty, as pretty as her mother.

"Sorry," Joseph said softly. Nobody was supposed to see his daughter's hair uncovered except her future husband. He was proud of his daughter. She wasn't dressed fancy like the modern world, but she was a lady nonetheless.

"It's okay, daed." Rebecca put her kapp back on quickly, her face still red.

Joseph sat down with Mary, and Rebecca took the seat across from them. The twins jumped into the seat with Rebecca, although they were a little crowded. The boys were nine and very slim, with curly brown hair. Maybe the boys didn't want to sit so close to these strangers.

"Why are those people wearing costumes, Dad?" one little girl asked. "It's too early for Halloween."

"Hush, dear," the man said. "They're Amish. They always dress very plain. I think it's part of their religion."

"I'm glad we aren't Amish. I would hate to dress that way every day."

"Pay her no mind," the man said, looking at Joseph. "She's not used to seeing people dress differently than she does."

"It's okay," Joseph said, smiling. "She's just curious."

He would never allow his own children to be so disrespectful to other people. Finally, all was quiet for a few minutes as the people finally got used to the "Pilgrims" on the bus.

"It will be nice to see my mother again," Mary said.

"I wonder if my cousins will even know me. I haven't seen them in so long," Rebecca said.

"I am sure they will," Joseph said. "It feels like we are going to a reunion and meeting our family for the first time."

Hours later the bus slowed and then pulled into the station. The bus was so dark on the inside; Joseph could barely see his children sitting across from him. Rebecca and Caleb whispered to each other and Benjamin just stared out the window. The driver turned on the interior light.

"All right, everyone, we have arrived at our destination. Don't forget your luggage. And thank you for traveling with Greyhound."

Joseph looked at his wife leaning against his arm, fast asleep. Mary had worn herself out the last week getting everything ready so that they could move. He was proud of her. For all the years she had been married to him, she had never once complained about not seeing her family that lived in another state. He knew she missed her mother, but she had always put their marriage first. Mary had moved to Pennsylvania to take care of her aunt Edna, who had passed away a few years after they were married.

"Time to wake up, dear." Joseph shook her gently with his free hand.

Mary opened her eyes and sat up straight. "I'm sorry. I didn't mean to fall asleep. I didn't realize I was so tired." She yawned.

"I figured you needed to rest," Joseph said gently. "Now let's get off this bus. I have been cramped up too long."

Very quickly the family reached the front of the bus.

As they exited, the driver said, "Good luck to you all." He then handed each of the children a sucker.

"Thank you," Rebecca said.

Joseph shook the driver's hand. "It was nice meeting you."

"I've got to get me some coffee before the next load leaves out," the driver said, getting up.

The family went inside the station and set their luggage down. They were the only passengers in the lobby. The bus driver poured himself some coffee from a coffee pot sitting on a table beside the vending machines. The driver waved at them a few minutes later as he left the station with his coffee.

Caleb found a television and stood before it, gaping at the cowboys riding bucking bulls across the screen.

Caleb didn't understand that there weren't many shows on television that supported a Christian lifestyle. It seemed like you couldn't watch anything on TV that didn't curse God's name. Joseph was responsible for what he let his children do as long as they were under his roof. It hurt deeply to see his son interested in the things of the world.

"You must not watch those worldly things, Son," Joseph said. "They are bad for you." Caleb ignored him, his attention too wrapped up in the electronic gadget.

Joseph pulled Caleb gently out of the way by the arm. Spotting a remote on a nearby table, Joseph grabbed it and punched buttons, trying to turn off the television. Rebecca laughed at him when the TV started changing channels before showing a menu screen. Why they made things so hard to operate, he didn't understand.

Finally giving up, Joseph laid the remote down on a coffee table. He walked to the cord hanging down from the television and unplugged it.

Caleb's face turned red; he lowered his head and didn't say anything.

"Joseph is right," Mary said, smiling. "Our heart is like a garden; we must be careful what we plant in it."

"Let's read a book while we're waiting for our bus." Joseph pointed to some comfortable-looking chairs.

Joseph sat down and got out his worn copy of *The Budget*. Benjamin and Rebecca opened their books. Caleb looked through some magazines he found in a rack on the wall.

Caleb had always liked modern things. But he was just nine. He had plenty of time to grow out of these worldly influences.

Poor Mary nodded off again. It had been a long day. The children fell asleep too. His eyes ached to close as well, but he had to stay awake. He didn't want them to miss their ride. Only when their last bus pulled out of the station would he rest.

He got out his thermos of hot coffee and poured himself a drink with the attached cup. The coffee tasted strong and bitter, but hopefully it would keep him awake.

Bowing his head, Joseph prayed silently for God to watch over his family and be with them on this journey. He had so much to be thankful for. God had prepared a table for them in the wilderness. Surely as God watched over Abraham and told him to move on, He would watch over Joseph's family as well.

He felt a nudge in his side. "Joseph, wake up," Mary said.

He sat up with a jolt. How long had he been asleep? His family was all staring at him.

"The bus is here," Mary said.

Joseph grabbed their bags. "Come on, *bopplis*," he said to the children.

"Daed still calls us babies," Caleb whined to Benjamin.

"You will always be my babies." Joseph patted each boy on the head.

On the second day of their travel, Caleb grabbed his father's arm and pointed out the window at several Amish men plowing their fields behind teams of horses. "Look, Daed!"

"We must be near an Amish community," Mary said, leaning

over Joseph to see out the window. Her eyes sparkled as she looked at the people plowing the old fashioned way.

Joseph's heart swelled in his chest at the sight of his fellow Amish men, even though he didn't know them. How he longed for a farm of his own. A man felt near to God when he worked the open land. There was nothing like watching a pair of horses as they pulled a plow, tearing the ground open so a garden could be planted.

On the third day of travel, the family finally arrived in Ohio at eight o'clock on a beautiful morning. Joseph had never been out of his home state before. The land was all flat, just like his wife had said. He didn't know if he would ever like it here for his heart still belonged in another state, but the farm land was definitely pretty enough.

His family was a little ragged looking and tired. Joseph knew he could use a bath: that was the first thing he was going to do when he got the chance. And shave—he could feel his mustache growing even though he wore a full beard.

Joseph smiled as he walked off the Greyhound. His wife and children followed him, the boys wide-eyed as they stared at all the people at the bus stop. As Joseph's feet hit the ground, he thanked the Lord for keeping his family safe.

One of the attendants opened the side door on the bus to let everyone get their suitcases. He retrieved their luggage, his wife helping him with a smaller bag. Each of the children had a bag apiece to carry their clothes.

Joseph looked over the crowd. His wife's brother had promised to send someone to pick them up, but he didn't know who it would be.

A short, partially bald gray-headed man came walking toward them, wearing sport shorts, a gold watch, and thick glasses. He held a thin paperback book in his hand. The novel cover had a picture of a cowboy sitting on a horse.

"Mr. Komer?" the man asked.

Joseph nodded.

"I thought so. You Amish people stick out like a sore thumb. I'm Jessie Fugate. I'm here to give you a ride to your brother-in-law's place."

Joseph smiled as he shook the man's hand. "I guess it is easy to pick us out of a crowd because of the way we dress."

"My van's over here." The man led the way.

"I live close to your family's place. Do most of the hauling for them, in fact. After you get settled in, give me a ring, and I'll take you wherever you need to go." When they reached a new looking, red minivan, Mr. Fugate opened the driver's door with his key and then pulled the trunk release.

Joseph loaded their luggage in the back while his wife and children got in. Then he took a seat up front. Mr. Fugate talked nonstop as he drove.

"I dropped off an elderly Amish lady a little while ago. She was traveling to visit her sister in Indiana. Since I was already nearby, this trip will be free."

Joseph had expected this ride to cost him money, so he would have a few extra dollars to spend now.

"I'm retired now, nobody but me and the wife. I love to help people. Our children don't come around and visit much, except on the holidays."

Joseph had never heard a man talk so much.

"My parents were Mennonites, similar to the Amish, but a bit more liberal. I attend New Wave Pentecostal church now."

Joseph didn't know exactly what the man believed, but he seemed sincere about his faith.

The road got narrower as they left the city. They passed rolling fields, some already planted with corn. Joseph knew they were getting close when he saw yellow road signs with a horse and buggy on them. It would be nice to get away from the interstate to just a good old country road.

After about thirty minutes of driving, Mr. Fugate turned off the highway onto a dirt road. They were deep in Amish Country now.

"I hope the church will accept me back as a member after all these years," Mary said.

"It would be horrible if they didn't, especially after we've sold every thing we owned," Rebecca said.

"We will pray that the church will accept your mother," Joseph said, "and that our family will be welcomed into the community."

Chapter Two

Mary sat up straighter as the minivan neared their destination. She hadn't been home in a long time. Her mother had visited her in Pennsylvania a few times for Christmas, and she had come down for her daed's funeral nine years ago, but she hadn't returned since. And even during the funeral, she hadn't visited the homestead. She was thankful that God had provided the opportunity for her to come back home now.

It would be good to see her family again. Her brother's farm was just ahead, and her Grandpa's house was five miles further. The place they had inherited was isolated, with no other Amish farms on the road beyond it, a fact Joseph loved. Too many neighbors made him feel crowded.

A man in a straw hat plowed the field off to the right, walking behind two mules that pulled a plow steadily in front of him. He was too far away for her to see who he was, but he looked familiar.

As the van turned into the driveway, the man in the field stopped and looked. Dropping the plow lines, he hurried towards them. When the man got closer, Mary realized it was her brother John.

The van pulled into her brother's farm off the dirt road and parked in the driveway. The house door burst open and children ran out to greet them, followed by Elizabeth, still in her apron.

"It looks like you made it," Elizabeth said as she pointed out to the field. "John was getting a little worried over you."

"Jah, it has been a long trip," Joseph said softly.

Mr. Fugate popped the trunk and Joseph started unloading their luggage. Rebecca grabbed her bag, her eyes looked like she was about to cry. Joseph shut the trunk gently and the van took off.

John reached the group, arms outstretched. Mary cried softly as they hugged each other. She felt the muscles in her brother's chest as he pulled her close. Her heart filled with joy as he held her. It was one of the happiest days of her life.

John pulled back and looked her in the eye. "I never thought I would see you again."

"It's been too long." She buried her head in his chest again, sobbing. She was so glad to see her brother. She couldn't wait until she got to visit the rest of her family.

Joseph looked away as his wife cried. He hadn't realized that she had been so lonely. Her five brothers and sister still lived in the area. Her mother, Sharon, lived with another one of Mary's brothers. When Mary's father died, Mary's mother had split the farm between her sons.

Joseph now realized why God sent them this way. While he had no family left in Pennsylvania, Mary still had plenty of relatives here. It must be God's will for her to be near them. He felt ashamed that he hadn't realized it earlier. He had been selfishly trying to hold on to land and a memory, but Mary had something much more important here. She had family. He looked over his own family, deciding he would thank God for them while he still had them. Each day he got to spend with them was a blessing; all too soon death would separate them.

"Come inside," John said. "You'll have to stay the night. We'll take you home in the morning. It's been so long since I have seen my sister, and I want her to meet the rest of the family. Do you mind, Joseph?"

"That'll be fine," Joseph said. He had hoped John would invite them to stay. It was too late in the evening for him to travel to an empty house that hadn't been lived in for a while. He would leave early the next morning so they would have all day to get settled in.

"All right." John pointed to the mules standing hitched in the field. "Mary, I need to finish plowing our garden. I've got a couple hours of work left."

"Hold on," Joseph said. "Why don't you go into the house and visit with your sister. I'll finish the plowing for you. I love working in the fields."

John stepped closer, looking deep into Joseph's eyes. "Are you sure?"

"Jah, go ahead." Joseph laid his hand gently on John's shoulder and then headed out to the field.

"I appreciate it, Joseph," John hollered after him.

After an hour of hard work, sweat flowed freely down his face. He moved his hand from the plow just long enough to wipe the sweat from his forehead. He had given Mary a gift by reliving her brother of his duties so she could spend more time with him. And strangely enough, it made him feel good on the inside.

Joseph looked up from the furrow and saw Mary sitting on the porch with John, Rebecca, Sarah, and Elizabeth. The younger children played in the yard while the grown-ups talked.

He couldn't wait until he got to plant his own garden for his family. It was scary moving here and trying to get a farm going with the money he had saved up over the years. A few minutes later, Joseph looked back at the porch.

Elizabeth had brought out refreshments for everyone sitting on the porch. John grabbed something from a tray, and the boys came quickly from the yard to get something too. Turning back to his work, Joseph started another row and plowed on slowly. When he finished the new row, he turned around quickly as something caught his attention.

Mary was walking slowly toward him, carrying a tray with a

pitcher of lemonade, two glasses, and a plate of cookies. It was such a blessing to look up from your work to see your wife bringing you some refreshment. Mary was very beautiful on the inside. He unhitched the mules from the plow, drove them to a big shade tree at the edge of the garden, and tied them to a tree. The mules dropped their heads to eat some grass.

Mary looked at him and smiled. "I figured you might be thirsty."

"I am." Joseph pointed down at the ground. "Thank you. Please sit with me for a few minutes."

She sat down beside him on the grass and poured them both some lemonade. He downed half the glass in one gulp. The sweet, icy liquid refreshed him all the way from his lips to his stomach.

Mary gave him a cookie. "Do you think you'll like it here in Ohio?"

"I already do." Joseph took a bite of a cookie; it was delicious. "I think it's God's will that we came here. I'm not going to move our family anymore."

Tears welled in her eyes. She squeezed his hand. "Thank you, Joseph."

"But if we're going to stay, we have to get a lot of things. We'll need a buggy and a horse first. And then a team of horses to work the farm with."

Mary's eyes sparkled. "One of John's neighbors has a buggy he doesn't use any more since he bought a new one. It's a bit old, but it's in good shape. John thinks we can get it for a fair price. It's being stored in one of John's barns here."

"That's a gut start." Joseph grabbed another cookie. It was weird how things kept falling into place for him. He felt like he was being pushed in this direction. God had shut all the other doors in order for him to take the right one.

"And John raises and trains horses now. He hasn't said if he has any for sale, but maybe we can get one from him."

Joseph squeezed her hand gently. "The Lord is going to work everything out for us."

"I think God has already worked everything out," Mary said, smiling. "I know you were afraid of the move, but we must be like Ruth in the Bible and journey on."

Joseph stood. "You're right, Mary. Now I must get back to work." He kissed her cheek and then headed for the mules.

As he watched his wife stroll back across the fields, he thought about how blessed he was. With her long dark hair, pinned under her cap, she looked younger than her years.

Joseph backed the mules up slowly and then drove them over to the plow. He hitched the plow back up and lowered the plow into the dirt. The freshly tilled dirt had a pleasant odor.

He liked being out in the fields. All alone, he could hear God speaking to him.

All too soon, he'd plowed the final row. Joseph put the plow across one mule's back, secured it with a rope, and then turned back toward the barn.

John met him at the open doorway. "Did they work well for you?"

"Jah. They're a gut team." While Joseph unharnessed one mule, John worked on the other one.

"You could have left that plow out in the field. I'll have to plow again tomorrow."

Joseph hung the harness up on a rack in the barn hallway. "Old habits. I don't like leaving anything out in the weather." His daed had taught him that. "Dew or rain can rust a plow."

John hung the other harness up beside his. "You're a smart man."

Joseph turned the mules out to pasture and then fed them some corn in a trough John had hanging on the gate.

"Would you like to see my new horses? I've just trained them to pull a buggy, and I've been meaning to sell a couple."

"I could use one myself. And I can pay full price."

John smiled. "Follow me then, and we'll see if any of these wild horses suit you."

John showed him a few of his animals, including a milk cow

named Daisy. At the horse corral, John pointed out a few of the horses he had for sale. The well-broken three-year-olds paced around inside the fence, eager to run free. He didn't like to be pinned up either, but liked wide open spaces.

A palomino caught his eye as she threw her head in the air with her white mane and tail blowing in the wind. Unless he missed his guess, she would be going home with him. He looked forward to a day when he could have his own successful farm with plenty of horses.

Mary walked up to Joseph and touched his hand. Joseph put his arm around her and gave her a hug.

"Which one do you like?" Joseph asked.

Mary looked them over, shielding her eyes from the sun with her hand. Mary pointed at a mare pacing with her head up. "That one reminds me of a horse Grandpa had. He called her Fiery."

She was a pretty thing, iron gray with black dapples, her mane and tail black mixed with white. The horse was pretty enough, but Joseph was looking for other qualities as well.

"She's not broke well yet," John said. He made a slight face. "She needs a little more work before she'll be ready to pull a buggy. I had thought about keeping her for myself on account of her color. But I would let you buy her for Mary."

"Is she wild-natured?" Joseph asked. He was afraid to buy a horse that might hurt his family by acting up.

"Nay, she's just very spirited. Her sire is one of the fastest stud horses I've ever seen. An English man owned him—won a lot of harness races with him. If you turn her loose, she'll leave the country with you."

Joseph looked at Mary. She had a disappointed look on her face. If the horse made Mary happy, that was all he cared about, even though he would have bought the palomino. "We'll take Fiery."

Mary smiled. "Joseph, you don't have to buy that horse on account of me. I was just thinking about my grandpa. I trust your judgment; just buy whatever you think is best for our family."

Joseph got out his wallet. "How much do we owe you?"

When he named the price, Joseph paid without hesitation.

"Denki, Joseph," Mary said, looking in his eyes.

Joseph nodded. "Now let's look at that buggy you were talking about."

"Come on, I'll show it to you," John said.

John led the way to a shed built onto the side of the barn. Joseph helped him open the double doors. Inside sat a black buggy that looked new, except for a bit of peeling paint.

Mary walked all around it, giving it a close inspection. She ran her hand down the side door, looking at the paint. "Looks like somebody left it out in the sun a lot."

"We'll take it, if that's okay with you, Mary," Joseph said. It wasn't a shiny buggy by any means, but he didn't need anything real fancy.

"I don't see much wrong with it," Mary said, nodding.

Joseph kissed her cheek. "Well, Mary, we won't be traveling in style, but it's a gut buggy."

"That is all that matters," Mary said softly. "It feels gut to have some kind of transportation for our family."

Joseph turned to John. "Can you tell me where I can get a harness?"

"I have an old harness you can borrow until you can buy a gut one. I have been using it train buggy horses with, so it's not in very gut shape." John hit Joseph lightly on the shoulder.

"I'll return it as soon as I can, danke," Joseph said.

The dinner bell rang. Mary put her hand on Joseph's elbow. "Let's go eat. And you can meet the rest of the family."

"Gut idea," John said. "My belly is growling already."

"I thought it was mine making the noise," Joseph said.

Now it was time to meet the family he had met before at Edna's funeral, but didn't really know. Hopefully they would all get along.

CHAPTER THREE

When Joseph reached the house, Elizabeth and her daughter were putting dinner on the table with Rebecca's assistance. The twins were being surprisingly good, so Mary was free to help with the dinner. John had one of the longest solid-oak tables that Joseph had ever seen. John must really care about his family's meal time to invest in a table that big.

They took their seats, John and his family on one side, Mary and all of her family on the other.

"Let's bow our heads and pray silently," John said.

Everybody seemed so humble as they bowed their heads to pray. When John said, "Amen," they all dove into the food.

"Since we haven't seen each other in so long," John said, "I should probably introduce everyone." He pointed to his daughter chatting away with Rebecca. "This is Sarah. She's thirteen."

Sarah's face turned red as she lowered her head quickly.

John pointed as his oldest boy leaning back in his chair. "That's Matthew. He's eleven," John said. "Mark is ten, and Luke is nine."

At least the twins will have somebody to play with, Joseph thought.

Mary introduced Rebecca, Benjamin, and Caleb.

"I like that all of our children have biblical names," Joseph said.

"People should know we are religious by our children's names," John agreed, smiling.

When Joseph thought he'd eaten all he could, Elizabeth brought out two lemon pies. Joseph made short work of the tasty dessert.

"Thank you for the wonderful meal," Joseph said. "We'd love to have you all over for dinner after we get settled in."

"You can count on it." John winked.

As soon as they all finished eating, they went out on the porch. The children played like they'd known one another all their lives.

Luke and Caleb ran up to the porch. Caleb presented a sable-and-white collie pup in his hands.

"Can we have him, Daed?" Caleb asked. "Luke said his daed is giving them away."

A dog would be nice to have around to watch the place and play with the children. But Joseph wasn't sure they could afford to properly care for the animal.

"I was planning to take the puppies to town and give them to the pet store after they're weaned," John said. "You can take however many you want."

"One boy pup will be enough," Joseph said quickly.

Caleb's face broke into a smile. "Denki, Daed!" Caleb and Luke went down the steps with a bound to play with the pup.

John leaned back in his chair. "Mary, I never thought you'd move back here. It's like a dream come true."

Mary smiled. "When I got the deed to the place, it came with a handwritten letter from Grandpa. He said that if I wanted a farm in my hometown, his was mine. With one condition: the farm had to stay in the family. And if I didn't take possession within ten years, the place would go to another one of his relatives."

"I didn't know that." John leaned forward.

Joseph shifted in his chair. "I took care of my mother's farm for years, assuming she'd will the place to me. But when she passed on, I learned that my father had borrowed a lot of money to buy new farm equipment, leaving us in deep debt. I didn't have enough money to pay it off, so the bank foreclosed."

Mary patted Joseph on the arm lightly. "Joseph had enough money saved for us to start over here, but just not enough to pay off the huge debt on his daed's farm."

"I'm so sorry," John said. "But I'm glad you and Mary are here with us. We'll do whatever we can to help you."

"We appreciate that," Joseph said. It was nice to know that Mary's family would help them, but he didn't want to be a burden on anyone.

Elizabeth stood. "I'll go check on the children and get them ready for bed."

"I guess I'd better call it a day too." John got out of his rocking chair.

Joseph and Mary followed John inside the house to the living room. The children were lying on the floor, playing board games. It was slowly getting dark inside the house. The gas lantern sitting on the mantel didn't give out much light.

Elizabeth came out of a bedroom. "I laid out some extra pillows; the boys can all sleep in here for the night. Rebecca can sleep with Sarah tonight; we just have one guest bed."

"That'll be fine," Mary said. "I'll help you put the children to bed."

Joseph took a bath in the guest room. As he shaved his mustache, he heard Mary and Elizabeth putting the kids to bed.

"Your fathers are very tired," Elizabeth said. "Don't keep them up all night talking."

"Can't we stay up a little longer?" Caleb asked loudly.

"Absolutely not," Mary said.

Listening to Mary talk brought a smile to Joseph's face.

Joseph couldn't wait to get to their own farm. They would have it rough for a while, trying to get the farm in operating condition. But at least they'd have privacy. Staying with others always felt a bit uncomfortable, no matter how short the visit. Maybe it was because he always felt like he was imposing on people.

Joseph crawled into the guest bed. Moments later, Mary came out of the bathroom, her long black hair hanging down her back.

"I've got the most beautiful wife in Texas."

Mary smiled. "We're not in Texas, dear."

"Tell nay one," Joseph said, laughing.

She joined him in bed and wrapped her arms around his neck. It felt good to be in a bed instead of a chair on a Greyhound bus. Sleep found Joseph quickly.

The first rays of sunrise awakened Joseph. Rolling over, he realized Mary had already risen. Joseph hadn't meant to sleep in till six. He was getting lazy in his old age.

Breakfast was on the table when he arrived. Elizabeth and Mary had cooked a little bit of everything.

"Gut morning, Daed," Caleb and Benjamin said simultaneously.

Joseph sat beside Mary. Mary's eyes gleamed with joy. He had never seen her so happy.

They joined hands around the table, bowing their heads in silent prayer, and then passed the food. Joseph heaped his plate high with eggs, gravy, and sausage. John pulled out a Mason jar and unscrewed the lid, inside was apple butter for the biscuits.

"You're a wonderful cook, Elizabeth," Joseph said. "John is a blessed man."

"Danke." Elizabeth hung her head.

Most Amish didn't like receiving praise. But Joseph's mother was a Mennonite, and she'd taught him to pay people compliments when they were deserved.

"What are you going to do today?" John asked.

"I'd like to go to the homestead and start moving in. Figure out what we need to get ready for winter."

"May we be excused?" Benjamin asked.

Joseph nodded.

"Can we go outside and play?" Caleb asked.

"As long as you don't go too far. As soon as your mother and I get packed, we'll be on our way."

The boys bolted out the front door, Mark and Luke on their heels. The door slammed shut behind them.

John smiled. "The young are full of life."

As Joseph started to rise from the table, John waved at him to remain seated. "May we have a minute, Joseph? We'd like to talk to you and Mary while the children aren't around."

Elizabeth looked at John funny.

"Is something wrong?" Mary asked.

"A lot of English people have bought land around yours. Several people have come here asking to buy Grandpa's property."

"It's not for sale," Mary said, her face turning red.

"I understand. But Mr. Stevens and his family are very wealthy. And they're used to getting what they want."

Elizabeth moved in her chair. "There are many rumors about members of the Stevens family being in trouble with the law. Some say they're involved with drugs."

"What are you trying to say?"

"I wouldn't be surprised if he tried to force you to sell."

Mary gasped.

"The farm that Mary has inherited is our home now," Joseph said, "and we won't be run off by anyone. God will prepare our way."

"Joseph, we will have to go to the grocery store and stock up on food real soon," Mary said.

"The bishop took up a donation for you a few days ago," John said. "The men stocked your kitchen cabinets with canned goods. And the women brought in clean sheets and blankets. I think they even stocked your refrigerator with a few groceries to tie you over."

"That was very thoughtful," Mary said. "Denki, I appreciate it."

Joseph was amazed at how generous the Amish could be. The church members didn't even know him, yet they had stocked his shelves with food.

Joseph grabbed a sugar cube and took it to the barn. The mare ran up to the fence and stuck her head over the rails. Joseph handed her the treat. Horses were like women; they needed to be spoiled just a little.

Hooking a rope to her halter, he led her into the lean-to where the buggy stood. The mare stood calmly while he harnessed her, though she threw her head up and snorted a lot.

After climbing into the buggy, he released the brake and slapped the mare on the back with the reins. Her hooves stepped slightly sideways as she danced her way out of the lean-to. Then she sprang out of the barn, eager to run.

He gently pulled her to a stop so he could lock the door to the shed. Then he drove the mare up in front of John's house to pick up his family.

A little terrier ran up, barking loudly. He nipped at the mare's heels. Startled, she reared, and then kicked her back hooves at the dog.

Matthew came running up. "Lucy! Come here, girl."

The trembling dog ran into Matthew's arms.

John hurried to join them. "Matthew, get that dog out of here. I told you to keep Lucy locked up. She's not safe around the young buggy horses!"

"I just wanted to play with him." Matthew sniffled and fled.

"You're going to get a whipping for this," John called after him.

"Nay harm done," Joseph said. "Nobody was hurt." He hoped John wouldn't be too hard on Matthew.

John nodded, taking a deep breath. "If you want a calmer buggy horse, I have an older one that's broke."

"Danke, but I'll keep this one. Mary already loves Fiery."

John touched Joseph's shoulder lightly. "It's hard to say nay to my sister."

Joseph grinned. "I guess you're right. Come on, boys," he called to Caleb and Benjamin. "We need to load the luggage."

The little they had didn't take long to load up, especially with so many people helping. John's family stood on the porch to watch them depart. Joseph helped his daughter Rebecca climb into the buggy.

"Denki, Daed," Rebecca said, accepting his hand up. The

twins had already dived into the back of the buggy, eager to be on their way.

Mary came quickly then. "I'll help you up," Joseph said.

"Always has to be the gentlemen," Mary said, smiling. "I hope all my sons turn out like their daed."

"A man should always be courteous in life. A man who wouldn't hold the door open for a woman is a sorry person," Joseph said.

"Come back anytime," John said. "We'll be down to check on you all in a few days."

"Denki, John, I appreciate your hospitality." Mary climbed in the buggy.

With a gentle slap of the reins, they were on their way. As Joseph drove, he enjoyed the lush green grass and rolling fields of spring flowers. The wide-open farmland contrasted sharply with the densely wooded Pennsylvania area where he grew up. A man could see for miles here. Horses and cattle grazed in the fields, the ground freshly turned over for planting.

He was so busy observing Mother Nature that he didn't hear the buggy coming up behind him until Fiery suddenly sped up.

The other buggy horse passed as they rounded a curve. John, sitting in the driver's seat, winked at Joseph, then slapped the reins to gain the lead.

Joseph wanted to see what his mare could do. The horses raced side by side, even with Fiery pulling a full load.

"Joseph, stop!" Mary grabbed his arm.

"Don't let him pass us!" Caleb shouted.

When Fiery had outrun the other buggy horse by a good ten feet, Joseph slowed the mare gently.

She tossed her head, sweat lathering her flanks. What a horse!

John stopped beside them. His horse looked like she had been driven hard.

"What's wrong?" Mary asked John.

"You forgot your puppy." John held up the collie by the scruff of its neck.

Caleb jumped out of the buggy and grabbed the dog. "Thank you, Uncle John."

"You're welcome. Gut day to you all." John turned the mare around and headed back home.

Caleb climbed into the buggy with the pup. "What should we name him?"

"I'd like to call him Pilgrim," Benjamin said. "After the people in those books Mamm reads us. We're journeying to a new land just like they did."

"I like it," Mary said, messing Benjamin's hair a little.

"This is one of the most amazing horses I've ever seen. Take us home, Fiery," Joseph flicked the reins on the mare's back.

When they reached the homestead, Joseph's heart sank. Waist-high weeds spread out as far as the eye could see. The barn and the small corral leaned badly. And the house needed painting.

On the positive side, the farmhouse was set in a valley with open fields surrounding it and giant pine trees along the west side. Behind the house stood a little wooden building that could be used to store tools. *What have I got myself into?* Joseph thought, looking around the farm.

As Joseph urged the horse forward, he noticed the front door of the farmhouse hung on one hinge. The roof was missing a few shingles and some planks on the porch were also missing.

He had never seen a place so run down in all his life. Still, God had given it to them, and he was grateful. They would make do with what they had.

He stopped the mare in front of the house. "Boys, put her in the corral and make sure she has plenty of water and grass." Joseph took off the harness and hung it on the back of the buggy.

The boys seemed happy as they grabbed the mare's lead rope. He helped Mary down from the buggy; her eyes were watching him closely.

"It's beautiful."

Mary smiled. "Well, it will be one day I hope."

Rebecca pointed to the house. "Let's go see what the house looks like inside."

Mary walked up to the porch with Rebecca. Joseph followed close behind. When they reached the front door, he swooped his wife up in his arms and carried her across the threshold. Mary laughed as he held her, looking up into his eyes.

After setting her down gently, he gave her a kiss.

"Thank you, Joseph," she said softly.

The living room had some rugged wooden furniture—all of which desperately needed paint.

"Think we can make a home of it?" Joseph asked.

"I'm sure of it," Mary said.

Joseph found tools in the shed to put the door back on both hinges and replace the roof shingles. The women cooked and cleaned while the boys played in the backyard with the pup.

Mary rang the dinner bell just as the sun was beginning to set.

As he made his way to the house, he smelled chicken frying. On the table sat soup, beans, fried potatoes, and cornbread.

Mary looked up as he walked in. "Grandpa took gut care of things. The gas stove just needed a gut cleaning. There is a natural gas well on this property, and grandpa always got free gas to heat and cook with."

"We are so blessed," Joseph said.

After a silent prayer, they passed the food.

"I think this is one of the biggest farms I've ever seen." Benjamin reached for the bowl of fried potatoes.

"Jah, we will have plenty of places to explore." Caleb looked up while putting butter on his cornbread.

"You boys had better not stray too far on a strange farm. You may get lost," Mary said.

"While the boys were playing," Rebecca said, "I picked out my room."

"That's not fair," Caleb said.

"The house only has three bedrooms. So you boys will have to share a room," Joseph said.

"I still think we should've gotten to pick our room," Caleb said.

"Now boys, we have to treat the womenfolk in this house a little more special, especially since we have them outnumbered," Joseph said.

After dinner, Joseph fed the animals while the women cleaned up the dishes and the boys got settled in their bedroom. Then the family gathered in the living room. It was a little chilly, so Joseph started a fire.

"Everyone, please sit close to me." Joseph grabbed his Bible; he sat down in a chair to read by the lantern light.

"That's a gut idea. We must not forget to read the Scriptures even in busy times." Mary wiped her hands on her apron.

Joseph opened the Bible to the Lord's Prayer in Matthew, chapter six, verse nine. He read in a strong voice. "After this manner therefore pray ye: Our Father, which art in heaven, Hallowed be thy name. Thy kingdom come. Thy will be done in earth, as it is in heaven. Give us this day our daily bread. And forgive us our debts, as we forgive our debtors. And lead us not into temptation, but deliver us from evil. For thine is the kingdom, and the power, and the glory, for ever. Amen."

It was one of the most beautiful Bible verses he had ever read.

Caleb looked up when Joseph had finished reading. "It's going to be kind of scary sleeping in a strange bedroom."

Joseph put the worn Bible down. "Tell you what. Let's all sleep in here tonight where it's warm."

The family perked up at once. "That'll be nice." Rebecca smiled as the boys jumped up.

"I'll make some popcorn," Mary said.

"Boys, help me drag a couple of mattresses in here. Rebecca, bring us some pillows and blankets."

"This will be so much fun!" Benjamin giggled.

They all lay in front of the fireplace, huddled together.

"I like that we're all spending the first night here together," Mary said.

"It does seem fitting," Joseph said.

Chapter Four

Joseph woke to the smell of breakfast cooking; he could smell eggs and bacon frying. Mary and Rebecca were already hard at work when he entered the kitchen.

"What a fine girl you're turning out to be, Rebecca," Joseph said, kissing her on the cheek. "It sure makes a father proud to have a gut daughter or son; it makes him feel like he did a gut job of raising them."

"Denki, Daed," Rebecca said, smiling. "If only the boys my age could see me like you do."

"They will soon enough," Mary said, flipping an egg in the pan.

The boys were still asleep, huddled up together. They had quite a night and had worn themselves out. Joseph would let them sleep a little longer.

"Be back, Mary. I'm going out to feed the mare. We have so much work to do today; don't really know where to start."

"Honey, are you forgetting what day it is?" Mary asked. She stood by the stove, a spatula in one hand and wearing an apron over her dress.

"What day is it?" Joseph asked. He hoped he hadn't forgotten a birthday.

"Today is Sunday, the Lord's day of rest," Mary said.

"I'm sorry. You're right, Mother. There will be nay work here today besides cooking and feeding the animals," Joseph said. "I have a lot to do, to be honest, but the Lord said not to work on His day. We must honor the Father."

"The church congregation won't be having service this Sunday, but the next. John said that all of my family will be at his house today for dinner at one o'clock. We're invited. It's been so long since I've seen my mother," Mary said slowly, watching Joseph's eyes.

"You said 'my family,' but you're wrong. They're 'our family.' Dinner will be fine." Joseph smiled and walked on out the door to feed the mare.

"He's a gut man, isn't he, Mother?" Rebecca asked.

"A very fine man; I'm so blessed," Mary said.

The mare came quickly for the corn Joseph offered to her. While she was eating out of the trough that hung on the fence, he tied her to the fence so he could brush her down thoroughly.

The mare was going to need some horseshoes very soon if they intended to use her as a buggy horse. Besides farming, farrier work was one thing Joseph was good at. He had done most of the horseshoeing for the people in their church district back home.

The collie pup, Pilgrim, followed him everywhere he went. The pup went up and sniffed at the mare's back legs. Joseph was surprised when she didn't kick. She just turned around and looked at the dog; maybe the last incident had taught her a lesson. Most animals just needed a lot of patience and a calm gentle hand.

"Come on, pup, we've some visiting to do today," Joseph said, patting the collie on the head. The dog followed him, wanting to play.

The children were seated at the solid oak kitchen table when he went inside. Mary's grandfather's house might be rundown and the furniture might be old, but the furniture was all solid oak, well-made by an Amish man. None of this nickel and dime furniture you saw at most places. While Mary finished setting the table, Joseph put up the mattresses they had slept on last night. Then he made his way over to the table.

"Can we eat now, Daed?" Caleb asked. "We're starving to death."

"Just as soon as we say the prayer, boys; all heads bowed," Joseph said. After a few minutes of silent prayer, he said, "Amen."

In seconds, the boys tore into the food and passed the dishes around. Joseph ate quickly, for he knew Mary was excited about seeing their family.

"I'll bring up the mare and have the buggy ready. You all finish eating and be ready to go," Joseph said as he was on the way out. "I have already brushed the mare down. A man shouldn't show up to meet the kinfolk with a badly groomed horse. What would it say about his character?"

"Denki, Joseph!" Mary said. She was acting like a little girl again, clearly excited and looking rather lovely.

"You're worth it," Joseph said. "All of you."

With that, he went to harness the mare. She could use a little practice anyway. By the time he was done with her, she would be a very well-broken horse. He would have it no other way.

A few minutes later, Joseph drove the mare and buggy, now fully hitched, right up in front of the house. He wanted Mary to be able to spend as much time as possible with her family today, and he didn't want her to be late for dinner. Setting the buggy brake, he went inside to get his family.

He hardly knew them when he stepped inside. Mary was wearing her best dress and looked mighty fine with her dark black hair shining. Rebecca looked awfully pretty too, a younger version of her mother. And as the boys picked up their straw hats, he saw that their hair had been thoroughly combed.

Mary caught him staring at her, and Joseph's face grew warm. "If Rebecca keeps turning out as pretty as her Mamm, I'll have to run the men out of here that come courting."

"Now, Daed, you're just saying that," Rebecca said, smiling now.

"He knows how to make a woman feel gut," Mary said, her eyes still beaming.

Offering her his arm, Joseph asked, "Shall we go now, Mother?"

"After you, my gut looking man," Mary said, laughing and taking his arm.

Joseph led the way outside to the buggy. He opened the buggy door and let everyone in, helping the women folk up, of course. It was the way of the gentleman. Only after everyone was inside did he get in. It was a beautiful day for a ride, and the sun was beginning to warm things up. There is nothing like bright sunshine to make a man feel good.

Taking the reins, he released the brake and set the mare off on her journey. She jumped quickly into her harness, lunging forward eagerly. It was all he could do to hold her back, but she wasn't broken in enough for him to let her work very hard right now. An animal had to be conditioned, building its endurance up a little at a time. If he overworked the horse too soon, he would break her wind, and she would never be good for anything again.

So he held Fiery at a slow pace, letting her move along at a medium speed. The sound of her hoof beats could be heard on the road. Mary sat close to him with Rebecca on the other side and the boys in the back.

"It's a shame really, but I've only met my mother-in-law a few times," Joseph said. "I've only met the others at your father's funereal after he passed on."

"I understand, Joseph," Mary said. "It's harder to travel for us Amish since our religion forbids us to own a car."

"I think living a simple lifestyle, even if that means not traveling much, allows the Amish to keep a humbler spirit," Joseph said.

"We don't even know what it's like to travel in a car everywhere," Rebecca said, smiling.

"Jah, we could have already been there by now," Caleb said.

"Be nice to have an open buggy, but we can't afford one right now," Joseph said.

"Open the side windows, boys, and let in some fresh air," Mary said.

"Will they have a big dinner today, Mother? I guess I'll probably meet a lot of cousins today whom I haven't met before," Rebecca said.

"Well, you shouldn't leave hungry anyway," Mary said, laughing. "I just wonder how my mother is getting along health wise; I might not have very much time with her left."

Joseph's heart almost broke to hear her talk. He held back a tear. He had just lost his mother recently, so he knew how she must be feeling. Many a night he had cried himself to sleep. "If you want, you can bring her out here with us for a week or however long you want to. That way she can visit with us."

"You don't mind, Joseph?" Mary asked, looking at him.

"Whatever makes you happy, my love," Joseph said softly.

"She can sleep in my room, if that's okay?" Rebecca volunteered.

"That'll be fine. I'm proud of you, Rebecca. You are turning into a beautiful woman, but you're beautiful on the inside too, where it counts the most," Joseph said.

All too soon, for it was a very pretty day for a drive, they saw John's farmhouse up ahead. The mare was just starting to sweat, and she hadn't acted up at all.

"A man can say one thing of John: when he breaks a horse to a buggy, he does it well," Joseph said with admiration.

"Well, we'll be there shortly," Mary said, smiling.

They were about a mile from John's house when they suddenly heard a screech of tires as a pickup truck came around the curve from behind them. They were on the highway. A few cars had already passed them, and some of the drivers had waved at the Amish family. The truck behind them was rapidly approaching; the driver sped up as he neared the buggy.

The truck suddenly swerved toward the Amish buggy, driving as close as it could before pulling away at the last second. The truck's windows were down, and the driver laid on his horn for all he was worth.

One of passengers leaned out the truck window. "Get out of the road, you crazy fool!" he screamed wildly at Joseph and his family. Then the truck sped by quickly and was gone.

"Joseph, they're trying to kill us!" Mary said, grabbing his arm.

It all happened so quickly that Joseph didn't have time to react. The mare was startled and broke into a gallop, racing ahead. Joseph was jerked forward and almost fell when the mare pulled the reins from his hands. She raced on down the highway, not slowing as Joseph made a desperate effort to get the bridle reins back. He finally grabbed them and held on for dear life.

Mary and Joseph arrived at John's house at a gallop, for Joseph couldn't get the mare to stop. She raced into John's yard, sweat rolling off her sides. People scattered, getting out of the way. Finally, the mare, seeing all the other calm horses, calmed down herself. She quit running and stood there in the yard, trembling slightly.

John quickly ran outside. "What in the world happened?"

"Two young boys in a pickup truck tried to run us off the road!" Mary said.

"They're probably not used to seeing Amish people down this far in the county. You all will have to be more careful next time!" John roared.

All kinds of people were gathered at John's house, and the porch was full of visitors and relatives. Joseph drove the horse behind a few more buggies in line, set the brake, and got down to help his family out.

The boys leaped down and ran off to play. Mary and Rebecca climbed down and walked inside, Rebecca holding her mother by the arm.

John met him there at the barn.

"Come with me, Joseph, and I'll show you where to stable your horse," John said. "A man doesn't know how long these women will want to visit. It'll be hard on the mare standing there a long time."

"I appreciate it; you're a gut brother-in-law," Joseph said to John, meaning it.

"Take any empty stall. That way you won't have to run her down in the field when you get ready to go," John said.

Joseph led Fiery into an empty stall and stripped the harness off her. The horse might decide to roll on the ground, which wouldn't be good with a saddle or harness on.

"I'll feed her right quick," Joseph said as he poured her feed from a feed sack he'd brought along.

By the time he was done, John had brought a small bucket of water for the mare.

"An Amish man takes gut care of his horses," Joseph said, smiling.

"Now let's go meet the kinfolk you didn't know you had," John said, laughing. "It's about time for dinner anyway."

"You need any help with anything?" Joseph asked.

"Jah, we're fixing to move some picnic tables outside when you all showed up. There are too many people to sit at our kitchen table."

"Be nice eating outside anyway."

When they got back to the others, they helped move the picnic tables. They just needed a few tablecloths and they would be ready to go.

"I think you all have met Joseph before at Edna's funeral, though we will save the introductions until after dinner," John said to his four brothers.

"Gut idea; I'm starving to death," one of them said.

"That one is Samson," John said, hitting Samson on the arm. He did look like a brute too, muscles bulging, his head full of curly blond hair.

The women finished bringing the food out. The eight tables were packed closely together, all of them full of people waiting to eat. Joseph found Mary and his bunch already seated. Mary's mother was sitting with them. She looked like an older version of Mary.

"Joseph, this is my mother, Sharon. I know you've met her a few times at the funerals," Mary said.

Sharon held Joseph's hands as she spoke. "It's gut to have you back with us, Joseph. I look forward to getting to know the rest of my grandchildren."

"Thank you, Sharon. You're welcome to visit with us for as long as you like," Joseph said. "It'll do Mary gut to spend time with her mother."

"I think Mother just wants to get away from me for a while," Mary's sister, Hannah, said, laughing as she hit Mary lightly on the back. She was seated at a table right behind them. She also favored Mary and was very pretty, but was a little thinner with blond hair.

"I can't blame her," Mary said. "She probably doesn't like your cooking. You used to burn a lot of biscuits when we were growing up together."

"Let's all say grace," John said, standing up.

"I'll say it today," Sharon said as she stood up. Most Amish say a silent prayer, but Sharon must have thought this was a special occasion. All heads bowed then, though the children were eyeing the food.

"Thank You, dear Lord, for bringing all of my family together on this beautiful day. Sometimes it seems that we take our family for granted as we all pursue our own dreams and wishes. Often, we realize after it is too late that our family is the most precious thing we have—God's gift to us. So please, dear Lord, let us all have a few more years together here, and we know we will have many more together over there. Amen."

"Thank you, Mother," John said. "Now let's eat."

Joseph looked at Sharon and saw that she had a few tears running down her face; it was clearly a day she had thought she would never see again.

The food was certainly good, but as Joseph ate, his mind

wandered to spiritual thoughts. A man must make time for every relationship in order for it to grow and prosper, especially the relationship a man has with God. It is with a humble heart that anyone will be accepted into God's presence.

There wasn't much small talk going on at the table, for Amish men and women love to eat. They certainly did enough to work up a good appetite.

Hannah rose from the table and went inside with a few more women. In a few minutes, they came out carrying a few pies.

"I brought you all an apple pie I made myself," Hannah said as she laid it on the table.

"Thank you kindly," Joseph said. "Mary certainly has a wonderful family."

Joseph thought he couldn't eat another bite. But then again, a man couldn't say no to a woman, especially one with a pie in her hand. He barely had time to slice it up into pieces for everyone before it was gone. The twins took the first pieces, and Joseph handed Sharon a piece.

A man needs to take good care of his mother-in-law, Joseph thought. A fine woman of good character was worth her weight in gold. They were few and far between. If a man was lucky enough to have one, he had to treat her well. Angels don't get to stay forever on this earth. Once a person has excelled at everything and passed every test, God calls them home.

John stood up again to speak; he was the oldest son and the host for that day.

"All right, everybody, it's been a little while since we've had Mary's family all with us. So starting with Mary, let's all stand up and introduce ourselves. And, Mary, once again, welcome home. We all love you." John sat back down.

Mary stood up and quickly and introduced her family. All eyes were on them now. The twins ducked their heads and didn't say anything. Rebecca's eyes seemed to sparkle as she sat up straighter.

"Now it's Hannah's turn," Mary said, laughing.

Hannah stood up, and everyone grew silent again. "My name is Hannah. I'm Mary's sister, and this is my husband Jeremiah. Stand up, dear, and let them see you."

Jeremiah stood up gracefully. He was a big man, broad of shoulders and back and strong as a mule. Mary had said that Hannah handled him quiet well. He was also very skilled at shoeing horses and did a brisk business where they lived on the far side of the county.

"Pleasure to be here," Jeremiah said. "These are our two daughters: Sarah, who is five, and Rose, who is four years old. Stand up, girls, and wave at your kinfolk."

"Father, do we have to?" Sarah asked. She looked just like her mother.

"Jah, girls," Jeremiah said. Both girls stood up and waved shyly.

"It's your turn next, Samson," Hannah said as she sat down.

"I'm Mary's older brother Samson," Samson said, standing up. "These are my children, Tommy, Johnny, Curtis, Paul, and the youngest is Zachary. Stand up, boys, and wave at your relatives." The boys quickly obeyed. It was clear that they were all well behaved.

"Last, but not the least, is my beautiful wife Carlonia. Stand up, dear, and show yourself."

Carlonia stood up; she was a striking, breath-taking beauty with blond hair. "Hello everyone," she said before sitting back down.

"You can sit down now, Samson," somebody said.

"I'll go next," Lewis said. "I'm Lewis, the youngest son, although Hannah was born after me. I have been married for a few years. These are my two children Scott and Amy. And then, of course, my beautiful wife Malena."

Noey was already standing before his brother was done. "I might as well get it over with. I'm Noey, married to Rachel, my childhood sweetheart. We have three daughters, Susie, Amber, and Chyanne, and two sons, Jacob and Nicholas."

"Herman, you're next," Mary said, for he was the only one left. Herman was the second oldest son in the family. With his tall frame and very heavy beard, he looked like a mountain man.

"I'm Herman, married to Linda. We have two daughters, Cyantta and Lexi, and three sons, Michel, Austin, and Stephan. Though I am pleased to announce that Linda said we are expecting another baby."

"Are we really having another baby, Daed?" Austin asked, "I just now got my own room."

"We'll have to pray it is a girl," Stephan said, laughing.

"Now, boys, mind your manners," Herman said.

"All right, children, you all can go play now. The introductions are over, and later we'll have some watermelon. Might even play some horseshoes, though I must say that me and Herman are the champs at horseshoes around here," John said, laughing.

"You're not supposed to brag," Elizabeth warned.

"There are sure a lot of names to memorize. Hope they don't expect me to do it overnight," Joseph said to Mary.

"You'll have plenty of time to get to know everyone," Mary said, patting him on the arm.

"We'll have the rest of our lives together, and may they be gut ones," Sharon said loudly. "I'm so proud to have my family back home together, all of you."

The children had run off to play, even before John had finished talking. A child doesn't have to be told twice to go play, most of the time. Joseph could see the men gathering to play horseshoes.

"I'll think I'll head over there and play horseshoes," Joseph said, wanting to be with the men. "A man can't get to know people by sitting on the porch."

"Go ahead; I'll catch up on old times with the womenfolk," Mary said.

The day passed quickly. The men stopped playing after a few hours to eat watermelon as the whole family gathered around. Then they went back to play a few more games. Joseph and Jeremiah were now the new champs.

"It's because they both shoe horses. They have the biggest muscles," John said.

"Speak for yourself," Samson said, flexing his muscles.

All too soon, the daylight faded; darkness settled slowly, stealing the sun's ray. The men called it quits and packed up to leave. Joseph didn't rush Mary. Today was her day.

Eventually, Mary and her mother found him. "Mother wants to stay a week with us to visit until next Sunday's service. They'll be having it here at John's house. I think we'll have to meet the Bishop and get accepted into the church then."

Joseph took Sharon's hand and gave her a slight hug. "You're welcome for as long as you wish to stay."

"Thank you, Son-in-law," Sharon said with a twinkle in her eyes. "I suppose we had better get moving before it gets too dark."

"You're right, Mother," Joseph said. "Have everyone get ready while I bring up the mare and hitch the buggy up."

Most of the buggies were leaving now. Some children were waving at each other, their hands out the windows. One last buggy pulled out for home, and Joseph and his family headed in the opposite direction.

There was just enough moonlight on the road to see ahead, although they traveled slowly. The children fell fast asleep as the mare pulled them along, snorting a little and throwing her head. She was clearly glad to be leaving.

Joseph went about a mile when suddenly he pulled the mare to a stop.

"What's going on?" Mary asked curiously.

"I got an Amish caution sign from John to show people to watch out for Amish folks driving buggies in these parts. I'm going to put it up here where that truck passed us," Joseph said, getting down with the sign and a hammer.

"You think it'll help?" Sharon asked.

"Well, it won't hurt to try," Joseph said.

He drove the sign down into the bank. Now the English would know that Amish people lived down this way and, hopefully, would watch out for them.

CHAPTER FIVE

After everyone went to sleep, Rebecca quietly got out of bed. She made her way over to her dresser. She had a small mirror there and a lantern. She found and lit a candle, hoping no one would notice the meager light. She loved her parents and knew why they had to move, but her heart wasn't fully in it. For one thing, she was thirteen, and she had always had her heart set on marrying her boyfriend, David. Now they were so many miles apart. And she didn't know if their love could endure the test.

They had pledged themselves to each other long ago under the apple tree in the school yard. David had kissed her there for the first time. Her mother would think she was too young for such feelings, but she would soon be fourteen, and she was changing into a woman fast. She remembered the sorrow in David's deep, blue eyes when she told him she was leaving.

He had bowed his head, fighting back the tears. "I'm going to miss you," he had said, looking deep into her eyes.

"I have your address. I will write you often," Rebecca had replied as they kissed goodbye.

"As soon as I'm done with school, I'll be coming for you," David had promised. "Remember, you pledged to marry me; never forget."

That was the last time she had spoken to him. She longed to hear his voice again and to see him again. It was hard being Amish and in love, when you weren't allowed to have a picture of your boyfriend. It would be awhile before her family would be completely settled in. They had so much to do. But she was going to write David and let him know that she had made it safely. Tomorrow, she would mail the letter.

Sitting down at her desk, she found a piece of paper and began. She did her best to be quiet. Her grandmother, Sharon, was asleep, and she didn't wish to wake her. She began:

Dear David,

It has been so long since I have seen you. We have arrived safely in our new home. The farm needs a lot of work. I never thought my daed would move since we have lived there all my life. I guess I took it for granted that I would see your face every day. My father kept our financial troubles we had to himself; I guess he didn't want us to worry. But I didn't even know that we didn't have enough money to keep the farm until it was time for us to move.

I wish I had of known. That way, I would have had a better chance at telling you goodbye. I don't think it was fair for him to move us all without any warning. My heart aches for you, more with each passing day. The pain is almost more than I can bear. Please promise me that you'll write me as much as possible. That way I can have something of yours to hold close to my heart. I do pray that you'll never forget your promise. And that we will be together some day,

Your true love,
Rebecca.

After addressing the letter, she put it in her dresser drawer. Combing her hair out lightly, she got ready for bed. She slid in quietly beside her grandmother. Rebecca lay there in silence, thinking of David. It was then that the tears came, and she could not hold them back. She sobbed softly.

"I take it you're crying over a boy?" a voice asked.

"Grandma, I didn't know you were awake," Rebecca said. "How did you know that I missed my boyfriend?"

Her grandma pulled her close, giving her a hug. "A grandma knows these things. Hush now, dear. Please don't cry. I promise that everything is going to be all right."

It was then that the rain came beating down hard outside; maybe listening to it would take her mind off her troubles. Rebecca fell asleep with tears running down her face.

Joseph woke up early to the smell of breakfast cooking. It was the dawn of a new day, and he had a lot to do. He must somehow get a crop in the ground and get everything ready before winter set in. That was one of the reasons they had moved so early in the spring.

It was true that they had family here that would help them, but Joseph wanted to be independent. The good Lord helps those that help themselves. In fact, some of the early ancestors of this country, when they had settled here, had arrived too late in the year to get in a good crop or gather enough firewood for winter. A lot of people had died the first winter in the freezing cold. A disease had also killed many of the early Pilgrims, but they had still come for a chance at a new life.

People didn't seem to realize that this country was founded on Christian folks who gave everything so that everyone could have a better life here. If a man believed in something, he would die for it if need be. That was the reason the Forefathers stood strong against their mother country, Great Britain, and demanded freedom. Somewhere in Joseph's bloodline, he could trace his ancestors back to these brave pioneer men. And the pioneer spirit still lived on in him and his family.

Joseph's mother was a Mennonite; they were similar to the Amish, but not as strict. So he was raised different than most Amish.

He had seen the best of two different religions, often visiting his Mennonite family. He believed that the quiet life, living as simple as possible, was the best way to be close to God.

The Mennonites had a lot more freedom and believed in electricity, television, and all the modern conveniences of the modern world. Most tried to live a plain life as the Amish did, and the women still wore their prayer caps on their heads and the men dressed plainly.

"Joseph, your breakfast is ready," Joseph heard Mary call, interrupting his thoughts for a moment.

"Be right there, Mary." Joseph pulled on his boots. His coat was hung on a wooden peg on the wall. Grabbing it and his hat, he hurried to the kitchen.

The family was all there when he arrived at the table. The boys were looking at him bright eyed and bushy tailed, as the old saying goes. He sat down beside Mary at the front of the table. Rebecca was rubbing her eyes.

"Gut morning everyone," Joseph said.

"Gut morning, Daed," the boys said at about the same time.

"You seem awful cheerful this morning," Mary said.

"It is the love of a beautiful woman and a family that makes me feel so blessed. We have suffered so much, the loss of my parents, yet we still have a lot to be thankful for," Joseph said.

"You're right; the sun always comes up in the morning. Never forget that, children," Sharon said. "Trust me. A woman my age would know."

"A man born of a woman…his life will be a few days, full of trouble," Joseph said. "All heads bow for grace. Thank you, Father, for bringing our family back together. Please, Lord, give us a few more years that we can be together. And for this wonderful meal. Amen."

Sharon looked at him weirdly, maybe for praying out loud, but didn't say anything. A man must be himself first. He felt there was nothing wrong with praying out loud. He just didn't want to offend anyone.

"Pass me the bacon, woman," Joseph said to Mary.

The food was very good, and he ate well. It would be a long day at work, and he needed a good start. When a man threw everything he had into a job, it went along a lot smoother.

"Daed, can we please get a television?" Caleb asked suddenly.

"Nay, we don't even have electricity," Mary said, laughing.

"I haven't seen much gut on television," Joseph said. "We must be careful what influences we put in front of our children. The Bible said to set nay evil thing before you. The way I look at it, we would not let anyone come into our home and curse our God. So why would I allow them to curse in my house through a television?"

"You're right," Sharon said as she reached for a biscuit. "Hollywood can't make a movie without putting something bad in it. They love to curse God's name in every movie."

"How do you know, Grandma? You've never even watched a movie," Caleb said, smiling.

"I watched a few when I was younger…had to sneak out of course," Sharon said, pointing a finger at Caleb. "Now don't be getting any ideas in your head, young man."

"The idea that Christian movies can do well is not catching on in Hollywood," Joseph said.

"It is a shame really," Mary said.

"You children behave while I'm gone," Joseph said. "I need to go help John the next few days finish his plowing and planting the fields. When he's done, I will have to borrow his mules to do our gardens. I won't be back until late this evening."

"It's gut that you're helping each other," Sharon said.

"A family is all a man has. He will take nothing else from this world, but their love," Joseph said softly.

Finished eating, he got up quickly and gave the children all a hug and a quick kiss on the cheek. "It is about time to hitch the mare up. She's coming along real well."

"Where's my hug, young man?" Sharon asked smiling.

"Sorry, Mother-in-Law," he said, hugging her.

"Mother will be just fine," she said, hugging him back.

Going out, Joseph made his way over to the corral to get the mare. The early mornings were still a little cool; full spring hadn't set in completely yet. It took him a few moments to realize that the mare wasn't there. Finally, he saw the gate hanging loose on one hinge. The gate must have fallen, and she wandered off. Grabbing a leash and some feed, he was getting ready to go after her. It had rained hard last night, and he could see the horse's hoof prints on the ground.

It wasn't until he was following them that he saw the other prints—a man's cowboy boots. Clearly, someone had let the mare out. There were big muddy prints that led right up to the gate.

Joseph walked inside the house to get the boys. "Come on, Caleb and Benjamin, you can help me catch the mare."

"Catch the mare? What do you mean? Caleb, did you lock her up last night?" Mary asked.

"Somebody broke the gate down and let her out. There are footprints of a man walking near the corral last night," Joseph said.

"Why would anybody do something like that?" Sharon asked.

"John said some of our English neighbors don't want us living here on this farm. My guess is they are trying to run us off," Mary said.

"I hope not," Sharon said. "Though someone did burn my daed's barn down when he lived here. We never did find out who did it."

"Well, I best be off and catch her before she gets too far," Joseph said. "Come on, boys."

Joseph walked back to the corral; the boys were following close behind him. They tracked the mare a good mile out in the back pasture of the farm. She was grazing quietly in the tall, knee-high grass.

"Gut thing she didn't go very far," Caleb said.

"A horse will usually just go far enough to get out of your sight," Joseph said.

He rattled the feed bucket with the horse feed inside. The mare came quickly to eat, putting her head into the bucket. Joseph slipped the bridle on her then. "Alright, boys, get up, and I'll lead you back." He helped both of them onto the horse's back, and then headed back to the house. He had lost a lot of time in fetching the mare.

He harnessed the mare up after feeding her some corn. The mare clearly liked attention; you never had to run her down. Most animals, when taken good care of, usually are just big pets. There is nothing like a horse that'll come to a fence, wanting an apple or a treat. Get them used to that, and you'll never have any trouble catching them.

"She's a gut horse, isn't she?" Benjamin rubbed her on the nose.

"Jah, we picked a gut one," Joseph said. "Though it costs as much to feed a bad horse as it does a gut one. The animal you can't do anything with usually gets sold at stockyard sales. There they sell pretty cheap, though you never know what kind of animal you're buying. Once you got the highest bid, it'll be too late to take the animal back. When they run them through the ring at the sales, you only have a few minutes to make your mind up. Kind of like marrying a wife—you may need more than a few minutes to make your mind up."

"We need to go to the stock sale sometime," Caleb said, biting down on an apple; the rest he shared with the mare.

"I think Caleb wants to find him a wife there and bid on her." Benjamin hit Caleb on the arm.

"You boys are too young to be thinking about a wife," Joseph said, smiling. "A lot of times, people will drug an animal to make it seem gentle. I have seen people buy a horse that was calm at the sale, but the next day, when the drugs wear off, you couldn't ride it. It's a shame really that people will stoop that low to sell a horse."

"They must not have any honor," Benjamin said.

Joseph finished hitching the mare to the buggy and took off.

The mare went to work with a jump, tossing her head. Joseph was driving out of the yard when he saw Mary come outside.

"Hey there, gut looking. Is anything wrong?" Joseph asked, wondering why she had stopped him.

"I brought you something to eat: two sausages and biscuits in case you get hungry…and some orange juice." Mary handed it to him.

"Danke, Mary," Joseph said. He leaned forward and she gave him a kiss.

He hadn't got to spend much time with her lately with so much going on. He rubbed her face gently. She was so pretty and always smelled good.

"Hurry back to me," Mary said.

Pilgrim had now woken up and came over and barked at him.

"As soon as that brother of yours will let me go, I will," Joseph said, smiling.

As Mary went back inside, Joseph slapped the reins lightly and was off, moving out to the road. It was still dark out, the moon giving off just enough light to travel by on the road. Pilgrim chased the buggy out of the yard, barking and biting at the buggy wheels; seemed like he wanted to go as well. A dog was important around a farm. They'll often keep the varmints from coming in your yard, such as raccoons.

If you didn't have a good dog running around in the yard, it was hard to raise chickens, for the foxes would get them. Every animal had a place and a job on a farm. It was hard enough to feed a dog and take care of it for it not to have a role such as protecting the other livestock. There were not too many animals a farmer could just keep for pets. The chicken that didn't lay eggs anymore was more than likely tomorrow's chicken and dumplings.

A deer and her fawn ran across the road in front the buggy; the mare snorted, startled a little. He would have to take time to go hunting later. Fresh meat would be good right now and would help his family out. God put all the animals here for our use. There was something about being out in the woods that made Joseph feel good. It brought an inner peace. To hear the animals creeping through the leaves on the ground and to feel the wind blowing through the trees was special. If a man was quiet enough, he could hear his own heartbeat at one with nature.

Joseph liked to keep plenty of fresh hog and deer meat. Fresh food seemed more natural to him and tasted better. *Surely it was the way God intended everyone to eat,* Joseph thought. People of the older generations lived this way, eating fresh food all the time, even people that were not Amish. It was a way of life for everyone. They also were more active than the new generation of people in the English world.

The mare plodded on, pulling the buggy. The only sound that could be heard was the steady hoofbeats of the mare. What a horse. Soon he could see John's farm up ahead. And then he heard the distant sound of a rooster as the cock decided it was morning time and gave his wake up call.

He was going to have to get him some chickens; a rooster's call was a pleasant sound. Nothing made a landscape prettier than a flock of chickens scratching around in the yard. He liked the Wyandotte breed for some reason and had always kept different colors of them.

One of John's collie dogs came running out with a bark, biting at the buggy's back wheels. He drove the mare inside the barn; then he quickly unhitched her, putting her in a stall that had hay in it. John wasn't in the field yet, so he went ahead and harnessed up the mules. By the time John came outside, he had already plowed up a couple of rows.

He spotted John coming across the field. John looked surprised to see him already at work. John's boys were now at their chores, feeding the animals and gathering eggs. John said something to the boys, and then they all came his way. It looked like it was time to go to work for all of them.

"Joseph, I didn't know you were out here," John said upon

reaching him. "Please come inside for some breakfast. It's on the table."

"Nay, thank you. I've already eaten," Joseph said.

"Either you're a gut worker, or you are just in a hurry to borrow my mules," John said, laughing. "Well, we have a lot to do anyway; we had best get at it."

CHAPTER SIX

Mary felt good to finally have a home near her family. Her grandpa's house was in bad shape. A house runs down pretty fast if nay one is living in it. Little things go wrong, things taken for granted, when nobody is around to fix them—like a hinge on a door coming loose, a plank in the floor that gives when you step on it, and loose shingles coming off the roof.

It would take a lot of work, but they were going to make this house into a home, a place even her grandpa would have been proud of. He had loved this farm and had taken very good care of it. He would be ashamed of the shape it was in now, though its rundown condition couldn't have been helped. She had gotten here as fast as she could, under the circumstances.

She was worried about Joseph, though she kept her fears to herself. He had lost his mother recently, and his father's passing only a few years back was nay doubt still fresh in his mind. He had nay other family now besides her and the kids. She had seen him grieve a lot in the past, though he had never blamed God for his loss. Sometimes his eyes were watery when he came back inside, and she could tell he had been crying.

"Life is full of loss and pain," he had said to her once. "Though we must make good of what time we have here on earth, and thank God for every minute He lets us be with our loved ones."

He had suffered so much. It didn't seem right for one human being to have to go through so much. She just hoped he would be happy here; they had nowhere else to go. It would be harder on him than her. She had grown up here, so it was familiar and comforting. The children had taken the move easily, an adventure to them. It didn't seem like too much could faze a child anyway. They were so happy.

She knew it would be hard getting settled in, starting a new life. They had only a buggy horse right now, hardly enough to get things properly squared away. They needed so many things. She knew her family and neighbors would help in any way they could; that was the Amish way.

Maybe in time, Joseph would come to like it here, and his heart wouldn't be so sad. Often she saw him staring off into space, a hurt look evident on his face. She couldn't tell what he was thinking anymore, though he never complained to anyone. Maybe that was the problem; he kept his feelings locked up inside too much.

The children were inside cleaning the house, which needed it badly. Walking outside to the shed, she found some paint. The pup was following her every move. He must be lonely as well; she patted him on the head.

It was very beautiful on their new farm, with flat green fields as far as the eyes could see. The land had just enough trees to make you happy. She stood for a minute, admiring the view. The wind shifted the bottom of her long dress gently.

Thank You, God, for this place, and please heal Joseph's broken heart, she prayed silently. His faith had always been a little different than hers, though he was a good man. A plain simple man at heart, he had left the Mennonite ways of an easier lifestyle and hadn't looked back. He truly loved their children. It seemed like that was the only time his eyes would light up anymore. It was truly hard to lose your family, nay matter how long we have had them.

Checking the paint, she was surprised to see how much of it there was. Her brothers had been getting ready to paint the house, but had decided against it. They probably figured she would never come back to live here, so they hadn't kept the house in good shape.

The paint had been sitting a couple of years; hopefully it would still be alright. Anything would beat the way the place looked right now, paint peeling everywhere; most of it was faded away. There is nothing that puts a new face on things like some new paint.

It was warm out, about fifty degrees already, and it was going to be a beautiful day. Though she hadn't planned this for today, she decided to paint. Maybe by the time Joseph got home, she would have it done. She was never one to sit around and not do anything. Being active was good for the mind.

Loading all the paint and a few scrapers in the wheelbarrow, she started off towards the house, Pilgrim still following her. It was such a beautiful day that she wondered if perhaps the children would want to go on a picnic later. There always seemed to be a peace while enjoying nature, especially on a sunny day.

Rebecca came outside as she neared the house. "What have you got there, Mamm?"

"I found some paint in the shed. I need you to help me, so change into some old clothes and come on."

"Oh, Mamm, are we painting today?" Rebecca asked.

"Let's surprise your Daed," Mary said.

The boys had come out then, along with Mary's mother, Sharon. "Benjamin, you and Caleb change clothes right quick. I need you to scrape the walls ahead of us, while me and Rebecca paint."

"I want to paint too," Caleb said.

"Me too! I can paint gut," Benjamin said.

"Maybe later, boys." Mary messed Benjamin's hair up. "Right now, I need you to use the paint scrapper."

Sharon still got around, but she was getting up in the years. She moved around slowly, hunched over just a little, but she managed to do everything she wanted to do. It had been Sharon's father, in fact, that had originally bought and built this farm. Her mother was in nay shape to keep a farm running by herself.

"I think I'll finish cleaning the house and then watch my grandkids paint," she said. "Later, I'll help you with dinner."

"I think I'll cook Joseph's favorite meal today, chicken and dumplings and apple pie," Mary said. "That is after we get done painting, of course."

"Father would be proud to see you living here and making a home out of this place," Sharon said.

"Thank you, Mother, I wish I could have spent more time with him," Mary said softly.

"You done the best you could. That is enough. To whom God gives a little, then a little is required," Sharon said as she started back inside.

"Come on, children, let's do some painting," Mary said. It was going to be a hard day, but a good one at that. "Hard work always pays off, children. Never forgot that. You will never get nothing done just standing there looking at it."

She couldn't wait until Joseph got home. She could picture his face when he saw how shinny the house looked with a fresh coat of paint. By then, she might actually need to be scrubbed down herself.

The two mules pulled steadily, sweat dripping slowly off their faces between their eyes. Still they labored on, tearing the earth open with every lunge. Behind them, hanging on to the plow for dear life, was Joseph. It was all he could do to hold the plow down so the mules could do a good job.

John had gone to the shade tree to wait his turn. He wasn't trying to get out of work; it was a matter of honor between the two men. A man should pull his own weight in this world. Joseph could see him stretched out on the ground, resting now. John's whole head glistened with water. He had dunked it in the stream to cool off.

A man had to work like this to eat, especially back in the old days when a plow and a mule was all you had. Now the modern farmer used a tractor and a plow. *They would never know what it was like to put in a long hard day at work,* Joseph thought.

The Amish man still lives like they always did—nay modern equipment, just a man against nature. By the sweat of the brow, a man shall earn his bread. It was true here. In the old days, when everybody lived like this before all the technology, you had to plow with a mule or starve in the winter. And you had to cut your own firewood with an axe or you could freeze to death in the winter.

Right now, his back hurt, feet hurt, and his legs ached. It seemed like he was aching all over. Maybe he would sleep well tonight. They were getting close to being done; it was just about dinnertime. He finally saw Matthew coming out to talk to John, his father. Joseph turned the mules around slowly; it looked like John was still asleep.

John looked Joseph's way quickly, probably hoping the other man hadn't caught him napping. Joseph pretended not to notice. They had both worked hard today. They had plowed five rows each and then traded out with each other.

John got up, fully awake now. "Joseph, come on in; dinner is on the table."

Joseph finished plowing the rest of the row, trying to keep the row as straight as possible. "What about the mules?"

John stepped to the back of the team and unhitched the plow. "Drive them over there—to that shade tree I was resting under. Getting out of the sun will do them gut."

Once they had the mules tied there, they took off for dinner. Joseph was sure hungry. A man that couldn't eat well when working with a team of mules hadn't worked hard enough.

"Clean up, men," Elizabeth ordered when they got inside the house.

"Follow me," John said as he led the way. In the back of the house, they had a small washroom with a sink and a small bar of soap. After a good scrub down with the bar of lye soap—hands, arms, and face—they were ready for dinner.

"Don't know who was the dirtiest," Joseph said, smiling.

"Dinner is on the table, men," Elizabeth called to them.

Making their way to the table, Joseph pulled out a chair and sat down. John sat down with a sigh at the head of the table. Elizabeth had put a new red and white checked table cloth on the table, making it look pretty. The table had the food already on it in some big white bowls, fried chicken, soup beans, corn bread, and wieners.

"Let's say a silent prayer, all heads bowed," John said. After a moment, John said, "Amen."

Joseph didn't have to be told twice. Elizabeth sat out some lemonade to go with their dinner. They were all seated around a very large oak table, solid wood chairs and all. An Amish man rarely buys anything that isn't real wood. For one thing, he'd just be throwing his money away.

The house was a plain house, nothing really fancy. It was pretty rustic looking, a lot of dark stained oak boards for trim. Sarah and her brothers were all eating very quickly, passing the food around the table. Sarah was going to make a very pretty woman someday.

"This is the best food I've had in a while," Joseph said, wanting to make Elizabeth feel good.

"You're just saying that because you're hungry," she said.

"Jah, right now just about anything would taste gut," John said, laughing.

Elizabeth gave him a stern look, and he shut up quickly.

"You all can stay one night sometime with my boys," Joseph said to Matthew and his brothers.

"Soon as we get all the plowing done, your place and mine," John said. "The boys can help plant the crops."

"What do you mean your place and mine?" Joseph asked John.

"Well, you helped me do most of my plowing," John said. "My boys are too small to help right now. So I'm going to help you get your fields plowed as well. We will trade work out."

"Thank you," Joseph said. "I'll need to borrow your mules until

I can buy a team later on. I think I have enough money to buy only one mule right now."

"The man I got mine from has a few more for sale. He raises them and trains them for a hobby," John said.

Joseph ate until he couldn't take another bite.

"Anybody want any dessert?" Elizabeth asked.

"Can't eat another bite, but thank you," Joseph said quickly, getting up. "It's time I get back to work. Are you coming, John?"

"Boy, Joseph is a hard worker," John said, laughing. "He pushes me harder than you do, Elizabeth."

Joseph made his way stiffly back to the field, John would be out in a few minutes. The pain would come tomorrow—or would try to. He would work the stiffness back out. By the time John made it outside, Joseph had the mules hitched back up to the plow. The mules looked like they had finally stopped sweating. He patted one on the side as it glanced back at him.

"Yelp, get up mules."

The mules took off slowly. He still had two more rows to plow. And then he would take a break and let John take his turn. It would feel good to just lie down for a few minutes.

A little later he had the rows done. John came forward to trade out with him. Finding the shade tree, he stretched out to rest. He had brought his hand-sized New Testament Bible with him to read. A man should talk to God on a daily basis. But right now, he was just too tired. He dozed off, straw hat lying across his face to help keep him cool.

The day wore on, and the sun descended, taking some of the heat of the day with it. It wasn't a real hot summer day yet, still being early spring. Nay matter how cold it was, if you worked hard enough, you would stay warm. Joseph was plowing again, and John was sleeping now.

Joseph could see John's children moving around doing their chores outside. He was just about done for the day. He saw John's daughter, Sarah, coming across the field, carrying refreshments. He could use something to drink right about then.

He plowed on down to the end of the row and left the mules there. John waved him over to the shade tree. Going over to them, he found a place to sit down and take a break.

"What have we got here, Sarah?" Joseph asked.

"I brought some homemade sugar cookies. Do you want some lemonade or milk?" Sarah asked.

"Lemonade will be fine. Hope it's cold," Joseph said.

"It's ice cold," Sarah said, pouring him a glass.

"Sit down, Sarah, and take a break with us." John laid a feed sack on the ground for her to sit on.

"Okay, Daed."

"She's going to make some man a gut wife someday. She's always concerned about other people," Joseph said.

"Denki, Joseph, I appreciate it," Sarah said, smiling. "It looks like the whole family is coming over now." Sarah pointed towards the house.

Here came her mother and her brothers, Matthew, Luke, and Mark. They made it to them a few minutes later.

"What are you all doing? Taking a break?" Elizabeth asked as she sat down on a feed sack as well.

"Jah, but we're out of feed sacks," John said laughing. "The rest of you will have to do like me and Joseph and sit on the ground."

"A little dirt never hurt anyone," Joseph said. It seemed to him that he and John had hit it off really well. It was certainly a blessing to have family you liked.

"Jah, you can't work outside without getting dirty," John said. "So you might as well get dirty first."

"If you're not careful, I'll let you do your own laundry," Elizabeth said.

"Boys, there are a few sugar cookies left, so help yourself," John said, ignoring her.

The boys didn't have to be told twice. They grabbed all of the remaining cookies and lemonade and made short work of them.

"Joseph, just as soon as we're done eating here, I think we'll call it a day. Give you time to make it home before it gets dark. Me and the boys will bring the team in. You can go on when you're ready."

Joseph downed his drink in one gulp. "I'll be on my way then; see you all in the morning."

"Will you be here in time for breakfast?" Elizabeth asked him. "You're welcome to come and eat with us."

"Denki, but Mary usually has breakfast fixed before I leave every morning. You children be gut. I'll see you tomorrow." Joseph messed Luke's hair up.

"We'll see you tomorrow then, Joseph," John said.

Joseph went to the barn to get his mare. She would be raring to go, nay doubt. It would feel good to get home, clean up, and see the family. A man normally doesn't stay away a long time from his family, but when he did, they were always on his mind.

"Come on, Fiery, let's go, baby," he said, leading the mare out.

It looked like she had been rolling in the hay. She was a little dirty; he would take better care of her later. The mare tossed her head like she understood. She was worse than a dog, always wanting to be petted. He was getting attached to the mare. A good horse is hard to find—much like a good woman. You don't replace them so easy, and some can never be replaced in a man's heart.

He felt a great loss over the passing of his mother. Though he knew it was something everybody had to go through if things proceeded normally. We must all say goodbye to our loved ones here on this earth. We must hold onto the blessed promise that we will all meet again in Heaven, a land where we will never have to say goodbye anymore. A loved one, who is a Christian when they die, is actually in better hands. Jesus said not to weep when a loved one passed, but to rejoice. That is hard to do for a fleshly man who feels earthly sorrow.

He finished hitching the mare, climbed into the buggy, and

was on his way home at last. It looked like Mark and Luke were riding the two still harnessed mules back towards the barn. They waved at him as he went by. He hoped the boys couldn't see the pain in his eyes.

Chapter Seven

David came in the house from plowing in the garden. His shirt was soaked with sweat, sticking to his back. Taking his hat off, he hung it on an empty peg of the wooden hat rack. His family was all at the table when he sat down. It looked like they were ready to eat diner.

His mother smiled at him. "David, you got a letter today from Rebecca." She tossed it in his lap.

David felt his face warm. "I'll read it later," he said, glancing at it.

"Way to go, son," Jim said. "She must really care for you."

For a second, David thought his eyes were about to tear up, but then it was gone. He nodded. "Denki, Daed, we've always been close."

He ate quickly. He was a few years older than Rebecca, having already turned sixteen. He was just about through with school; this was his last year. Not even his parents knew that he couldn't read very well. It was embarrassing. When he was younger, he had had trouble focusing. All he had wanted to do was play.

Rachel was Rebecca's best friend, and they both knew his secret. He would go there now and get her to read the letter to him. He knew Rachel wouldn't tell anyone. And she would be glad to hear from Rebecca as well.

"May I be excused?" David asked. "I'm going to go show Rachel the letter. She keeps asking about Rebecca."

"Go ahead," Jim said. "You can take the buggy if you want."

"I'll just ride Jumper," David said. "I have to put him up anyway."

"Alright, son, but that work horse is a little slow," Jim said.

"Well, if that doesn't beat all—our little boy in love," Margate said, laughing.

"It is sad though since they moved so far away," Jim said. "You might not see each other again."

"Well, if it is really love and God's will, then they'll see each other again," Margate said. "The heart knows nay boundaries."

"Denki, Mamm, you sure are an inspiration to talk to," David said, getting up.

Going outside, he walked over quickly to Jumper and mounted up. With a gentle kick, he was on his way. David rode him hard. He was pushing old Jumper for all he was worth. The horse still had the harness on his back. David would unhitch him later. Finally, he made it to Rachel's house. He rode into the yard, scattering chickens everywhere.

Rachel was sitting on the porch with her mamm, Ruth. He stopped the horse right in front of them, tying the tired animal to the porch rail.

"Well, I declare, David," Ruth said. "And what has brought this visit on?"

"I have heard from Rebecca!" David waved the letter. "I was going to share it with Rachel."

"Well, I'll go inside and give you two some privacy," Ruth said. "I'll bring you out a snack in a few minutes."

"Denki," David said, looking at Rachel.

"Sit beside me, David," Rachel scooted over on the porch swing.

"Sure," David said, sitting down and noticing her dark brown eyes and brown hair. Odd…he had never noticed it before. The girl was, in fact, a striking beauty. The boys will be swarming after her soon enough, like bees after honey.

David pulled the letter out and showed it to Rachel.

"You haven't opened it?" Rachel asked, looking deep into his eyes.

David hung his head low and didn't answer.

"I am so sorry, David," Rachel said. "I had forgotten that you couldn't read."

Ruth came out then with some brownies. "Hope you enjoy." She put the tray down on the small table in front of the swing. She left hastily with just one backward glance.

"I'll read it for you, David," Rachel said, tearing the letter open carefully. "And when we write her back, I'll put a letter from me in there as well."

"Denki," David said with a sigh.

Rachel read it slowly to him. He kept his head down, hanging onto every word.

"Read it one more time," David said when she was done.

He sat there in silence for just a few minutes. And then he put the letter in his shirt pocket. "How I wish I knew how to read. It's embarrassing to have to get someone to read and write for you."

"David, I promise you; I don't mind. And I'll not say a word to anyone about this." Rachel put her hand on his arm, which startled him for a second.

"Denki, Rachel, you've always been very trustworthy," David said. "That is what I have always liked about you."

"David, I've got an idea," Rachel said. "When I write back for you, why don't we take our time? I can teach you to write and read. Our teacher often said that you were smart, just had trouble paying attention."

"Do you really think I can learn?" David asked, munching on a brownie. They were quiet good. "These are great brownies, by the way."

"Actually, I was the one that made the brownies," Rachel said with a smile. "Of course you can learn. If you can learn math, then you can learn to read and write."

"If you are willing to teach me," David said, "then I am willing to learn."

"Tomorrow, then, about this time, we have a date," Rachel said.

"What kind of a date?" David asked, confused.

"A date between friends," Rachel said with a laugh.

"Alright, then it is a date. And with the best looking girl in the school nay doubt," David said, laughing. "I had better be on my way."

He rode out a lot slower than he had come. He looked back to see Rachel watching him from the porch. It was getting dark fast. Soon the darkness had stolen the light, and only the shadows remained.

Joseph was halfway through the yard in the buggy when he noticed that something was different about the house. A glistening coat of fresh paint was visible through the dim light. It looked like Mary had found something to do as well. A man should take pride in his surroundings. It reflects his character.

He drove the buggy in under the lean-to where it would be dry, then unhitched the mare. He turned the horse out in the pasture. She was soon rolling in the field, trying to dry the sweat off her back.

Joseph saw Mary setting the plates on the table when he came through the door. He could smell a pie of some kind; it smelled good.

"We have been waiting on you, Daed," Caleb said.

"You all should have gone ahead and eaten," Joseph said.

"Not without you, Joseph," Mary said softly.

"Danke, I think I need a bath first. I believe dirt is even coming out of my ears," Joseph said, causing his children to laugh.

"Just go ahead and wash up. We'll wait for you," Mary said. "Just don't take too long. The children may eat your apple pie that I made you."

"I'll be right there," Joseph said, going to wash up.

He was indeed dirty; he pulled his shirt off fast and washed up. Soon, with a clean shirt, he looked halfway decent at least.

They were all seated when he made it back to the table. Sharon was there as well. Bowing their heads, they prayed silently before they ate.

"What are we having?" Joseph asked.

"Chicken and dumplings—your favorite," Mary said, smiling at him.

"She usually wants something from me when we have chicken and dumplings," Joseph said.

"Now, Joseph, be nice," Mary said, smiling.

"It is gut to be home. Pass me some soup beans; a working man has got to eat," Joseph said.

Sharon handed him some beans. "How is the plowing going at John's place?"

"Pretty gut. It might take a few more days, though, to finish," Joseph said.

"Are we going to have a big garden?" Benjamin asked.

"Jah, we'll grow anything that you all want to eat this winter," Joseph said, looking at Mary. She looked rather stunning today.

"This place definitely looks a lot better since it has been painted," Joseph said. "Thank you, Mary…you sure make a house a home."

"We were wondering if you were ever going to notice," Mary said, laughing.

"We helped paint too," Caleb said.

"Gut job, boys. I'm proud of all of you. You too Rebecca, for I see fresh paint on your hands."

Joseph didn't eat all he could. He was saving room for the hot apple pie. It went good with milk. Finally, he had enough to eat; he couldn't eat another bite.

"Now I have to see about my bath. I can't stand this dirt any longer," Joseph said, getting up. "It was a very gut dinner, Mary."

Suddenly the sound of an automobile could be heard pulling into their driveway.

"We have company, Daed, an English man, driving a long black car," Caleb said. He was standing by the window, looking out.

"You children stay inside; me and Mary will go out and see what he wants." Joseph walked out on the porch along with Mary.

The man was tall and slim, wearing a cowboy hat. Silver spurs jingled on his boots as he walked. He was wearing black jeans and a long sleeved red shirt. His hair was dark black, speckled with grey, and his moustache was roughly trimmed. He had a silver ring on a finger and a gold watch on his wrist.

The big, black Cadillac had a small gold bull mounted on the hood. Joseph noted a sticker on the front that read, "You mess with the bull, and you get the horn."

"Hello, my name is David Stevens. I own a part interest in the bank in town. I hear that Mary was willed this farm. The fact that it joins mine is one of the reasons I have been trying to buy it."

"What do you want with this old farm?" Mary asked.

"To be honest, I'm going to start breeding race horses. And I need some more pasture," Stevens said.

"Please sit down, Mr. Stevens. And we'll get you something to drink," Joseph said.

"Is he bringing us a welcome cake?" Caleb asked, opening the door.

"No, this is not a social call. I have not brought a cake."

"Go inside, Caleb," Joseph said.

"I'm here to make Mary an offer on this place for fifty thousand dollars. It is more than fair, I think. You all are the only Amish that live down this far in the county. And this is not the best neighborhood in the world for raising children. You would be better off farther up north, where all the other Amish farms are. I know how isolated you must feel here."

"This place is not for sale," Mary said.

Mr. Steven's face suddenly turned red. "Not for sale? Anything is for sale if the price is right. I may go up to seventy-five thousand, but that is it. You had better think my offer over and be quick about it. I can make things hard for you at the bank in the future!"

"We do not believe in borrowing any money," Joseph said. "We do welcome you as a neighbor, but the farm belongs to Mary, and it is her decision."

"A woman doesn't know anything about running a farm. You had best talk some sense into her!"

"She may not know how to run a farm, but I do. Mr. Stevens, if you do not want any lemonade, then you can come back later when you are more civil. I have worked hard today, and I have to get up early in the morning," Joseph said, extending his hand for him to shake. "You can come back anytime. You will eventually find out that we are gut neighbors."

"And we are planning on staying," Mary said.

The man did not take Joseph's hand. His face had turned red again. "You can keep your blasted lemonade. You probably made it yourself anyway!"

"Nothing wrong with that," Joseph said as the man stormed off. The car backed up, swinging around, and took off very rapidly.

Sharon was standing on the porch now with the children. "What was that all about?"

"We just met Mr. Stevens, our neighbor. And he didn't bring a welcome to the community cake," Mary said. "In fact, he was trying to get us to sell the farm to him."

"Don't pay him any attention," Sharon said.

Joseph looked at Mary. "The more people try to take this place from you, Mary, the more it makes me want to fight back. This place is your inheritance. And if they get the deed to this property, they will have pried it from my dead fingers!"

"That's the spirit. I am proud of both of you," Sharon said, looking at Mary.

"Maybe they don't realize how stubborn Amish people can be," Mary said, laughing. "We have been enduring persecution for many years, mostly over our religious freedom."

Joseph was heating water up in a pan on the stove's burner to bathe with. They had a private bathroom that joined their bedroom. The children used another located in one of the other bedrooms. Both bathrooms had a bathtub and a small sink. Some folks weren't as fortunate. Joseph felt blessed to have natural gas here to heat with; a lot of Amish people didn't have this or running water inside—even though Mary had to use a hand pump to get the water flowing. It did make it easier on the women; they had enough to do anyway. Joseph was carrying the cold water inside, pouring it in the tub while his bath water was warming up.

The Amish here weren't against using natural gas. They just didn't want electricity in their homes. It would make it too easy to get a television for one thing. Most people didn't realize that the more modern conveniences they had, the harder it would be to get to Heaven. We must come out from the world and be a separate people. It is the one goal in life that we all need to achieve. It is what we are all supposed to be working on anyway.

In the quiet of the day out in a field or in the woods all alone, that was where you could hear God's voice. Although most people just weren't listening.

Mary came in then, getting ready for bed. She looked rather lovely. "I was going to take a bath too, Joseph."

"Sorry, my lady, you can go first. I'm pretty dirty anyway," Joseph said. He loved this strange woman for some reason.

The water was steaming now; Mary checked it to see how warm it was. "Go ahead and tuck the children in for the night while I get ready."

"I'll be right back," Joseph said, walking down the hallway.

"Alright, children, everybody please get in bed, and turn those lights off. You're running up the electric bill," Joseph said, going into the boy's bedroom.

"Daed, you know we don't have electricity," Benjamin said, smiling.

"Alright, you Amish children, blow out your candles and go to bed. You're running up the light bill," Joseph said.

He made sure the boys had enough blankets and gave them both a hug and a kiss.

"Gut night, Daed," Caleb said.

"Gut night, Son. Now I have to check on your sister," Joseph said, going out the door.

Rebecca was putting her book up on the small table beside her bed when he came in. She was lying in the bed and had her blanket pulled halfway up on her waist. When she turned back around, the blanket slid down.

"Are you okay, Rebecca?" Joseph asked, straightening her blanket.

"Jah, we just had so much going on. We haven't had time to do anything as a family," Rebecca said.

"Just as soon as we get the planting done, we can relax a little. We may go fishing or on a picnic—whatever you want to do," Joseph said. "But if we don't get the planting done in time, we will be in trouble this winter."

"Okay, Daed, I can handle it a little longer," Rebecca said as Joseph kissed her cheek. "Gut night, Daed."

"Gut night, Daughter. You are my favorite daughter anyway," Joseph said laughing.

"I'm your *only* daughter, Daed," Rebecca said, laughing too.

Joseph shut the door slowly, looking back at Rebecca as she settled in. It seemed like his children had grown up so fast. He dreaded the day his daughter would leave him for a life of her own.

Mary was in the bathroom now, looking very lovely. God made many beautiful things, and one of them was a woman. Mary was so pretty that she took his breath away. The prettiest flower God ever made was a woman, and Mary was a bright red rose.

"What are you thinking, Joseph?" Mary climbed out of the tub, grabbing a bath robe.

"How pretty you look tonight and how sore my back is," Joseph said.

"Joseph?"

"Jah."

"Shut the door," Mary said.

Chapter Eight

Rebecca came inside the house from doing her chores and saw her Mother standing by the kitchen table, looking through the mail.

"It looks like Rachel has written you a letter." Mary handed Rebecca a thick envelope. "I guess you do miss her. I never thought it would be so hard on you to leave your friends behind."

"It will take some getting used to." Rebecca took the letter. "I'll sneak to my room and read this right quick."

"Okay, Rebecca, if you need anything, please let me know," Mary said. "When you get a little older, your daed and I will talk about letting you go back and visit one summer."

"Do you really think daed would let me visit?"

"Only time will tell," Mary said. "The only hard part is that we don't have any kinfolk there for you to stay with. Maybe you could stay with Rachel. We have known their family for a long time."

"Denki, Mamm," Rebecca said, hugging her.

Rebecca made her way to her room and read the letters slowly. Rachel and David both had written her a letter; it looked like Rachel had done the writing. It felt good to hear from them. How odd...she had forgotten that David couldn't read and write very well. Perhaps Rachel could actually teach him to read. The idea of teaching him had never entered her mind before.

All David had written was a poem; something he had heard from school, nay doubt:

Oh, how my heart bleeds for thee,
But between us, is a deep blue sea.
I count the days, I count the time
Until once again you are mine.

It was silly of him, to write such a thing...and yet so sweet.

Sticking the letters in her apron pocket, she went to help her mamm fix dinner. Tonight, when everything was done and her grandma asleep, she would write back to both of them. They would be glad to know that, if all went well, she might be able to visit them next summer.

Every girl in Rebecca's class had liked David, including Rachel. But he was never interested in anyone but Rebecca. It seemed like absence does make the heart grow fonder, for she felt a deep pain in her chest for David. And she could not explain it. Maybe this is what love feels like—a terrible ache that could only be healed by reuniting with the one you love. If so, then she had it bad.

Her mamm came through the kitchen later. Rebecca was reading the letters again, standing in front of the kitchen window.

"Is everything alright, Rebecca?" Mary asked as Sharon came in from the living room.

"Jah," Rebecca said, putting her letters away.

"I think all young girls go through this stage," Sharon said, smiling. "At about the same time they discover boys."

"You will be fine, dear," Mary said. "Now let's set the table, for we have a lot of hungry people on our hands."

Joseph got up early to do the feeding before church. The last few days had kept him busy, leaving before daylight and arriving home right at dark. They had done a lot of planting at John's farm.

Joseph's house was now complete on the outside. Mary seemed happier than he had seen her in a long time. Spending time with her mother had helped her a lot. Mary had been working on painting the inside of the house. The entire house had a makeover, being washed and scrubbed. The solid oak floor was shining as well. There were a few places where the floor was weak, but Joseph could fix those easily enough.

It is usually a woman's gentle touch in a house that makes it look like a home. Mary had sewed some curtains out of some new material. She had also put some new rugs on the floor. That was some of the things a man appreciates, but wouldn't think up himself. A woman sees things that a man cannot. She can take flowers in a field and a vase and go a long way towards decorating. The good Lord made all of them in His own special way. Thank God for women; man would be lost without them.

Mary had breakfast on the table when he finished the chores. Everybody was sitting at the table, waiting on him. After a quick prayer, they were ready to eat.

"It is time to attend church service at John's house," Sharon said passing the gravy.

"As soon as everyone gets done eating, we will be ready to go," Joseph said.

"This past week has gone by so fast. I'm going to miss you, Mother," Mary said, getting up.

"Don't worry, we'll have a lot more time together," Sharon said. She grabbed Mary, giving her a hug.

Joseph saw tears in Mary's eyes. "I'll hitch the team up, Mary." Joseph left quickly so they could have a few minutes alone.

The next week would be pretty busy. It would take a few more days to finish up the planting at John's place. And then they would start on Joseph's farm. It would be good to get a crop in the ground. He really did appreciate John; his brother-in-law had helped Joseph out a lot. After all the planting was done, he could take time to find a mule.

The mare came quickly for the treat he always gave her, a small sugar cube. She nibbled it up out of his hands. Strapping the lead rope on her, he led her into the lean-to. Once there, he brushed her down good, letting her eat grain out of the trough. He didn't want to visit the church congregation with a dirty horse. That wouldn't say much good about his character.

In a few minutes, he had her harnessed up and hitched to the buggy. The mare seemed to love his attention. As long as she kept acting the way she did, she would never have to worry about a home.

"Get up, Fiery," he said, flicking the reins gently on her back.

Fiery came through the yard, wanting to run, but he held her back. She would need her strength once the buggy was fully loaded.

Stopping the buggy in front of the house, he set the brake, and then stepped out to get his family. Pilgrim ran out, barking at him in welcome. Mary had seen him pull up, so she was already coming out the door with the rest of the family. Joseph opened the buggy door, and the boys climbed in first. He stood there to give the women a hand.

"Are you going to miss me, young man?" Sharon asked him, while he was helping her up.

"Nay, I'm not," Joseph said loudly.

"Why Joseph, how rude," Mary said.

Joseph climbed inside, released the brake, and they were off. It looked like the women were a little mad at him.

"What did you mean?" Mary asked.

"It will be hard to miss someone when I'm asking her to stay another week with us. You all haven't got to spend much time together, so I'd be pleased if she stayed another week. Though it is up to your mother," Joseph said, laughing.

"Will you stay, Grandma?" Rebecca asked.

"If Mary wants me to, I will. I just don't want to be a burden on anyone," Sharon said. "I do like spending time with my family. We have missed so much together."

"It's settled then." Mary laughed, grabbing Joseph by the arm.

The sparkle had come back into her eyes. "And here I thought Joseph was in the dog house tonight."

The children were all laughing at him now.

"You're going to make daed sleep in the dog house?" Benjamin asked. "We don't even have a dog house."

"It is a gut thing then. It would be cold out there tonight," Sharon said, laughing with the children.

It is a lonesome ride by yourself if you travel very far. A man has plenty of time to think and pray and be one with nature. He has nothing else to do.

Sharon pulled out an old worn Bible. "Let me read you children something," she said, finding her page. "This Bible belonged to my husband that passed on years ago; he bought me the bookmark."

She read, "'Blessed are the peace makers: for they shall be called the children of God. Blessed are the meek and lowly at heart: for they shall inherit the earth. Blessed are they that mourn: for they shall be comforted.'"

"That was a comfort…just what I needed to hear." Joseph tried not to think about his mother who had passed on as a tear rolled down his cheek. He hoped nay one would notice, though Mary squeezed his hand.

"I thought so," Sharon said softly, closing the Bible.

"Look, children, we're here," Mary said as they pulled into John's yard.

The drive to John's farm seemed a short one, especially when shared with family. They had now arrived for the church service. Joseph got behind the long line of buggies, waiting to be parked.

"This place is packed out with more people than the last time," Caleb said.

"It's because of the church service," Sharon said. "People come for miles around to worship. Our church service isn't held in one particular building. Every other Sunday, we have church at one of our member's house."

"What will they do if they can't fit everyone into the building?"

Benjamin asked. "It looks like there are too many people here as it is."

"If the population gets too large, a portion of those further away will branch off and start a new community and a new church," Sharon said.

"I hope they give us plenty of time to get our house fixed before they want to have a church service there," Joseph said.

"I'm sure they will," Sharon said.

He had spent all day Saturday helping haul benches, getting everything set up for the service. There was a lot of work that went into each service. And there was always a dinner afterwards, everyone pitching in of course, bringing their favorite dish.

"Something smells gut," Joseph said.

"Me and Rebecca baked a few apple pies," Mary said.

"I'll have to try some then," Joseph said, smiling. "It is truly an inspiration to see that people care so much about God that they dedicate the whole day Sunday to Him."

"The Sunday we don't attend service is our time to visit each other," Sharon said. "When you don't have so many distractions in life, it makes it easier to do these things."

"When we were growing up, we had nothing else to do besides work," Mary said. "Visiting church and the neighbors for fellowship was a break that we truly enjoyed."

"Jah, life goes by so quickly. Our time will be up before we know it," Sharon said. "All that our loved ones will have is the memory of every time we did something with them—like a visit when they are sick, giving them a card, or a flower. The children will remember each time we took them fishing and camping. God has placed each individual child in our life for a purpose. He has trusted us to bring them up right in His ways."

"You're right," Joseph said. "I've seen what it's like in the modern world, with people always rushing everywhere. They simply do not have time for each other. I don't want to live like that, not any longer."

He finally made it to the front of the house, and he pulled the mare to a stop. Joseph let them out in front of the house.

"I'll put the mare up," he said to Mary.

"Danke, Joseph," Mary said. Leaning up, she surprised him by kissing him on the cheek. The boys had already run off to play with the other children.

Soon as he had the women folk unloaded, and Joseph circled around to put the buggy up and the mare in a stall. Some people just turned their horses out in the small fenced field, but Joseph wanted his mare out of the sun to let her rest.

Since it was warm out, the service was being held outside. When it got colder, they would have church on the inside of the house, moving everything out to set up the church benches.

Some of the older Amish families had their doors fixed inside for that purpose. The home owner would spend the day before getting ready, cleaning everything and scrubbing all the floors.

Joseph walked over to join the church service, looking for his family.

He could see Mary sitting in the back across from John and his family. "Sit over here," Mary said, waving.

They had gotten there late; it was time for the service to begin. Making his way over, he sat down across from Mary. She looked so happy to be here among her own people.

The church service was held with the females on one side and all the males on the other. The rough, heavy oak benches were backless and very uncomfortable.

"It is time to get the service started. All heads bowed for prayer," Bishop Moses Beiler said.

Joseph looked at the twins, Benjamin and Caleb, as they looked around at everybody else. This was as new to them as it was him, having church for the first time with all these strange people. Rebecca too was looking around. She was sitting with the other young girls her age, across from the older boys. He truly hoped they would like living here for their mother's sake. In time, maybe it would feel like home to them.

Soon the service started with some singing, without instruments. Joseph missed the music. He loved hearing a guitar and a piano. Here among the Amish, music wasn't allowed. A few hours later, the preaching began. Two preachers spoke, and both of them were long winded. They certainly took their time.

Deacon James got up next, opening up his Bible. "I would just like to ask a question today. What do you value the most in your life? Is it something that will pass away with time? Or will you be able to take it with you when it is your time to depart this life? Some just don't realize the value people have on their lives until they are gone. We take each other for granted it seems, always figuring that we have more time. We can always visit our family tomorrow.

"It's hard for anyone to understand another person's grief until you have felt the same. Life is filled with sorrow, pain, and mourning—though not all of it is that way. For God also said that there is a time for laughter, joy, and peace."

"We must always be thankful for what we have, our blessings in life, and not worry so much about what you don't have. Being content is the secret to happiness. It doesn't mean you don't care, but that you have faith in God to meet your needs. We're going to have to go through some things here on this earth; it's just part of life. 'He that endures to the end shall be saved.' We must be like Job in the Bible, and if nothing else, just keep plowing on. 'Though God slay me, I will not curse his name.'"

Joseph saw Caleb doze off and then finally Benjamin. He turned around to see Mary pointing at the boys from across the aisle; the service was about over now. Joseph touched the twins on the back of the neck to wake them up.

"What in the world?" Caleb jumped.

Joseph touched his finger to his lips, motioning for them to be quiet.

Finally, Bishop Moses stood up again. "We have some new

people with us today, Mary and her family. We are rejoicing because our sister Mary has come home again. Make sure you take time and speak to them before you leave, and of course, dinner is ready for us all. Stand up Mary, and let everyone see you."

Mary stood up then as all eyes turned upon her. And then she sat back down quickly, her face a little red.

"Joseph shoes horses, so if you need any work done, you know where to find him. I think some of the brethren have been taking their horses to another district. Now it is time to eat."

"Come on, Joseph, I am starving to death," Mary said getting up. "Follow me, children."

They had the food laid out on three big long tables, joined together in a row. The tables were covered with white tablecloths and loaded down with food. They got in line to get their food, Mary joined now by her sister Hannah. She gave Mary a hug. Jeremiah, Hannah's husband, and their two girls, Sarah and Rose, were right behind her.

"It is gut to see you all," Hannah said. She turned to look at Sharon. "Mother, are you coming home with me this week?"

"I guess not," Sharon said. "Joseph has requested that I spend another week with him and their family. We haven't seen each other in so long—it seems like ages."

"After I get my crop in the ground, we'll have a sleep over," Joseph said. "And you all can come over and spend the night with us, every one of you."

They moved through the line, getting their food. Joseph was surprised about how many men asked about shoeing their horses. He was going to have his work cut out for him.

One old man, Amos, who looked like he was too old to shoe his own horses, came up to him. "Joseph, do you need anything for your farm? I have a few animals, but not much money. Maybe we could trade out some livestock for your work?"

Joseph felt sorry for the man. He did need a few things, though, and trading work for goods was something he was used to back home. "What do you have?" Joseph asked.

"Well, I have lots of chickens and a few pigs. I mostly fool with small animals."

"What kind of chickens have you got?" Joseph asked.

"I've got some Silver Laced Wyandottes. They are one of the best brown egg layers that there are. I need shoes put on two of my work horses. But I have nay way of bringing them to you. I actually live about three miles from here."

"Twelve hens and two roosters, and you have a deal," Joseph said.

"I would have given you a few more chickens. Can you be there tomorrow evening?" Amos asked.

"I'll be there, about the edge of dark. A farm is just not a farm without a rooster crowing in the morning," Joseph said.

"Gut, I'll set out a lantern or two in the barn so you can work," Amos said. "I'll tell you something, Joseph. I like to see a mare running loose in a field with a baby colt and a pair of beagle hounds chasing a rabbit, barking with every breath. It is the small things in life that we take pleasure in; God has created them all for our enjoyment."

"You're right, Amos. We must have a lot in common. I'll see you then," Joseph said, shaking the older man's hand.

Mary had already left to find a place to sit and eat.

He made his way over to Mary's table to talk to everyone. Hannah and her family were sitting there beside Mary at the next picnic table. And sitting behind Mary was Samson, his wife, Carlonia, and their five boys. It looked like a small family reunion was going on.

He missed his mother and still felt a deep pain in his chest. He wished he could have one more day with her just so he could tell her how much he loved her and just hug her neck one more time.

Joseph sat down beside Mary and ate his food. She reached over and squeezed his hand when she saw him looking downcast.

The boys finished eating and went to play with the other children, and Rebecca wandered off with Sarah. Soon, the young men would be noticing the two girls, for they were changing into women fast.

"I'll be back in a minute, Joseph," Mary said, getting up. "I'll get us a piece of apple pie that I made."

"You truly are a gut woman, Mary," Joseph said, smiling.

Mary was back soon with two plates of dessert filled with apple pie and a few other treats.

John and Deacon Moses were making their way over to him now. It was time to meet the Deacon. Moses was of average height with a long black beard mixed with gray. He was a little heavier than most of the Amish men. He had preached his whole sermon in the German language which he knew well. The Bishop sat down beside Joseph on the picnic table bench.

"Mary, John tells me that you wish to join the church. You left early in life when you were married, so you were never baptized here. Are you going to stay here with us or go back to Pennsylvania?" Moses asked.

"We have nay place else to go. Joseph's parents have both passed on and left nay farm behind. We are here to stay," Mary said, laying her hand on her husband's arm.

"What about you, Joseph. Someone mentioned that you were raised in the Mennonite faith. Do you want time to consider our ways?" Moses asked, looking him in the eye.

"Nay, I've been baptized in the Amish faith long before the children were born, me and Mary both. A quiet life is all I seek now, a place to earn a living, raise a family, and be close to God."

"That's what I like to hear." Moses smiled as he hit Joseph on the arm. "At the next church service, we'll baptize you, if that's all right?"

"That'll be fine, Bishop," Joseph said.

"Brother Moses will do, for you are one of us now," he said, shaking Joseph's hand.

"Danke, Moses," Mary said. "We're all part of a community again, a dream of mine that has come true at last."

Sharon had tears in her eyes as Mary spoke. "It is gut to have you home, daughter. And you too, Joseph; you are making a special place in my heart."

"It's gut to be home," Joseph said. This was his home now and he knew it.

"I guess we had better help load the benches, Joseph," John said.

"Gut idea," Joseph said. He looked up to see the other brethren already at work packing them.

All too soon, the fellowship had passed, and folks were getting ready to leave and go home. It had been a good day and a rather large turnout. The few people that had missed the church service would get a house call by Bishop Moses. Finally, every bench was loaded for the next service, and the place was soon empty of nearly all the guests.

Joseph went to get the mare and hitch her up. It was late in the afternoon, and he wanted to get home quickly to spend a little time with his family, maybe sit on the porch and enjoy nature.

Hitching the mare up quickly, he drove up to the front of the house to pick his family up. They were ready to go now. Setting the brake, he jumped down and helped them all inside. Elizabeth came out with a picnic basket of food, some left over chicken, potato salad, rolls, mashed potatoes, and two pies.

"Saved you from cooking," she said to Mary as she handed them up.

"Thank you," Mary said. "I appreciate it."

Joseph brought the reins down on the mare's back, and they were on their way home. The mare made good time, though she was sweating some. As they neared their home, Pilgrim came running out to greet them, barking with every breath.

"I think Pilgrim missed us," Caleb said.

He let his family out in front of the house, and then Joseph drove down to unhitch the mare. He turned the mare loose in the field, giving her a little bit of grain. After eating, the mare went over and rolled in the dirt. It looked like she was glad to be home too.

Now it was time to relax, so he walked back to the house quickly.

"What do you want to do this evening?" Mary asked as he walked up on the porch.

"Nothing besides eat some leftovers and watch the children play." Joseph grabbed a rocking chair on the porch.

He was worn out and the porch had a great view. Mary went inside to warm up the food a little later. Though they didn't cook on Sunday, they would often warm their food up, cooking it the day before. This is actually what it said to do in the Bible.

He leaned back to relax for just a minute.

"Daed is sound asleep in his rocking chair," Rebecca said, looking out on the porch.

"Let him rest. He can eat later," Mary said. "He has been pushing himself too hard. I think he's worried about not getting the crop planted on time. The rest will do him gut."

CHAPTER NINE

Joseph was sleeping in his bedroom when something woke him up. Pilgrim was barking with every breath, making the worst racket there ever was.

"Joseph, there is something out there," Mary said, shaking him.

He got up and grabbed Mary's grandfather's old .22 rifle. He had cleaned the gun out earlier, and got it working again. "It's probably, just some wild animal prowling around."

He started to go outside when he saw the light. It was shining brightly on the house windows. The light was shining on the living room windows and the front door. Stepping outside, he looked to see where the lights were coming from. He could see the lights high up on the hill in the front of the house. It looked like somebody was shining three spotlights aimed at the house.

"What's going on?" Mary asked. The children were standing there in the doorway behind her, watching him.

"I think somebody is trying to scare us," Joseph said.

"Well, it's working," Rebecca said, coming out on the porch. "Earlier, I saw grandpa walking around outside."

"You couldn't have seen him; he's dead," Mary gasped, stepping outside.

"It was him, Mother. I looked right at him," Rebecca said loudly.

"This place is too scary. I wish we had never moved here. We are already seeing ghosts," Caleb said.

Joseph watched a coyote run through the wooded area. Nay

doubt he was scared off by the men with the lights. Suddenly Joseph had an idea.

"It's just a coyote after our chickens," he said, laughing.

Raising his rifle, he began to shoot at it. The coyote was too far away for him to hit it, but it ran away rather quickly. He emptied his gun at it, right there on their front porch.

The lights suddenly blinked off; it looked like a few shots had accidentally gone over their heads. They heard somebody yell. Then a few minutes later it sounded like a four wheeler started up, and the men quickly sped away, whoever they were.

"Let's go back inside, children. I don't think the coyotes will be bothering us any more tonight," Joseph said jokingly.

"Why Joseph, I almost thought you were enjoying that!" Mary said shocked. "And besides, we do not have any chickens."

"Well, the coyotes didn't know that. Gut night, woman," Joseph said going inside.

The family left out at daylight after feeding all the animals. The horse moved along steadily on the dirt road, making a soft sound. Joseph pointed out four deer in the bottom. The skittish deer took off abruptly, their tails held high.

"Joseph, I heard there were some coyotes packing lights last night," Sharon said, smiling.

"Jah, you'll be surprised what you might find out here. The children are even claiming they're seeing ghosts."

Sharon laughed then. "Well, maybe the coyotes learned them a lesson last night."

John was going to plant his fields during the next few days. So they all had come to help. The more that helped, the quicker it would be done. Then they would have to start plowing up Joseph's fields. They would need a big garden to carry them through this winter.

It was going to take a lot of hard work to pull them through.

He tried to keep most of his worries to himself. He didn't wish to worry his wife and children.

Joseph glanced back at the boys, they had fallen asleep. Soon the short ride was over, and the horse pulled the buggy on into John's yard.

"I'll let you ladies off at the door," Joseph said, stopping in front of the house.

"Thank you, Joseph," Sharon said as he helped her down.

"Wake up, boys, we're here," Mary said, shaking them.

The boys climbed out slowly, still half asleep.

"Now I got to put the horse and buggy up," Joseph said as they all walked off toward the house.

He put the mare up quickly, leaving the buggy parked outside the barn. Then he headed toward the house to find John. The women and kids where already inside. John met him at the door.

"Come on in, Joseph. We're getting everything ready," John said.

"Anything you need me to do?" Joseph asked, looking inside the house. The rest of them were getting the garden seeds ready.

"You can hitch up the two mules each to a plow of its own," John said. "I want to run two plows. One will lay the rows out while the children plant. The other mule will run behind him, covering the seeds up."

"Gut idea," Joseph said. "That should make it go a lot quicker."

"It makes a man appreciate a gut mule. An animal that will get down in the dirt and sweat it out with you is worth something," John said, chuckling.

"That's for sure," Joseph said, walking off.

Plowing made the ground soft, easy to work with. Plowing usually took two mules to a plow, if you were plowing it for the first time that year. Farmers would come behind then with one mule and one plow for the planting, laying out the rows as straight as possible for the seeds.

It usually cut a hole in the loose dirt three or four inches deep.

Then once the seeds were planted, you could run another mule and plow beside the row that you planted, holding the plow closed so that it would cover up with dirt what you had just planted.

Going out to the barn, he hitched the mules up. Driving one mule on out to the field, he went back for the other mule. By the time the rest of them made it to the field with the seeds, he had everything ready. Before they reached him, Joseph picked the reins up, and set out laying a row off, trying to look good in front of his wife.

Mary and Elizabeth were carrying the garden seeds along with John and all the children. They put the seeds down under a big pine tree in the middle of the field.

"You women can help plant for a while until it gets close to dinnertime," John said.

"Men are always worried about a meal," Elizabeth said, smiling.

"Alright, everyone, gather around. I need to show everybody what to plant and how far apart," John said. "Put four or five corn seeds to each hole, sometimes they all won't come up."

"Why are you planting so much corn?" Caleb asked.

"We're going to plant our garden first, but I'll need enough corn to feed all of our animals this winter. We might even have a little extra to sell," John said.

"I think we're going to be hoeing corn in our dreams," Elizabeth said, laughing.

"Man, that Joseph is a gut worker," John said, turning to Mary. "I can't keep up with him. Is he like this all the time, even at home?"

"Jah, I can't get him to be still. He pushes himself too hard," Mary said.

"He's probably got a lot of worries on his mind," Elizabeth said.

"Well, it's not easy setting up on a new farm," John said. "A man has a lot to do before winter sets in. Once you make it through the first winter, things might be easier next year. After you have a barn and all your other buildings built."

Joseph came back down the other side of the garden row. He had already laid off two rows. Mary waved at him, trying to get him to come to her, but he just at her. He turned the mule around and started back, plowing off another row.

"Well, we'd best get to planting. Joseph isn't going to let up," John said, laughing.

"He will at dinnertime," Mary said, laughing.

"You're probably right," Elizabeth said, smiling.

"Any man would like your cooking, my dear," John said.

"He's just saying that." Elizabeth laughed.

"Come on, children. I'll show you what to do," John said, leading the way; everybody followed him.

"I'll work with the girls," Elizabeth said. "Come on, Sarah and Rebecca—you too, Mary. Let's see if we can out work these men."

Joseph turned around a little later to see all his family planting. Caleb and Benjamin waved at him. He nodded back. A man plowing can't turn loose of a plow. It takes two hands to plow. He had looped the bridle reins in a circle around his neck. It made a pretty sight, the two families helping each other in their time of need.

Helping each other, coming together in love, that was what a family was all about. And that was what the Amish belief was based upon. It should be that way for any Christian, no matter what religion. Most people didn't have time for each other, as they all pursued their own selfish dreams.

Usually, a couple of John's brothers helped him plant and plow, but they lived so far away in buggy miles; Joseph was a lot closer. It would make it easier too when John came to help him.

Joseph thought a lot when he was plowing in the fields. A man needs time to think and pray. That is usually when you could hear

God's voice. At one point, he turned his back on his family as an image of his mother appeared in his mind. A tear rolled down his cheek. He missed her so bad, he couldn't stand it. *Why, God, did You take everything from me?* Everything he had held dear was gone, his mother, father, and now the farm he had grown up on.

The children now had a row planted; all the boys were working with John. A little later, John grabbed the other mule and began covering up the row they had planted. Joseph pushed on, not stopping. After a while he lost track of time.

"It is time to eat," John yelled, waving at him.

Joseph dropped the plow at the end of the row. Driving the mule on down to the shade tree, he tied her up there. John had brought some corn along, so he fed the mule a small ration of corn. The animal was going to need her strength.

"When I come back, I'll water the mules," Joseph said. "A short break will cool them off." The mule had sweat running all down its side. Joseph brushed her down real quick, knocking some of the dirt off her.

"You are a strange man, Joseph," John said. "You are always trying to care for an animal."

"A righteous man takes gut care of his beast," Joseph said. "That was one thing my father taught me. A man that doesn't take gut care of his animals doesn't need them."

"Well, let's get washed up for dinner," John said.

Going inside, they got in line. The boys were all there scrubbing down. Matthew was working the hand water pump so they could wash their hands.

"I have never seen my boys so dirty." John rubbed Luke on the head.

"Oh Daed, I was just about clean," Luke said.

Joseph waited until John was done washing, John handed him a bar of lye soap to scrub down with.

"Joseph, I have never been without running water in my life," John said.

"I thought you didn't have electricity," Joseph said. "Do you use it in your barn?"

"Nay, I don't have any electricity on the place," John said. "I have always had to run and get my own water."

"A man can bring five gallons at a time," Joseph agreed, laughing.

In the old days, they made their own candles to light their homes with. People had to rise at daylight and get their work done, taking full advantage of the sunlight. For when it got dark, you had nothing to do except go to bed.

Work while it is day, for when the night comes, nay man can work. The Amish still live their life by these principals. True, it is a humble and a plain life, though he doesn't need much. Wanting something and needing it are two different things.

After scrubbing well, Joseph dried his face quickly on a towel. It was time to eat now, and he was very hungry. He made his way to the table. The others had already sat down to fried chicken, soup beans, cornbread, fried potatoes, and corn on the cob.

"A man doesn't get enough to eat here," Joseph declared, sitting down. "There is something wrong."

John cleared his throat; his clothes were still dirty though his face and hands were clean. "Let's bow our head for a prayer."

Soon everyone was done praying. John helped himself first at the head of the table and then passed the food to Joseph and on down the line. Joseph helped himself to a generous helping of beans and chicken. It was delicious.

"It seems like the Amish women really know how to cook," Joseph said.

"I tell you, Joseph, the way you're plowing we may get done a day sooner." John put butter on his hot corn bread.

"I have to go to Amos's farm tonight when we're done. He has two horses that he wants me to shoe."

"Joseph, there is nay way you can get all that done before dark." John passed the corn.

"I'll shoe them in his barn. He has some lanterns that we can use for light." Joseph helped himself to some fried potatoes.

John just shook his head, looking at Mary. "At least stay with us tonight, so we can get an early start in the morning. It'll be too late to have the women out after dark. And be hard on them getting up so early."

"Denki, we'll accept," Joseph said. "Anyway, he is going to give me some laying hens for my work. There is nothing I like better than hearing a rooster crow on a farm."

"Why? They're more annoying than anything." Elizabeth smiled.

"Women just can't see the beauty in a gut rooster," John said.

Elizabeth got up, ignoring John, and went into the kitchen. She came back with two pies. She had a pink apron on. "Does anybody like lemon pie?"

All the boys sat up quickly. "Sure we do," Benjamin said.

"I thought it would take two pies." Elizabeth placed them on the table. Getting a knife from her apron pocket, she cut the pie into many pieces.

When everyone got a piece, there was none left.

"Well, they certainly liked your pies," Mary said, laughing.

Joseph stood up and walked over quietly and looked out the window. John didn't pay him much attention at first, but soon the door shut softly behind him.

"Where is he going now?" John asked Mary.

"Back to work," she said, laughing.

John just shook his head, laughing. "Mary, that husband of yours is killing me. I can't even take a break with him around."

"Well, he doesn't believe in letting moss grow under his feet," Mary said, smiling.

"Well, let's go back to work, boys. When you women get the

dishes done, you can come out and help us," John said. Getting up quickly, he walked back outside with the boys.

The day was passing quickly, Joseph working steadily on, everyone trying to keep up with him. He saw Sarah and Rebecca packing out some refreshments. John waved at him to come and eat under the pine tree.

Joseph didn't have to be told twice, he met them there.

"Let's sit down and take a break Joseph. This is a gut shade tree as any," John said.

"It is not that dirty in the green grass, along the roots of the tree," Elizabeth said pointing.

"We are all dirty anyway, it doesn't matter," Sarah said sitting down.

Everybody was sitting down on the ground now. Sarah handed out some paper plates. The sugar cookies and lemonade, didn't last long.

Sharon was sitting on the front porch watching them. She had joined them for dinner, but hadn't been moving around much today.

"I think Mother is tired," Mary said.

"She is getting old," John said.

"Denki girls, the cookies were delicious." Joseph downed the last of his lemonade, handed his cup to Mary, and went back to work.

A few hours later, John stopped just a little bit early. "I have got to give everybody time to take a bath," he said, laughing. "We usually don't have this much company, though we do enjoy your help."

"Gut, I will hitch the mare up and be on my way. I need to go shoe Amos's horses," Joseph said.

"The children can stay here and rest," John said. "Mary, run along with Joseph if you want to. It will give you all some time alone."

"Are you sure?" Mary asked.

"We can handle the children," Elizabeth said, smiling. "Or at least, we think we can."

"We won't be any trouble," Benjamin said.

"It is settled then. Be on your way," John said, laughing. "A man needs to take his wife out on a date when he can."

"Why John, you haven't taken me on a date in ages," Elizabeth spoke up, her eyes flashing.

"Well, we don't have a babysitter that lives nearby. You know that, dear," John said, his face turning red.

"Then we will have to take turns and let you all go on a date," Mary said, laughing.

"That just might work," Elizabeth said.

"Let me grab the buggy, Mary, and I'll be right back," Joseph said, walking off.

He came quickly with the buggy and picked Mary up. A few minutes later, they were on their way. "When we get back, I need to take a bath," Mary said as they were leaving the yard.

Joseph nodded. "Hopefully things will be better when we get settled in our own home."

"We will just have to be patient. We will have it soon enough. Though this will be fun, all of us sleeping over here tonight. The children will have so much fun."

"They should sleep well tonight anyway," Joseph said.

The mare made fast time of the short drive. She was getting used to this buggy work. The only time he had seen her act up was when the dog had scared her. Mary looked pretty sitting close to him. It reminded him of when they were dating.

He could see the farmhouse up ahead; they were about there now. Amos was standing by the barn door when they pulled up. Joseph drove past him and stopped at the house.

"Mary, go inside and visit with his wife while I shoe his horses," Joseph said. "It won't take that long. You need to sit down and rest anyway. You have been on your feet too much today."

"What about you, Joseph, are you tired?"

"I will be fine," Joseph said. "Denki for coming with me. It would have been a lonesome ride back by myself."

Dropping her off at the front door, he made his way over to the barn. Amos had two of the prettiest work horses he had ever seen tied in the barn hallway. They looked like miniature draft horses.

"What kind of horses are those?" Joseph asked.

"They are Haflingers, son," Amos said. "Miniature work horses most don't get over fourteen and a half hands, but they have the draft size. They can pull too. Actually anybody looking for some work horses would be better off with these. Man could always raise a mule out of them if he wanted. You see, Joseph, a mare will replace herself if bred, a mule can't. I don't have any sons. I have five daughters. They have all moved so far away that they are not much help to me."

Joseph nodded, getting his tools. He started to work on the first horse, picking its hoof up. He stood off to the side, not directly behind the horse in case it decided to kick him.

"You think people will start using these types of horses?" he asked.

"Jah, I say they will, especially when they figure out that these horses can do the work of the bigger ones, but on less care."

Joseph finally finished shoeing both of them, which took him about an hour to do. He had been shoeing for some time. Surprisingly both horses worked out well. They didn't move, even though it was the first time they had been shod. They were definitely gentle horses.

"How much would a horse like this cost?" Joseph asked Amos.

"They are not any higher than other horses right now. The prices have dropped a lot on horses now. Come on, I'll show you a two-year-old stud horse that I have for sale. I have just started working him in the harness."

Joseph followed him to the stalls. There he was, a young Haflinger stud. He was light red in color, with a blaze face, flax mane and tail, and four white stockings. Amos led him out of the barn for Joseph to see on a lead strap. He turned him around in the aisle, so he could see both sides.

"I am too old to deal with a stud, and I hate to cut him. He is a registered horse. I'll sell him to you cheaper, if you will breed my mares for me in the future."

"How much are you asking for him?" Joseph asked. When Amos told him, he made a slight face. "It is a little more than I was planning to give for a mule."

"Tell you what, Joseph. You can work out the rest of the money if you want. I do need a little help around here, planting our garden."

"I was really planning on a mule. John wanted me to look at one with him," Joseph said, smiling.

"Well, a man should please himself first," Amos said, laughing.

"What is his name?" Joseph asked, rubbing his hand down the horse's back, which was a mistake.

"I call him Lucky," Amos said.

"Well Lucky, you now have a new home," Joseph said. "Now what about my chickens? When can I get them?"

"I already have them loaded up, son. I put them in some feed sacks. They are laying by your buggy," Amos handed him the lead rope. "Take him on."

"I don't have enough money with me right now," Joseph said, hesitating.

"A man is as gut as his word," Amos said softly.

He tied the stud horse up behind the buggy and then loaded the chickens up inside the buggy. He was now ready to go.

"Hang on a minute, Joseph?"

"Jah," Joseph said, he was getting ready to leave.

"Come back and see me anytime, son. You are always welcome," Amos said.

"I will bring the whole family next time," he said, shaking Amos's hand.

Fiery, the mare, kept glancing back at Lucky tied up behind her. Though she couldn't see him on account of the buggy, she knew he was there. The two horses kept neighing back and forth at each other. Mary was coming his way now; suddenly she stopped.

"What is going on, Joseph? What are you doing with that horse? I thought we just came here for some chickens?" she demanded.

"That we did, woman," Joseph said, smiling.

Amos laughed then. "I made him a deal he couldn't turn down."

His wife said, "Men!"

Joseph tipped his hat to her. "Gut day, ma'am."

With a flick of the wrist, the reins fell softly on the mare's back. They were on their way. "We will have to travel a little slower so the stud horse can keep up," Joseph said.

"What are we going to do with him tonight?" Mary asked.

"His name is Lucky. And we will put him in John's barn tonight. I will take him home tomorrow after we are done planting."

"I guess you know your own mind," Mary said, laughing at him.

"That I do, woman, that I do," Joseph said, pulling Mary closer to him.

"You would think we are still courting," she said.

Joseph laughed then.

"What is it?" Mary asked.

"Honey, if we were still courting. You wouldn't be asking so many foolish questions."

She swatted his hand playfully. Joseph stopped the buggy and gave her a long kiss, looking deep into her eyes.

"What was that all about?" she asked with a twinkle in her eyes.

"I just wanted to see if you still moved me...the way you used to," Joseph said.

"Well, do I?" she asked, waiting.

"I don't really know, but if I could get another kiss, I could make my mind up."

"Just one?" Mary teased as they continued their journey.

"Well, maybe two or three," Joseph said.

"Mary, do me a favor when we get there. I'll put Lucky up in the barn. Don't tell anyone that I bought him, okay? I just want to see John's face when he finds him in the barn."

"Alright," Mary said, snuggling up against him. She seemed very tired.

Joseph didn't say anything else. He could see Mary was dozing off. Soon she fell asleep and slept all the way back.

It would be good to get back and get some rest.

Riding on through the darkness in silence, he drove the buggy under the shed. John had it fixed so you could drive a horse and buggy in on one side, leave the buggy there, and take the horse out the other open side. It was actually a good idea, especially when it was raining outside. It allowed you to take care of your horse sheltered from any bad weather.

Mary was still asleep in the buggy. Joseph set the brake and then climbed out. He took the mare inside, giving her feed and hay. His next move was to take the stud horse inside, putting him in an empty stall. Once he threw him some hay and a grain ration, he filled up a five-gallon bucket of water and placed it inside.

John had a bucket holder made on the wall to hold it firmly in place. A man doesn't want anything loose lying in a horse's stall. Sometimes an animal can be accident prone. If it can be done, most of the time an animal will figure out a way to get hurt. Goats would run their heads through a wool wire fence only to find out that their horns refused to let them back out.

He had just about forgotten about the chickens. Going to the buggy, he got the chickens and put them inside an empty cage behind the barn. They would be alright there until he left tomorrow. Once he had everything done, he went to get Mary.

He saw somebody inside the house place a lantern up next to the window. It was pretty dark out now.

Shaking Mary lightly, he woke her up. "Get up, Mary. We are here."

"I can barely walk," Mary said as he helped her down from the buggy, leading her inside.

Now it looked like he had the makings of a small farm going on. Though right now, he needed some sleep.

Chapter Ten

David hitched his daed's mare up after chores. He was heading out to visit Rachel again for his first lesson. He still felt a little awkward about being taught to read at his age, but he knew it was something he needed to do. He longed to be able to write Rebecca a letter and tell her how he felt without Rachel looking at him funny.

The horse pulled him along slowly, the small buggy bouncing some as he left the yard. Rachel had mentioned in school that they could go fishing on their farm while he was learning to read. The pond was real close to her house, so they would have some privacy. Rachel's daed didn't like to turn her loose with a boy unless he could watch them.

Rachel was waiting on the porch when he pulled up to the house. A picnic basket was in her hands. *She looks very pretty*, David thought as he got out of the buggy.

"My mamm fixed us something to eat, some leftover chicken, potato salad, and baked beans," Rachel said.

"You're making me hungry," David said. "Now are we ready to fish?"

"After you, my fair prince," Rachel said, smiling. She hesitated when David suddenly frowned.

"Enjoy your meal, David," Ruth said, coming out. "And have Rachel back before dark."

"I will, ma'am," David said. "I don't like traveling in the dark. I don't have a gut light on my buggy. Either that, or me or the horse can't see very well."

"Well, at least you have a sense of humor," Ruth laughed as she started back inside the house.

David helped Rachel inside the buggy, and then they were off. Rachel, he noticed, was sitting quiet close beside him in the open buggy.

"Have you heard from, Rebecca?" David asked as they approached the pond.

"Nay, it unusually takes about a week to hear from her," Rachel said. "It is so beautiful out today. It makes you feel glad to be alive."

"God is all around us," David said sincerely.

"Are you planning on joining the Amish faith?" Rachel asked, touching his arm to get his attention.

"There has never been any doubt in my mind. I would like to do a few things first—like drive a car," David said. "Now, what are your plans?"

"I just want to get married someday and raise a gut family that is close to God and each other," Rachel said. "I think that is more important than anything else."

"I will have to get you a date with Jim Bob," David said. Jim Bob had liked Rachel since they had been real small. Rachel, however, had never wanted anything to do with him.

"Hey! That's not fair!" Rachel punched him playfully in the arm.

"We're getting to be gut friends," David said as Rachel touched his hand without thinking. Their fingers joined for just a second. It sent shock waves through his arm.

"We are best friends now," Rachel said. "Ever since Rebecca left, I spend more time with you than anyone else."

"It's kind of odd, a boy and a girl being best friends," David said. "Anyway, I do hope the fish are biting today."

"Now David, keep your mind off the fishing," Rachel said. "Remember, we're going to be studying between bites."

"Jah, my teacher," David said teasingly. "I think you would actually make a gut teacher. You really care about others."

They pulled in beside the pond. David stopped the buggy back near the trees to give shade to the horse. He went over quickly to help Rachel down. "Don't forget the food."

"You are going to be hard to teach anything," Rachel said, smiling. "It seems like food and fishing is all you worry about."

"Well now, a man has got to eat," David said, grabbing their fishing poles.

Mary rolled over to wake Joseph up, but he was gone. She was a little puzzled as she got up and went into the kitchen. The children were all up now.

"Have you seen Joseph?" she asked John. "He's not in the bedroom."

"Maybe he's feeding the stock or getting the mules ready," John said, smiling. He walked over, opened up the door, and then stepped outside on the porch. Mary and Elizabeth followed John outside. "I don't see him," John said.

Mary looked out in the field, finally spotting him in the distance. He was plowing with the mule.

"What's got into him, Mary? He hasn't even eaten his breakfast," John said.

"I'll take a plate to him," Mary said.

"Won't he come inside and eat?" Elizabeth asked.

"I doubt it," Mary said.

It was amusing to watch John's face trying to figure out how he felt at how hard Joseph was working. John considered himself a hard worker, and he didn't like anybody to outdo him. Joseph wasn't trying to; it was just the way he was.

Mary knew Joseph was at peace working in the fields.

"Well, let's eat before our breakfast gets cold," Elizabeth said, leading the way back inside.

Sharon was already at the breakfast table. She must be feeling better today.

"Gut morning, grandchildren," Sharon said.

"Gut morning, Grandma," the children said.

"Where is Joseph?" she asked, looking around.

John sat down at the table and just gave a grunt. They all ate fast, especially John. When he was done eating, he pushed back his chair and walked away quickly. The door slammed shut behind him.

"Children, let's go help John this morning," Mary said, pushing back her chair.

The family followed John to the barn to help him get started with the chores.

John was harnessing up the other mule inside the barn. He had run a rope from both sides of the barn wall, which was tied to the mule's halter on each side. In this way, he could keep the animal in the center of the aisle.

It looked like Joseph had been working for at least an hour by himself, judging by the amount of work he had already done. Mary noticed Joseph was looking their way a lot, a smile on his face.

John bent over, checking the mule's back shoes. Lucky suddenly put his head over the stall door, and nudged him with his nose. John jumped about three feet straight up in the air and let out a yell. When he calmed down, he turned to regard the strange horse in his barn. Mary had forgotten all about Lucky. They all were laughing so hard at John that they could hardly breathe.

Joseph had stopped the mule out in the field and was leaning against the plow, laughing. The mule turned around and looked at him.

"Where did that horse come from?" Caleb asked as the children crowded around to look at the new horse.

"Joseph bought him off Amos last night," Mary said, still laughing. "It had slipped my mind."

"He is a beauty," John said. "Though...he is a little small."

"Oh! I forgot to take Joseph something to eat. I'll be right back," Mary said, walking off.

Sharon had come out on the porch and was sitting in a rocking chair. "What's all the yelling about?"

"Joseph bought a horse last night and hid it in the barn. I think the horse scared John to death. When he bent over, it gave him a nudge in the rear end. John jumped about three feet straight up in the air."

Sharon started laughing, and that got Mary started all over again as well. When Sharon's laughter finally died off, she said, "Mary, I haven't laughed that hard in a long time."

Mary fixed Joseph's plate and took it to him. He stopped the mule, sat down on the plow, and ate his breakfast right there. She had stacked the plate high for him and brought him a cup of milk. Joseph cleaned the plate, eating every bite of food. He was sure hungry.

Joseph handed the plate and cup back to her. "Thank you, Mary, now I must get back to work."

"Can't you take a break?" Mary asked.

"We've got too much to do today, but it has started out right. A merry heart does well like a medicine."

Getting up, he grabbed the reins, steadying the plow, "Get up, Betsy!"

With a flick of the reins on her back, the mule pulled on.

That evening, they quit a little early since Joseph had a lot of the work already done. The buggy finally pulled out for home, traveling at a steady pace. On the buggy floor were some feed sacks, with a laying flock of chickens inside. Tied behind the buggy and traveling easily was the Haflinger stud horse.

"I'll be glad to get a hot bath and a bed," Joseph said. "I have trouble sleeping anywhere else; it just doesn't feel like home."

"I know what you mean," Mary said, shifting beside him.

The miles passed slowly. All was quiet except for the children talking softly. The sound of the mare's hoofs on the dirt road slowly ate up the miles.

The wind was blowing slightly, and the sun was warming up the earth gently. The grass was never more beautiful than right after a long cold winter.

"I can feel God's gentle presence here," Joseph commented to Mary. Sometimes he kept his feelings to himself, but this was too overpowering. It needed to be shared.

"God is always here," Sharon said softly.

"Jah, I believe He is, Mother," Mary said.

"I think spring is God's favorite time of the year; it is a time for a new beginning," Sharon said. "The earth looks dead in the winter, so barren. Yet with spring's gentle promise comes life—a resurrection of all the dead seeds in the earth that will spring forth into life. We must die out to sin in order to live."

Arriving at the farm, Joseph let them off at the house. He went quickly to put the animals up. He didn't have a good barn in working order, so he turned the stud horse loose in the corral. He turned the mare out in the pasture to let her eat some grass.

The corral was the best place for the stud; it was built out of a solid wood pole fence stacked high for a corral. It was solid enough to keep a stud horse in. A stud couldn't be trusted around a mare that was in season, and they've been known to go right through fences to get to the mares.

Joseph made sure the horses had feed and water before he went to get the chickens. He put the chickens beside the shed in the lean too. He would have to make a chicken house and a wire pen later. It might brighten the place up now with all of the animals on the farm.

Joseph walked over to the corral to check on Lucky. The horse came closer, and put his head over the fence. He was built of solid muscle, though he was very gentle. Mary and Rebecca came walking out to join him.

"How are my two favorite women?" Joseph asked, smiling.

"We're fine, Joseph," Mary answered.

"You really like that horse, don't you?" Rebecca asked.

"Jah, he has been worked very little. I'm looking forward to training him. Hopefully, by this time next spring, he will be doing all of our plowing."

"You think he's big enough?" Mary asked curiously.

"He's plenty big enough; it's the heart that counts. Later, I'm going to buy another horse, a mate for him. That way we can tear some ground up." Joseph rubbed the horse between the ears as he spoke.

"I haven't seen Daed treat a horse this way before," Rebecca said, smiling.

"Joseph, come inside; we can eat some ham sandwiches before it gets dark," Mary said.

"You all go on. I'll be there in a few minutes," Joseph said. He pulled an old wooden chair up next to the fence and sat down. A man needed time to relax.

He watched that horse settle into his new home until it turned dark, and then he went inside. The ham sandwiches were cold, but still good.

Joseph and Mary woke to the sound of sirens outside. Their small yard was filled up with a fire truck and cars from the local sheriff's department. It took Joseph a few minutes to get outside. Someone was banging very hard on their front door, trying to wake them. Joseph opened the door and saw the county sheriff, John Clemons. He was of medium height, not heavy, with brown curly hair and dressed in full uniform.

"Do you realize that your barn is on fire? Somebody driving by saw it and called 911!"

Joseph grabbed his hat. "Nay, I did not!" He could hear the children running to the door behind him.

"Mary, please keep the children inside with you. I'll go see what's going on."

"What is your name?" The sheriff asked.

"Joseph Komer."

"Come with me, Joseph. I'm sorry that we didn't arrive in time to save your barn."

"It was in bad shape anyway. I think it was about ready to fall."

The chief firefighter came forward then. "I'm afraid all we can do is keep it from spreading to your other buildings. We sprayed all your buildings down with water to keep the fire from spreading."

"Thank you, I didn't even know it was burning," Joseph said.

Joseph stood there watching the fire. It was burning high; the flames were almost twenty feet over the barn. Suddenly the barn started leaning and fell quickly, making a very loud noise. It also sent red sparks flying everywhere.

Mary came out with the children.

"Stay back, ma'am," the sheriff said.

Mary nodded her head and took them back to the porch.

"Joseph, do you know anybody that would want to harm your family?"

"Why do you ask?" Joseph stepped closer to him.

"Come with me, and I'll show you something," the sheriff said, leading the way.

Laying behind the shed was a red gas jug. "Is this yours, Joseph?"

"Nay, I have never seen it before."

"That was what I was afraid of. I haven't touched it, hoping to get some fingerprints off it. Joseph, this fire was set deliberately; I think somebody was trying to burn you out. Do you know who it might be?"

"Some of our neighbors don't want us living here, including Mr. Stevens. I couldn't say for sure who it could be."

"Well, I know Stevens. They are likely to do anything, but we will have to get proof. I have been trying to catch them in their dirty deeds for years. Actually, this makes the second barn that has been torched on this farm. One burned down before you all moved here years ago."

"It is not our way to press charges against any one. Our religion teaches us that we must forgive."

"You've got to be joking. You mean if I can prove this on Stevens, you wouldn't even press charges?"

"Nay sir, I would not," Joseph said honestly.

"Well, I could press them anyway," Sheriff Clemons said.

The fire chief waved at the sheriff then, and he turned around. Suddenly something caught Joseph's eye. There on the ground lay something very shiny. Picking it up quickly, he put it in his pocket after looking at it. He didn't want anybody to know about the clue he had just found. He would have to give the situation a lot of thought, and prayer.

"Did you find something, Joseph?"

"I thought I saw something shiny, but it wasn't a quarter though." He wouldn't lie about what had happened, but he didn't have to volunteer any more information either.

"Joseph, if we find out anything, we'll let you know. I'm going to talk to a few of your neighbors; maybe it will put a stop to this nonsense. If you need anything, just let me know. I firmly believe that every man has a right to his own beliefs."

Finally, all was quiet again as the vehicles left. Joseph went back on the porch to tell everyone what was going on.

"They won't burn our house down, will they?" Rebecca asked.

"I hope not, dear. God will watch out for us. We just need to trust Him more," Joseph said.

"Well, let's try to get some sleep," Mary said. "Though, I don't think we will be able to."

CHAPTER ELEVEN

Joseph got up early to feed the animals. Today, he was going to work on the roof, replacing the bad shingles. The floor inside the house needed to be fixed as well, but first he had to stop the leaks.

Grabbing his tools, he climbed up on the roof and started working. The day wore on; he could see the children playing now. They didn't have that many chores yet, just taking care of the animals. When he got the fields planted, all of their work would increase.

A child needs a few chores to help them learn responsibility. A child should be motivated and challenged. Once they come of age and leave home, school is out. They will be a product of what was taught to them. The seeds sown in their hearts must be planted with great care.

"I got you a few more shingles," Caleb said, throwing them up on the roof.

Joseph jumped, startled, his thoughts interrupted. "Denki, be careful climbing up and down the ladder."

The women were inside, preparing for dinner now. A few hours later, the roof was making the house look almost new.

"Joseph, do you know what day it is?" Mary asked suddenly, looking up to him from the yard.

"Nay, I do not." Joseph hammered a shingle down.

"It is Friday, and Bishop Moses is supposed to drop by to talk to us," Mary said.

"Why?" Joseph asked.

"It's the custom that the bishop talks to you before baptism to make sure we know what we're getting into," Mary said. "It is a big thing being baptized into the church. The church leaders of the community want to make sure that we know all the rules of the Ordnung."

"I'm ready. We are both baptized members of an Amish church in my hometown," Joseph said.

"I know, Joseph, but every community is different," Mary said.

"A church should be like a big family, all working towards making Heaven their home someday."

Mary just nodded her head and walked away, checking on her flowers.

Joseph was busy working a few minutes later when suddenly Pilgrim started barking, charging at a buggy coming into their yard. Joseph saw the bishop and a church deacon get out and approach Mary. It was time to meet the bishop. He climbed down off the ladder and made his way over to them.

They were sitting at a little table on the porch, enjoying the sunshine.

"Do you want to go inside?" Joseph said.

"Nay, it's fine out here. The sunlight is gut for the spirit," Bishop Moses said. "By the way, this is Deacon James; he travels with me a lot."

"Gut to meet you," Joseph said, shaking the man's hand.

The man was tall and skinny as a rail with a very long beard. He was a well-dressed man. It looked like he had pressed his clothes, for there were nay wrinkles in them.

"Are you all staying for dinner? It will be ready in about an hour," Mary asked.

"Nay, we have some more places to visit," Moses said.

"Mary, please bring us some refreshments," Joseph said.

"That would be gut," James said.

Mary went inside and came back with a tray loaded down with

lemonade and peanut butter cookies. "These are Joseph's favorite snack."

"I knew I smelled something gut," Joseph said, smiling.

"You are a blessed man," James said, grabbing a cookie.

Moses ate his cookies and drank his lemonade, and then cleared his throat. "Mary, are you sure that you want to join the church? Once baptized, you will be a full member. We expect a lot from our members—attendance at church and helping each other when needed. I know you were in an Amish church back in Pennsylvania, but we are stricter here. We try to keep out all worldly influences and live as plain as possible."

"I grew up in the Amish faith," Mary said softly. "And I have been baptized in another Amish church. I am ready to recommit my life to God."

"We are sure you are, Mary," Moses said.

"Now what about you, Joseph? This is a lot different from the Mennonite faith. Are you sure?" James asked.

"I'm ready; the world has nothing for me. I truly wish to live as plain as possible and raise my family in God's ways," Joseph said sincerely.

"We will give you a try, Joseph. You will be under observation for a while, but then again so are many of our members. You will be alright if your heart is pure," Moses said as he stood up.

"Only God can see the heart in all of us," James said.

"How are you all doing with the farm here? Any money problems?" Moses asked.

"It is hard getting everything in working order," Joseph said. "Sometimes I feel like we are scraping the bottom of the barrel."

"That sounds like the woman in the Bible whose oil never ran out," James said. "It doesn't mean that your oil might not get a little thin. Or that you might not have to scrape the bottom of the barrel. It just means that it won't run out with God's help."

"Life is often a battle of your faith and your will. To give up on God would be easy, but he that endures to the end shall be saved,"

Moses said. "To endure means that you are going to go through some rough times here on this earth. He that puts his hand to the plow and then looks back is not fit for the kingdom of God."

"Sometimes it is all a man can do to hold on to the plow," Joseph said. "I think God must have been a farmer to mention a plow."

"I think I have my Scripture now for this week's sermon," James said.

"What would that be?" Moses asked, smiling.

"There is a time for everything in the seasons, a time to plant and a time to take up what was planted," James said.

"He is ready alright," Mary said.

"We are sorry to hear about your barn burning. Is there anything we can do to help?" Moses asked.

"Nay, the barn needed to be torn down anyway," Joseph said.

"Joseph, do you think that someone is trying to cause your family harm?" James asked. "You haven't done anything to offend anyone have you?"

"Nay, I don't think so; maybe they are trying to run us off. I haven't offended anyone that I know of," Joseph said. He didn't want to worry anyone, especially the deacons, about his problems. He wanted to make sure he knew who it was that had been bothering his family before he said anything.

"If you need help, let me know," Moses said.

"Denki for coming out. Your Scripture quotes were spiritually uplifting," Joseph said.

"God always knows what we need," Moses said.

They were getting ready to leave when a brown and dusty UPS truck approached the farm quiet rapidly. The driver pulled in and stopped, getting out with a long package and a clipboard.

"I am looking for Joseph," the driver said as Joseph walked toward him.

"That'll be me," Joseph said, smiling.

"Sign right here." The driver handed Joseph the clipboard to sign. "Have a good day," he said, taking the clipboard back. He climbed in the van and left stirring up dust.

"Did you order something, Joseph?" Mary asked curiously.

"No, not that I can remember." Joseph laid the package down on the porch and opened it up with his pocket knife. Inside was his daed's Marlin thirty-thirty hunting rifle and a note from Bishop Adam back in Pennsylvania.

Joseph,

I know you left me this rifle as a gift, and I appreciate it. But I didn't feel right accepting it. I know this gun meant a lot to you and was the only thing you had left that belonged to your daed. Please write and let me know that your family is doing okay.

You will be in our prayers,

Adam.

"Are you sure that a hunting rifle is a good idea around your family?" Moses asked.

"Jah, it's the only thing I have left that belonged to my father," Joseph said. "And I love to hunt."

"Well, you be careful around these children." James frowned. "We don't want anybody to get hurt."

Soon the bishop and deacon were on their way, leaving as quickly as they came.

"Do they always act so stern?" Joseph asked Mary, handing her the rifle.

"Just until they get to know you and figure out your intentions," Mary said. "Sometimes they may not seem very friendly, but they mean well."

"Well, the Bible says to know those that labor among you, so we have to honor that," Joseph said. "Mary, put the gun up in a safe place until I can do something with it. Now I must get back to work; call me when dinner is ready."

Joseph stopped an hour later to eat and then went back to work. It was dark outside now. When he finally came down, he had the roof fixed.

Now he could move on to other things.

Going inside, he had two things on his mind, a bath and a bed. The water they had inside was pumped with a hand pump in the washroom. They did have gas heat, a blessing in itself, and a gas cook stove. They also had a fireplace in the house as well so they could burn wood. A lot of Amish still had a coal and wood stove.

"I have already heated your bath water," Mary said.

"What a woman," Joseph said, smiling.

"You have worked hard today," Mary said.

"I was thinking about what the bishop said," Joseph said. "We should take time to count our blessings, not our possessions. If a man has food on the table and a roof over his head, he is blessed."

"I think not worrying shows our Heavenly Father that we trust Him to take care of us," Mary said. "Sometimes people just don't realize how blessed they truly are."

It was a beautiful morning. Mary had breakfast on the table when Joseph woke up—the way he liked it. Walking barefoot into the kitchen on the oak floor, Joseph sat down to eat.

Sharon had gotten up and joined them as well. "Gut morning, Joseph," she said cheerfully.

"Gut morning, Mother," Joseph said.

The family was all there now, the twins and Rebecca.

"What are you going to work on today?" Mary asked.

"Nothing. Today is a holiday," Joseph said. "On Monday we will start plowing. I'm going to take the boys deer hunting on our farm today. We could use some fresh meat."

He didn't tell them that they needed fresh meat bad. Another man might share all his financial difficulties with his wife. He felt that sharing the burden with his wife might make her worry, and he thought it also showed distrust in God. How much money a man has is between him and God. Of course Mary had done all the cooking, so she had to know about the meat running low. Hopefully, she would think he had been too busy to go buy some more.

"My father built a tree stand on the far side of the property," Sharon said. "There is a stream nearby. I honestly don't know what kind of shape it is in. You can actually do better hunting higher up, because the animals can't smell you."

"You're right, Mother. We'll go there and check it out," Joseph said.

"Will we get to climb up in a tree house?" Benjamin asked.

"If we can find it," Joseph said. "Now I have to harness Lucky up right quick, we will take him with us. When you boys get done eating, please feed the mare and the chickens. And tie Pilgrim up to keep him from following us."

A few minutes later, they headed out for the woods, moving slowly. A lot of the land was flat, though it had a lot of trees here. A deer can hide about anywhere; they usually travel more in the morning and evening. Joseph was leading Lucky while Benjamin and Caleb rode the stud horse.

Joseph carried his daed's old thirty-thirty rifle, which was a good gun in the brush. He didn't want to shoot a gun that would fire a long way in this wide open territory.

"Boys, let me give you a lesson about gun safety," Joseph said. "Too many people have been hurt hunting, and it is mostly due to negligence. A bullet can travel a long way, some up to a mile. A man should never point a gun at anything unless he plans to shoot it. And keep it pointed at the ground when you're not using it."

"Do we get to shoot today?" Caleb asked.

"It will be a few more years. First you must know how to handle them safely," Joseph said. "Always look behind your target;

where is the bullet going to go if you miss? Is there a bank behind your target, something there to stop it?"

"It makes sense," Benjamin said.

The going was slow, and they traveled quietly, for a man must sneak up on his prey. Getting close to where the tree stand was, Joseph tied the stallion to a big tree well out of gun range. They would go the rest of the way on foot.

Maybe the deer wouldn't spook if they smelled the horse, he didn't know, but they were not going to take any chances. A deer can smell well, especially if the wind is blowing right.

"You know, boys," Joseph said. "The American Indian would stretch a deer hide over themselves to make the deer think he smelled one of their own. Every animal meant something to the Indian, and they never killed unless they intended to eat it. And like the Indian, we must give denki to God for providing the meal."

"I wouldn't take a deer's life for nothing," Benjamin said.

"I don't think he would even kill a deer," Caleb said, smiling.

"Come on, boys, let's go," Joseph said, helping them down off the horse. Sometimes he thought too much, but it was through the thoughts that God speaks to a man.

Joseph stopped in the trail. "Boys, let's pray a silent prayer before we hunt. It is God that sends the wildlife our way. He knows our needs, and that we will not be wasteful."

Then they were on their way, traveling quietly. The boys were still sleepy. It was still dark out. He could barely see the trail in front of them. Joseph grabbed his light. He didn't want to use it unless he had to. The trail loomed on ahead of them and looked mysterious.

"The woods seem scary," Benjamin said.

"Jah, a man seems afraid of the dark, what you can't see," Joseph said. "It is easy in the woods to feel like you are the one being hunted. You could very well be. A bear is an animal a man doesn't want to tangle with. Bears have been known to sneak up and attack a man in the woods."

They finally reached the tree stand. Holding his light up, Joseph made sure that the boards to climb with were secure and that the tree house was in stable condition.

"Alright, you all go up first. I will hold the light for you," Joseph said.

Benjamin kind of held back until Caleb stepped up. "I'll go first."

Joseph pushed him up a little to get him started. "Just don't move around a lot until I get up there."

He strapped his gun around his back out of the way. Soon they all made it up. And it felt cozy, blocking off the wind. It was a small building, built out of rough lumber, though it was stained. It had benches built around the sides and places to shoot from. The boys had each brought along a blanket and a small pillow. The darkness was still upon the land. It would be a while before daylight fully set in.

"You all can rest until daylight, if you want," Joseph said.

They sure looked tired right now. Soon they dozed off. Morning would be here soon. Joseph stared out into the darkness. He heard sounds everywhere of animals moving, but he couldn't see anything.

A man should spend time with his children and try to do something with them at least once a week. Too quickly they will be gone. You may have more time with them, once they are on their own, but it is not the same.

It is a good feeling to have a little child call you daed. To them, you can do nay wrong, and you are a hero in their eyes. You are the one they come running to when they are hurt, needing your help. And it is a special time when they will listen gladly to your advice, for a father always knows.

We have a Heavenly Father that looks after us as well; we can find His advice in the Bible. He said He would never forsake us, but go with us all the way.

Joseph finally dozed off, sleeping with the gun in his hands away from the boys. Finally, something woke him; he came awake with a jerk. And out in the field, something was moving.

The boys too were now awake; Joseph motioned to them to be quiet. A few does were drinking from the creek. All was silent, except for the birds as they sang good morning to God above. A few squirrels came out to play, running through the tress to the ground. A few hours passed. The deer grazed, eating of the spring grass before wandering off.

A few turkeys came down for water, followed soon by a gobbler. The boys were now looking at a book they had brought along and chewing on some leftover sausage biscuits that Mary had sent along.

"God bless the women. They sure know how to make a family more comfortable, even in the wilderness," Joseph said.

"They sure do," Benjamin said, smiling.

He enjoyed the time spent with his boys, even though they had to whisper. You had to be quiet when hunting, or you could scare off the game.

Suddenly a doe appeared, followed by a young buck not far behind. It was time. Swinging his gun up slow, Joseph waited until the buck got closer. The deer was about a hundred yards out now. The boys were moving slightly, trying to see what was going on. Joseph became still, sighting in until the shot was his. A shooter knows after a while when he has a good shot. He could see nothing but the deer's side as he shot behind the front leg into the body.

At the shot, the doe left the country moving on. A lot of turkeys hit the air, flying very rapidly in every direction for a few feet. The buck ran about fifty yards after the doe and then went staggering down to the ground.

"Come on, boys, I got him!" Joseph said. They backed slowly down the ladder to the ground.

Joseph took off, walking fast, anxious to see the deer.

"Which way did he go?" Caleb asked, trying to keep up.

They followed a small blood trail to the stretched out deer, a beautiful small spike buck.

"You all stand back; let's make sure he is dead." Joseph nudged the deer with his rifle. "This will be some gut eating, boys. We must thank God now for providing the deer."

Joseph and his sons bowed their heads in a silent prayer. "A man shouldn't shout out loud at the heavens anyway; it isn't right. It is the little things we do in life that please God—like a prayer before a meal, giving denki always that touches His heart."

"Is he dead, Daed?" Caleb asked, looking closely at the deer.

"Jah, you boys go back down the trail and bring up Lucky. Do you think you can handle him?" Joseph asked.

"Sure, Daed, we'll ride him back," Benjamin said.

The boys took off, walking quickly. They were back soon with the horse, both of them riding him.

Joseph had a harness already on him and a swingle tree tied to the back.

"Boys, I think that deer will weigh about two hundred pounds," Joseph said.

"How are we going to pack him home?" Caleb asked as they slid off the horse.

"I have already thought of that, son. We are going to let Lucky pull him." Joseph hooked a tarp under the deer and ran a chain around his front shoulders, hooking it to the swingle tree. "It is better to use your brain instead of your back. You boys get back on him, and we will be off."

The twins climbed up quickly on the horse. Joseph grabbed the plow lines and walked behind the deer to guide the horse. And with a flick of the plow lines against Lucky's side, they were off.

The horse blew loudly, looking back at the deer behind him. And then he went on, tossing his head slightly like it wasn't anything. Joseph stopped once as Caleb climbed up to get their supplies out of the tree house. And then they were on their way.

Joseph was surprised to see a car in their yard when they got back. He walked down to greet the guest, leaving the boys with the deer. A tall man got out of the car; it was Mr. Stevens.

"How are you doing, Joseph?" Stevens asked. "I heard about your barn burning. What will you do now?"

"We will build another," Joseph said.

"I know this must put you in a hard spot financially. So I'm going to raise my offer to a hundred thousand dollars," Stevens said. "I shouldn't have lost my temper last time. That is no way to do business."

"I'll tell Mary about your offer, but I don't think she'll be interested," Joseph said. "Would you like to come in and have breakfast with us? We have plenty of leftovers."

"No thanks, I am late for the bank anyway," Stevens said. "If you change your mind, let me know."

With that, Stevens was gone, the car being driven just a little fast.

CHAPTER TWELVE

Mary was busy fixing dinner for everyone. She stepped outside on the porch for some fresh air. The cook stove was getting a little warm. Sharon was sitting on the porch, a steaming cup of coffee sitting beside her.

"I'm out here enjoying the sunshine," Sharon said.

"It is nice," Mary said. "Have you seen Rebecca?"

"She is hanging the washed clothes out on the line to dry," Sharon said.

Mary turned in that direction and spotted her daughter coming. "Rebecca, did you hang the clothes up high enough so Pilgrim can't get to them? A dog will tear your clothes off the line and play with them."

"Jah, I put them up as high as I could," Rebecca said, carrying a laundry basket.

"We need one of them pulleys that we can turn by hand and run it out to a tree higher up," Sharon said. "That way we can move our clothes back and forth. It lets you put your clothes twelve feet off the ground and tied down with your mother's clothes pins."

"I heard some of the Mennonite women say that their electric bills were getting so high that they couldn't afford them," Mary said. "The way we dry our clothes, there is nay electric bill."

Mary was happy to see Joseph coming in from hunting. It looked like the boys had a deer with them; they could use some fresh meat.

She knew Joseph tried to hide things from her, to keep her from worrying. Though, like Joseph, she had great trust in God. She knew things might get a little rough, but God would take care of them.

Joseph stopped the horse in front of the house, letting them look at the deer.

"He's a big one," Rebecca said, standing on the porch.

"I have been craving some deer meat," Mary said.

"Deer meat should be gut fried in butter and onions, a recipe handed down by my father," Sharon said.

"We will have to try it. Now we have to skin him out. Come on, boys, I need your help," Joseph said.

"I'll bring some hot water in a pan to put the meat in," Mary said.

Joseph drove the horse under the lean-to. He threw a rope across a beam, then using the horse, they pulled the deer up in the air. Once they had the deer off the ground high enough to work on him, they tied him there. Joseph set to work skinning out the deer and gutting him. Soon the shoulders and meat were skinned out.

In a little while, the meat was ready to go to the smoke house. Mary decided to fry some for dinner. Too often, the meat in grocery stores have so many preservatives in it that it doesn't taste like fresh meat. And it's not as good for you health-wise. In fact, buying foods with too many preservatives in them means you often lose the nutriments that God intended for you to have.

Later that evening, an old truck with a rusted horse trailer pulled up into the yard. An older man was driving with two younger men sitting beside him. Joseph counted three horses inside; two had their heads stuck out the back of the trailer. In the back of the truck were three pretty Nubian milk goats.

"I'm Russell Watkins," the man called, getting out of the truck. "We're looking for a man named Joseph that shoes horses."

"That will be me. What are you doing with them goats?" Joseph asked curiously.

"We're taking them to the market to sell," Russell said. "Feed is getting so high that a man can't afford to feed them."

"Can we have one?" Caleb asked.

"Shoe these horses for me, and I'll give you all three goats," Russell said, smiling.

"It's a deal. Bring the horses to the shed, and I'll get started," Joseph said, shaking the man's hand.

Since they had provided the shoes, all he had to do was put them on. It was an even trade; shoeing a horse usually cost about fifty dollars. It is what each of the goats would have sold for at the market.

"How did you all know I shoe horses?" Joseph asked as he finished shoeing the last horse.

"Amos was telling people at the hardware store about your services. If you had some business cards made up, it would help your business. We had a little trouble finding the place," Russell said.

"Come back anytime, boys—except Sundays. We are not permitted to work then. It is the Lord's Day," Joseph said.

"We will spread the word," one of them said as they got in their truck.

"Danke kindly," Joseph said, as they were pulling out.

One man had his window rolled down. He nodded his head, and then they were gone.

Joseph and Benjamin were finishing up the feeding before it turned completely dark outside. Benjamin suddenly pointed out to the corral. It looked like there was a light moving around, maybe somebody carrying a lantern. Joseph saw Mary's daed walking in the field behind where the old barn had stood.

"It is grandpa! Rebecca said.

"He's real!" Benjamin yelled.

"Let's go see," Joseph said. "It's just somebody playing a prank on us more than likely."

"I'm not going over there," Benjamin said. "You go check it out, Daed."

"All right, I'll be right back," Joseph said, walking forward slowly.

The pranks had been going on long enough; it was time for them to stop.

Joseph came around the side of the dark corral where the light had been. Looking down in the moonlight, he saw the tracks. A ghost does not leave tracks. Suddenly he bumped into someone in the dark. For a minute, four hands were grabbing, trying to keep their balance. Then something hard hit Joseph on the head. The earth suddenly met him as he went down into the blackness.

Mary heard Benjamin yell for help and came running. Rebecca and Caleb were right behind her.

"What happened, Benjamin?" she asked.

"Daed saw the ghost and went after it. I heard them struggling in the dark," Benjamin said.

"Joseph, where are you?" Mary called.

They heard a moan a few minutes later and rushed forward. Joseph was laying on the ground, not moving.

"Hold the lantern up, Caleb, where we can see," Mary said.

The light revealed Joseph, coming around now. He had a small knot on the side of his head and maybe a black eye that would be revealed in the morning.

"What happened, Daed?" Rebecca asked, kneeling bedside him. She took his hand.

"I bumped into someone in the dark. I think he had one of them metal flashlights, and he hit me with it."

"Are you able to walk, Joseph?" Mary asked.

"Jah, once I get to my feet, I think I will be all right," Joseph said.

"I am sorry about all of this. Maybe we should sell this place, Joseph. There have been too many bad things happening to us. The barn burning and now this." Mary was crying slightly.

Joseph wiped a tear off her face when they helped him to his feet. "Nay, Mary, this place is yours, and we will never sell. I have prayed about this. I honestly don't think they meant us any real harm, or they would have burned the house. They are just trying to scare us away. It was somebody dressed like an Amish man, and he looked just like your daed."

Mary and Rebecca helped Joseph walk slowly into the house. "Just get me to bed, and I'll be alright. And children please don't tell anyone what happened. I don't want to worry anyone," Joseph said.

It was a beautiful day for church and time to be baptized into the faith.

"I know this is a dream come true for you, Mary." Joseph said as they pulled out of the yard with Fiery pulling the buggy.

"Jah, it is," Mary said. "We will finally be part of this community. I feel like I have come home."

Sharon patted her hand lightly. "You are home, my daughter."

"It is hard to believe that Daed and Mamm are getting baptized at their age," Benjamin said, smiling.

"You never get too old to do God's work," Joseph said to the boys.

"A willing vessel is all we must be. God will do the rest; just look at Moses," Sharon said. "I have never seen anyone get baptized with a black eye. What happened to you, Joseph?"

"I bumped into something in the dark," Joseph said.

"It will be nice to be part of a church family again," Mary said.

"I may go visit Hannah this week," Sharon said.

"You can stay with us as long as you want," Joseph said.

"Thank you; though I think I'll stay with Hannah this week. She lives so far way that I don't get to see her much."

"Okay," Joseph said, pulling in for the church service. "You all go ahead. I'll be there shortly."

The service started quickly, and men and women were still taking their seats when he got there. After two hours of sermons, Mary and Joseph knelt to answer the Bishop's questions.

"Joseph and Mary, do you vow to keep your faith? And follow all the rules of the Ordnung for the rest of your lives?" Moses asked.

"Jah, we will," Joseph said.

"I will," Mary said.

"Did Mary black your eye, Joseph?" Moses asked, smiling.

"Nay, I did not." Mary's face turned red.

"Joseph is the first man I have baptized with a black eye," Moses said, laughing. "Well, let's get on with the ceremony."

The deacon's wife removed Mary's cap. The bishop laid his hands on Joseph and Mary's heads, saying a silent prayer for them. And then the deacon poured water dipped from a bucket into the cupped hands of the bishop. The bishop let the water flow onto each head as he baptized them in the name of the Father, the Son, and the Holy Spirit. Each new member was presented with a holy kiss on the cheek, a symbol of brotherly fellowship.

The service continued on for a little while, and a few more songs were sung. Moses went forward, standing behind the small wooden pulpit. "Church is dismissed. And then of course dinner will be served on the ground," Moses said, smiling. "A man should never leave a meeting like this hungry, either spiritually or physically."

"I will say amen to that," Samson said, chuckling.

A lot of people shook their hands after the service, welcoming them into the family.

Most of Mary's family was there, and they played horseshoes until the church congregation left. Joseph and Samson beat everybody at horseshoes until they were finally beat by Jeremiah and John. The day had passed so quickly, but it always does when spent with family and friends.

Mary went to tell her mother goodbye; Sharon had climbed in the buggy with Hannah. Jeremiah stopped their buggy beside Mary before they rode out of the yard. Mary had tears in her eye as she gave her mamm a hug.

"I will be back soon; don't worry. I'm sure we will have more time together," Sharon said as Benjamin, Caleb, and Rebecca gave her a hug.

"I'll get the buggy ready," Joseph said to Mary.

A few minutes later, Joseph and his family pulled out for home. They rode the rest of the trip in silence. It looked like Mary was deep in thought. Arriving home, Joseph and Caleb turned the mare out in the pasture; soon the animals were all fed and had fresh water.

"Come inside when you get done with the chores," Mary said, standing on the porch. "I warmed up some fried chicken, mashed potatoes, and soup beans."

"It sounds gut. We are done anyway," Joseph said. "A woman shouldn't have to cook on Sunday."

"That sounds like a plan, Joseph," Mary said, smiling. "Now let's go eat."

After a silent prayer, they all dove in. The meal wasn't bad warmed up. Mary brought out some snacks later as they sat on the porch watching the sunset. Pilgrim was lying beside Caleb. It felt good to relax a little. Rebecca brought out a checker game, and beat the boys at checkers. All too soon, the gas light was put out. The darkness had arrived, and tomorrow they would start plowing their own land.

Joseph was on his knees praying when Mary came in their bedroom to get ready for bed. She had her hair down and was a striking beauty with her long dark hair.

"How blessed I am," Joseph said, looking at her as he got up.

Mary gave him a swat with her hand. "Now you are just saying that."

Soon everyone was in bed, except for the dog, Pilgrim, as he whined making his rounds. Tomorrow would come early.

Rebecca sat in the shed, reading the letters that Rachel and David had just sent. It had been two weeks since she had received a letter. At first, the letters had come every week. *Surely I am not losing him*, she thought. It was hard having a relationship with someone who lived so far away.

She couldn't call him, and she couldn't see his face. All she had was the letters, and now they had slowed down. She tried to comfort herself, thinking that if this was really true love, then it would last.

As soon as David became of age, he would come for her. There were a few boys in school that wanted her attention, but she would never look at another boy.

She read David's letter first. It was another poem. He had written just a few words of his own. It looked like Rachel was doing well with him. Nobody else had ever been able to teach him anything—though nay one had given him private lessons before either. Still, for some odd reason, David's letters were half as long as they used to be.

Rachel's letter was next.

Dear Rebecca,

I wish you could see the look on David's face as he learns to read. We are spending three evenings a week together fishing at the pond, which is the only place I can get him to study. We are also catching a few catfish; David is an excellent fisher. It is kind of odd, but since you have left, he has become my best friend.

I think you will be pleased when he learns to read. He told me he was doing it so he could write you a letter. I feel so sorry for him. He is almost grown and doesn't know how to read and write, but he is learning, fast. He is ashamed of himself, and keeps it hidden from his mamm and daed.

It seems like the miles between us get longer every day. And I fear we will never see each other again. It is not like living in the modern world were people travel so easily in cars. We have such limited mobility. I do hope we see each other again before we get married. David has developed a special place in my heart. I hope we can be together soon.

Your dearest friend,
Rachel

Suddenly a strange feeling hit Rebecca. She could see it as plain as day. Rachel was trying to take her boyfriend from her. They were spending too much time together. And Rachel had always had a crush on him.

She read the line again about him developing a special place in Rachel's heart. And then the tears came. Sitting there on the bale of hay, she cried her heart out. She should have known that it would come to this. Why did they have to move so far away? By the time she made it back home, David would be practically engaged.

"Rebecca, is everything alright?" Her father opened the door, and she jumped, startled.

"Oh Daed, I didn't know that you were there," Rebecca said, crying more now. She couldn't stop the tears.

"Jah, I was finishing up my chores. I didn't mean to barge in on you." Joseph pulled her to him, giving her a hug. "Come now, it can't be that bad can it?"

"It's just that I miss Rachel and David so much," Rebecca said.

Joseph held her while she cried. "Hush now, and as soon as school goes out, I will let you go visit. Hopefully, I can raise the money somehow."

"Do you really mean it, Daed?" Rebecca asked.

"A father should never lie to his children," Joseph said. "The only thing that slows us down is lack of money. I never make a promise I can't keep."

"Daed, I really do appreciate it," Rebecca said, hugging him back. "I know we're having a rough time, so this means a lot to me."

"Rebecca, do you think that you might have feelings for David?"

"I do love him, Daed," Rebecca said, looking him in the eye.

"Well, it's in God's hands," Joseph said. "If it is His will, then it will work out. You do seem a little young to be worrying about such things."

"Oh Daed," Rebecca said, smiling, "what girl doesn't worry about such things?"

"Come on, dear," Joseph said. "Let's go see if your mother has that cake baked that I smelled earlier. We will sit outside on the porch and have a talk."

Chapter Thirteen

Joseph awoke very early. It was still dark out, and somebody was banging hard on his bedroom wall on the outside. Pilgrim was barking with every breath. Mary was shaking him now.

"Joseph get up, there is someone banging on the wall outside."

Joseph dressed quickly and then made his way outside cautiously. He was wondering what was going on. Surely someone wasn't trying to break in on them. Suddenly a figure lunged at him; Joseph threw a punch as he screamed.

Mary came running to him, carrying a lantern in her hand. "What is wrong, Joseph?"

Joseph now saw what had scared him. John was bent over double as he laughed.

"I can't believe you lazy people are still in the bed," John said, smiling. "I wanted to beat Joseph up this morning; I didn't think he would try to hit me though."

"You scared me a little," Joseph admitted.

The children had now come outside.

"Well, you can't work on an empty stomach," Mary said. "I'll go start breakfast now, since we're up before dawn. Come on children; let's go back inside."

"I brought both mules over to plow with; they're hitched up and ready to go," John said.

"You can leave the mules here until we are done plowing if you want," Joseph said. "I will take care of them and give you a ride home in our buggy."

"Gut idea. Now let's go eat." John was still laughing slightly.

They sat around and talked until breakfast was done, drinking some hot coffee. Then after breakfast, they were off to the fields to do some plowing. The big, powerful, black mules were soon tearing the earth up, leaving behind a trail of broken loose dirt. Joseph held some dirt in his hands, letting it run through his fingers. It looked like very rich soil.

"It will probably take about two weeks of work to get done, one to plow and one to plant," John said, stopping the mules beside him.

"Jah, I will be glad to get it done," Joseph said. "Next year, Lord willing, I would like to have my own team of horses to plow with."

"You had better say some prayers, if you plan to plow with a pair of Haflingers," John said, laughing at him.

"They will out pull your mules next year," Joseph said.

John snorted. He was a mule man.

"Take a break; I'll plow some." Joseph grabbed the reins.

They worked on, stopping only to eat and take a break. As darkness began to take over the land, Joseph decided it was quitting time.

"Caleb, you and Benjamin go hitch the horse up to the buggy, so we can take John home," Joseph said.

"Alright Daed," Benjamin said. The boys were back a few minutes later, Caleb driving the buggy.

"We will ride with you, so you will have company on the way back," Benjamin said.

John walked slowly to the buggy. "Every bone in my body is sore, I believe."

"I know the feeling," Joseph said, climbing into the buggy.

With a flick of the reins, they were on their way. They could barely see the road, except in places that the moon favored. The house was up ahead now.

"I appreciate your help, John." Joseph drove him up in front of his house.

"We are a big help to each other," John said. "Are you all coming in for a few minutes?"

"Nay, we had better get back and take a bath. Plowing comes early it seems," Joseph said.

"Try to be up in the morning Joseph. Don't sleep in on me." John laughed as he got out of the buggy.

"I'll be up," Joseph said, smiling. He brought the reins down, and the mare took off.

Joseph was working on the pasture fence on their farm.

He could see what had happened by the tracks. Somebody had ridden a four wheeler up next to the fence and cut it down with a pair of wire cutters. The property here joined Ron Harmony, a neighbor who raised cattle, and some of his cattle had strayed onto Joseph's property.

Joseph and the boys were running the cattle back out now. Pilgrim was trying to help, though he did put the cattle scooting fast. It was a sight to watch the dog work, almost tirelessly going after each cow that tried to run off.

"He'll make a gut herding dog," Benjamin said, pointing him after another one.

"It is what he has been bred to do," Joseph said.

"What are you going to do about the fence, Joseph? Should we tell the sheriff what is going on?" Mary asked suddenly.

Joseph jumped; he hadn't realized that Mary had come up behind him.

"I will put it back and that is all," Joseph said. And he did, not say anything about the fence to anyone.

Joseph was putting his tools up in the shed when he saw some empty beer bottles. Maybe whoever had been sneaking around on their farm had been drinking in here. While grabbing the beer bottles, he accidently spilled some beer on his shirt. He would have to change his shirt and throw the nasty beer bottles away.

Stepping outside, he was surprised to see Moses and Deacon James sitting there in their buggy.

"How are you doing, Joseph?" Moses said. "My wife sent some banana bread over. I figured we would come over and check on you."

"Denki," Joseph said. "I just got to throw these empty bottles away. Step up on the porch, and I will join you in a few minutes."

"Something sure smells funny," James said. "What is that you're carrying, Joseph?"

"It is just some empty beer bottles that someone left in the shed. I'm throwing the bottles away." Joseph walked up to the garbage barrel and threw them in.

"You mean somebody sneaked in your shed with you all living right here? And drank four or five beers?" Moses asked.

"I guess so," Joseph said.

"How odd." James cleared his throat, glancing at Moses.

"Well, let's enjoy the banana bread," Moses said. "We will discuss this later. It just looks bad—a new church member with a black eye, carrying beer bottles."

Joseph got up early and hitched Lucky up to the plow. Today was Wednesday, and John was supposed to help him plow today. When John arrived a little later, Joseph was in the field plowing with Lucky. The little horse was plowing as good as a mule. He was built solid and was all muscle. You couldn't tell it by looking at him, but he was a working machine.

"It is about time you let that little pony earn his keep," John said.

"Jah, he hasn't been worked much. I'm trying to condition him in a little at a time."

Lucky was covered with sweat. He looked at the mules kind of funny, tossing his head.

"He doesn't know what to think about your ugly mules," Joseph said, laughing.

"Well, if you are done playing, put him up and let's get to work," John said.

Joseph finished plowing the row he was working on. It usually took two horses or mules to turn your ground up to be plowed. One horse couldn't plow alone; it put too much strain on him. Lucky had done well by himself, but if he had a mate to him, they would be all the plow horses he would need.

Stripping the harness off Lucky, he turned him loose in the corral. The horse went over and lay down in the dirt and rolled over, trying to dry the sweat off. Joseph had been driving him a little with plow lines each evening, teaching him how to drive. It took great patience to train a good work horse.

As John came down to the end of the row, Joseph went to meet him.

"Joseph, I need to ask you something," John said. "Bishop Moses came over and asked me if I knew if you drank beer. They saw you carrying beer bottles out of the shed."

"Jah, somebody left some empty bottles in there," Joseph said. "I hope it didn't make me look bad."

"I think they are going to have a church meeting about it. I told him you didn't drink," John said. "It is a gut thing that you have already been baptized before this happened."

"Denki John, for speaking up for me," Joseph said. "There is something I need to get your advice on. I have a little extra wood. Do you think that we all could pitch in and build Sharon a two room house? We can build it right on the back of our house? Mary misses her Mother so much, and I think Sharon would be more comfortable in her own place."

"I will talk to my brothers and see what they think. It would make it nice if she was closer. Hannah lives so far away."

"Thank you; only don't say anything to Mary until we know that we can do it. I don't want to disappoint her."

"You are a gut man Joseph, and I rarely say that...just stay away from those beer bottles," John said, smiling. "I do think Mother would like it here. I will take off early today; it will give me time to get in touch with my brothers. We will start in the morning, if at all possible."

Mary was ringing the diner bell. They had switched out plowing several times already. The mules looked beautiful today, and yet as ugly as ever. When a man can see beauty in a mule, then he has a good heart indeed, either that, or he is in love.

The goats came running along the pasture fence following them. The young Boer Billy goat hit the fence with his horns.

"He will make a mean goat," John said. "How many goats have you got, Joseph?"

"I have fifteen nanny goats, and one Billy goat," Joseph said. They had now arrived at the porch, walking quickly for dinner.

"Most people don't want to pay Joseph with money. They keep giving him animals for shoeing horses," Mary said.

"They all say they don't have much money, and Daed won't turn them down," Rebecca said, smiling.

"Well, a man can always start eating them," John said, laughing.

"You can't eat my goat," Caleb said as he came outside.

"Don't forget the chickens; we've got a lot running loose on this place. Joseph won't let the other chickens in the pen with his Silver Laced Wyandottes," Mary said.

"They will eat everything in your garden," John warned.

"We will have to butcher some of them before the planting," Joseph said.

Benjamin rolled his eyes. "There is nothing I hate worse than killing chickens."

"You are not the only one," Caleb said. "I think I would rather clean out a horse stall."

"You boys have your chores done?" Joseph asked.

"Jah sir," Benjamin said.

"Gut, then we are ready to eat," Mary said. "I made John's favorite food: catfish."

"Where did we get catfish?" Joseph asked, smelling the soup beans.

"Rebecca took the boys fishing this morning down at the pond."

"We caught eight big fish," Benjamin said.

"Well, we truly are blessed," Joseph said, smiling.

"Our grandfather stocked that pond years ago. I had forgotten all about it," John said.

Dinner was served on the long oak table. The curtains were all open, taking advantage of God's natural light. Actually, sunlight is the only light you don't have to pay an electric bill on. The oak wood floor was sparklingly clean. It looked like Mary had been hard at work; their laundry was hanging out on the line to dry.

"All heads bowed for the blessing," Joseph said, sitting down.

Soon everyone was done praying, and the food began to make its way around the table.

John grabbed the soup bean bowl and helped himself. When everyone was done eating, Mary brought out some fresh cupcakes.

"Thank you, Mary. You are a gut cook," John said as he grabbed another one. One thing about him, he wasn't ashamed to eat.

"You are welcome, my big brother," Mary said, laughing.

They sat around talking for a few minutes after dinner, catching up on the community news. There wasn't much that got past an observant man, and John clearly paid attention.

"We had better work a few more hours, I have to leave early this evening to take care of something," John said.

"It's not like you to run off from work this early," Joseph said teasingly.

John gave him a stern look and didn't say anything. Going outside, Joseph and John hit the fields for a few more hours of plowing and then quit for the day.

Joseph was taking care of the mules as John pulled out in his buggy, going home. His horse, a fancy trotter, left the yard very rapidly.

David arrived early for his tutoring lesson. His dog, Flint, an Australian Shepherd, was with him. Sometimes he had trouble getting away from the dog. He had opened the buggy door, and Flint had run and jumped in. He didn't have the heart to throw him out. He was red and white spotted, a very beautiful dog.

He had brought a picnic basket this time, wanting to surprise Rachel. She had always brought their food before, which was nice of her. He didn't know what he would do without her. She had just turned fourteen, but she was very mature for her age.

Rachel came out on the porch when the buggy pulled up into the yard. Flint stuck his head out the side of the buggy.

"I see you brought your dog with you," Rachel said, scratching the dog's ears.

"I couldn't get away from him, but he is gut company."

David got out to help Rachel get in the buggy.

"You all take your time," Ruth said. "If you catch us some catfish, I will invite you over for dinner, David."

"We will do our best." David helped Rachel in.

"David, if I didn't know any better, I would think that you are trying to be my son in law since you come over here so much," Ruth said.

David felt his face get warm.

"Mamm, please don't tease him, you know he cares for Rebecca," Rachel said.

"Don't pay me any mind." Ruth handed Rachel her spelling books.

It didn't take long to get to the pond. David jumped down quickly to help Rachel. Flint had already dived out and was exploring. Rachel stumbled and fell into David's arms. He grabbed her, knocking her cap off in the process.

David looked at her, long brown hair, which hung down to her waist. She was beautiful. The little girl he had grown up with was not little anymore. He was spell bound by something he couldn't control.

Leaning forward, he kissed her lips, and she kissed him back passionately. He never thought he could have such feelings for her; she had always just been a good friend.

After a moment, she pushed him back. "David, we must not do this. You are a gut friend, but you are courting Rebecca. You must decide what you are going to do. Until then, we must remain friends only."

"You are right. I do respect you for that," David said. "I got carried away for a minute when I saw your hair uncovered. That is something only your husband is supposed to see. You will make some man a gut wife."

"Alright, let's go fishing then," Rachel said, not looking at him.

David nodded, getting their fishing poles. The rest of the day, he did not enjoy. There were too many thoughts raging through his mind.

Mary was cooking breakfast when she heard something coming from outside. Joseph hadn't been up long and was getting ready for the day. Pilgrim was barking up a storm outside. She had never heard him bark that loud before. She heard a lot of voices. It sounded like a lot of people were outside. Maybe John had brought his whole family with him today.

Stepping out on the porch, she saw a few buggies pulling into the yard, and two wagons loaded down with wood. It couldn't be, but it was; most of her family was here. Maybe they had come to help Joseph with the plowing, but why so many? John was in front with Elizabeth and all their children. They were followed by the rest of her brothers. Everyone had come except for Hannah, who must have stayed with Sharon, though her husband, Jeremiah, was among those outside. They all came on and stopped in front of the house.

"Have you got breakfast ready for all of us?" Samson asked.

"I didn't know there were going to be so many of you. We were only expecting John."

"What kind of brothers do you think we are?" Lewis asked, smiling.

"What is going on?" Mary asked.

"We are going to build Sharon a two room house. Joseph asked us to help," Lewis said.

"We had better get started." Herman stopped his wagon loaded down with lumber and set the brake. Herman's wife, Linda, jumped down along with their children.

The farm was swarming over with people that were related to her.

"You should have plenty of help for dinner." Noey stopped behind Herman with the other wagon of lumber. Down jumped Noey's wife, Rachel, his three daughters, and their two sons.

"I already fed everyone this morning; I knew you weren't expecting them. And Joseph wanted this to be a surprise," Elizabeth said.

Joseph was standing there, not saying anything, just watching her face. She had forgotten her manners in all the commotion.

"Oh danke, Joseph, this is the best surprise you have ever given me," she said, grabbing his arm.

"You are worth it, my dear," Joseph said quietly.

"Where is Mamm and Hannah?" Mary asked John.

"We don't want her to know until it is done," John said.

"Well, we had better get started," Samson said, leading the way.

Joseph and John started plowing; the rest went to work building the two room house. It would be just a small place, but one person doesn't need all that much room. Her mother would have her own privacy and be near her grandchildren.

Mary looked back at the house a few hours later. Some people were sawing boards, a few were carrying wood, and some were doing the framing. Benjamin and Caleb were helping pack boards, along with John's three boys. It felt good to see a family working together so well.

The women were inside, preparing dinner. Elizabeth sent Rebecca and a few of the girls out with refreshments, and the cookies and lemonade disappeared fast. Mary went inside and got some lemonade and cookies for Joseph and John. She made her way slowly to Joseph, trying not to drop the tray.

"How are my two favorite men?" Mary asked as she gave them a drink.

John smiled at her, "Just fine, Mary."

"Joseph, about them chickens you wanted to kill later, I could really use them today," Mary mentioned.

"Take whatever you need. Just don't touch my Silver Laced Wyandottes. Get the boys to catch the chickens. Throw some corn in the crib, and they should follow."

"Okay," Mary raised up on her toes slightly and kissed Joseph on the cheek. "Denki again, Joseph."

Chapter Fourteen

Joseph nodded and went back to work. As Joseph plowed, he looked at all the kinfolk. There was so much going on. The smaller children were playing outside. It looked like five women were helping Mary cook dinner. At one point, Joseph heard Mary holler at Caleb and Benjamin to help her. Corn was thrown in the crib; the extra chickens went in after the corn, and the butchering began.

Most English women shy away from things like killing chickens, but to an Amish woman, it was just a way of life.

He saw Caleb coming to the crib with the hatchet; Mary had elected him to cut the chickens' heads off. Elizabeth came out with a big wash tub. Carlonia, Rachel, Linda, and Malena followed Elizabeth outside, carrying buckets of hot water. They soon were busy plucking the chickens and preparing dinner. With that many Amish women cooking, a man should eat well anyway.

Malena was an excellent cook; her favorite dessert was Oreo pie cake. Carlonia often baked friendship bread, banana bread and other treats. Sometimes she mailed them to her kinfolk.

Joseph smiled, watching every one giving of their time. He had always found a joy in giving what he could afford to people who were in need. He had never out given God. God had always paid him back. Giving of his time, a time set aside for each other, was one of the best gifts he had ever given.

Mary probably didn't have a lot of years left with her mother, so Joseph wanted them to be near each other. He knew how it felt to lose a mother; it was not easy by any means.

He plowed on a little longer and then switched out with John. Mary waved at him now as he walked across the plowed field to her.

"Joseph, can you set up some picnic tables? There are too many of us to eat inside. The table isn't long enough," Mary said.

"Sure." Joseph slipped through the rail fence.

Samson walked over to meet him. "You need any help, Joseph?"

"Sure, we need to set up a few tables for dinner."

"Nay problem. The quicker we get it done, the sooner we can eat," Samson said, laughing.

It didn't take long to move the picnic tables out to the center of the yard. John's girl, Sarah, came out with some tablecloths she had brought.

"Dinner is just about ready, Joseph," Sarah said.

"Denki, Sarah, you're the best," Joseph said.

"It will be hard to keep the boys away from you in a year or so," Samson said.

Sarah just smiled; she was going to be a beautiful woman someday.

"The most important thing is that she is a lady," Joseph said as Sarah was walking off.

"The heart does matter the most. A woman should be pretty on the inside first," Samson said.

Mary stepped out on the porch and rang the dinner bell. The women were carrying the food outside, fresh fried chicken, along with all the trimmings. Everybody came forward, anxious to eat. Soon they were all seated.

"It looks like the framers got done before the carpenters," Herman said.

The small two room house was just about done; it stood erect, lacking some flooring and a roof.

"We'll be done with it before dark," Lewis said.

Joseph cleared his throat. "Let's bow our heads for grace." All heads bowed for a few minutes of silent prayer. "Amen," Joseph said after a long moment.

Mary had sat down beside him with their children. "Will your mother like it here?" Joseph asked.

"She had better, or we built a house for nothing," Jeremiah spoke up.

"How did you get away from Hannah?" Mary asked.

"I told her that Joseph needed help today. She thought we would be plowing," Jeremiah said. "They'll both be surprised."

"Everyone is welcome to spend the night here," Joseph said.

"We will make you a bed somewhere," Mary said, laughing.

"Thank you, but we'll probably all go back tonight," Herman said. "Feeding comes early in the morning, and we all have a lot to do."

"We took a break from our planting to build mother a room," Noey said.

They sat around a while, everybody eating well. Mary seemed so happy to be spending time with her family.

"What about dessert?" Samson asked as Herman laughed at him.

"I'll be right back," Mary said. She came back with enough fried apple pies for everyone.

After a few minutes, Samson went back and grabbed two more pies. "In case I get hungry working," he said to Mary with a grin.

"He doesn't do enough work to get hungry," Herman said.

"He is one of the hardest workers I have ever seen," Carlonia said, taking Samson by the arm.

Herman just laughed and didn't say anything else. Sometimes it is best not to rile a woman.

"Well, let's go back to work. We still have a lot of plowing to do," John said standing up. "We may get done today."

Joseph got up as well. "Yes, we had better get started."

"We should have the rooms under roof today," Herman said.

"Joseph may have to finish up the rooms, and put something in them to heat with."

Samson went and got two big windows wrapped in plastic. "I bought the windows for mother. These should give her enough light in the rooms."

"That will work," Herman said, smiling.

"We already have the door up if you want to see," Noey said to Mary.

"Well, let's go look right quick before we start working," John said.

Everybody got up ready to work and walked around to the back of the house. The two rooms they had built for Sharon had a side door to them. Sharon wouldn't be able to walk from her rooms into Joseph's house, but she could walk around and come in their front door.

"This will be like having her own apartment," Mary said as Noey walked them inside.

Lewis was busy putting down a hardwood floor. The rest were working on the roof and rolling out the insulation for the walls.

"I've about got the floor down," Lewis said. "Next I will start putting the insulation up. Joseph, we will leave the wall boards for you to put up. We are not going to have time to finish them." He was the best carpenter in the bunch, especially when it came to the trim work.

"I'll finish the rooms up in my spare time," Joseph said. "I think Sharon will like these rooms."

"Jah, she will have it looking like a home in nay time," John said. "Now we had better get back to the plowing."

Joseph and John walked back to the field to finish the plowing.

"Yelp, mule, get up." John grabbed the plow.

As the evening wore on, they stopped once to take a break. The women came out at different times to see if anybody needed anything to drink.

They were getting close to finishing the plowing. "I think

we can be done in a couple of hours. We may have to finish up tomorrow," John said.

"Jah, we're cutting it close," Joseph said, leaning on the plow. "It looks like the men have the roof on the house anyway."

He saw them loading up their tools and the extra lumber that was left over. Soon Samson and Jeremiah came the edge of the field, watching.

"They're probably wondering what is taking us so long," John said, laughing.

Samson's mules were bigger than the mules John had. Jeremiah also had a big pair of mules, breed out of a draft horse, and they were wider than most mules. They were standing there talking, pointing their way. Samson unhitched his team of mules, driving them forward; he hitched them up to a plow. Samson followed Jeremiah with another plow he had brought with him.

"It won't take long now," John said, smiling.

Joseph went out to meet Samson and Jeremiah.

"Where do you need us?" Jeremiah asked, stopping his mules.

"You can start plowing over there on the far side of the pasture, and we will work our way over to you," Joseph said.

"Gut idea. It won't take long now," Samson said, flexing his muscles. He took off.

With three teams of mules plowing, they made good time. Row after plowed row kept bringing them closer, and they didn't stop any to talk. It was getting close to dark. One hour and fifteen minutes later, the plowing was done. They stopped in the middle of the field to let the mules rest. The mules were all lathered up.

"Thank you," Joseph said. "You don't know how much I appreciate you."

Samson laughed. "You take gut care of Mary. That is all we can ask."

"Well, let's put the mules up, and head for home," John said. "It is about dark anyway."

They made their way stiffly back to the house. Samson and

Jeremiah hitched their team of mules back up to their buggies. The rest were rearing to go. Their families were getting in the buggies and two wagons.

Mary went around to all her brothers and gave them a hug.

"We will be back soon," Herman said, returning her hug.

Lexi, Herman's daughter, came forward and hugged Rebecca and Mary. She was a small girl with blond hair and blue eyes.

"Lexi you are very pretty," Mary said.

"Denki, Mary," Lexi said, smiling. She went quickly to the wagon and climbed in.

"We had best be on our way, Mary." Herman gave the team a loud slap with the reins.

"God bless you all." Mary waved as they were pulling out.

The buggies rolled by, children waving. Turning around in a circle in the yard, they were on their way. Mary stood there and watched them leave; Joseph and the children stood beside her. Mary's family left the yard and went out of sight.

"Have you had a gut day, Mother?" Joseph asked.

"Jah it has been a very gut day," Mary said, taking his arm.

"Well, boys, let's get the animals taken care of, and then we can have the rest of the evening off," Joseph said.

Soon all the farm animals were fed and watered and the chicken eggs gathered. They made their way into the house where Mary was heating up some bath water.

"Have we got any left-over chicken?" Joseph asked.

"Jah, there is plenty," Mary said, smiling.

"Gut, just warm it up. Nay sense in you cooking anymore today. You have done enough," Joseph said.

Joseph was surprised to hear a loud knock on their door.

"Who could it be at this hour?" Mary went to the door and opened it.

Deacon James was standing there, holding his hat in his hands.

"Please come in, James," Mary said.

"I am sorry to bother you at this hour, Joseph. Have you all got a minute? I need to talk to you and Mary alone." James stepped inside, hanging his hat up.

"We can talk at the table," Joseph said. "The children are all in bed."

"I am sorry to be the bearer of bad news, but the church deacons voted against you, Joseph." James sat down in a chair.

"What has he done?" Mary asked, leaning forward.

"When we came out here the last time, he was seen carrying beer bottles," James said. "It is where he has been a Mennonite for so long that some church members are afraid that he hasn't truly adopted our ways."

"I was just throwing the empty beer bottles away. Somebody left them in the shed." Joseph put his head down on the table. He wasn't going to tell James that somebody had been playing pranks on them.

"The thing is, Joseph, some people believe now that you are a drinking man," James said.

"What will they do?" Mary asked.

"Your family is allowed to come to church, Mary—except for Joseph. He has been put on probation until the bishop says otherwise. I hope you do not miss church, Mary, on account of this." James stood up, sliding his chair back in under the table.

"We won't be back to church, me or my children!" Mary said, crying now.

"Do you believe Joseph is innocent?" James asked.

"I know he is," Mary said.

"My family will be at every church service. I will make sure that they don't miss." Joseph shook James's hand. "I will sit outside in the buggy while they attend church service."

"Well, you have a gut attitude anyway," James said. "That means a whole lot." He grabbed his hat, put it on, and left quickly.

"Joseph let's pray together before we go to bed," Mary said, grabbing Joseph's arm.

"Why is everybody against me, Mary?" Joseph followed her

into the bedroom. He kneeled down beside the bed to pray, holding back the tears.

"It is just that they don't know you." Mary kneeled beside him. "Once they see that you are a gut man, they will accept you."

Soon the prayers were said, and the little house was quiet. The gas light was put out. All was still now, because they had all worked very hard today.

Mary awoke before dawn and got up; it was time to make breakfast. It was still early spring. She was looking forward to planting some flowers around their home. She was surprised about how far along the farm had come in such a short time.

She couldn't wait until her mother could be with them. Joseph had made it possible by getting her brothers to help. She was so proud of Joseph; he had always given so unselfishly all his life.

She fired up the gas stove up; she was grateful for it. There had been many times that she had to cook on a wood stove in her life. Natural gas was something that they were allowed to have, though the Amish religion forbade electricity. Life has too many distractions. How can we hear our Heavenly Father with all the noise in a house?

Not long afterward, she had their breakfast on the table. Rebecca was still asleep; the girl usually helped her with the cooking. She must have worn herself out yesterday. Mary stepped out on the porch for a moment; there was a cool mist in the air.

Going back in the house, she knocked loud on their bedroom door. "Come and eat, Joseph." She heard him getting up. "Rebecca, breakfast is ready. Boys, get up please." She knocked on all the bedroom doors as she went down the hall.

She heard feet hitting the floor; the children were coming. "You should have woke me up early, Mother. I would have helped you cook," Rebecca said as she sat down at the table.

"I figured you needed some extra rest," Mary said as the twins sat down rubbing their eyes.

"Gut morning, Mother," Benjamin said.

"Morning, Mother," Caleb said.

"Gut morning, children," Mary said.

Joseph joined them at the table. "I sure have a lot of work to do today."

It was then that the rain came. The rain came slowly as they ate their breakfast. By the time everyone was done eating, it was pouring outside.

"Joseph, you are going to get wet today," Mary said, laughing.

"It may quit directly. Anyway, is it supposed to rain all day?" Joseph asked Mary.

"How do I know? You are an Amish man now, and we don't even have a radio," Mary said, laughing.

The children laughed with her. Caleb about fell out of his chair.

"I thought you might have heard the weather report from your brothers," Joseph said.

"They are all Amish men," Rebecca said, laughing.

"Alright, I quit, I am just used to my Mennonite ways. I grew up with a radio, and we always knew what the weather was going to be," Joseph said, getting up.

The rain was even louder than before, beating down now. It sounded like a bad storm had rolled in. Joseph was looking out the window, watching it rain.

"I know what the weather is going to be today," Caleb said loudly.

"What is it?" Joseph asked.

Caleb cocked his head, listening to the rain. "They are calling for lots of rain today," he said, laughing.

"That reminds me of a weather rock I saw at a flea market," Joseph said. "At least the man said it was a weather rock. You just set it outside, and when you see snow on it, then it is snowing, wet it is raining."

"I have never heard of a weather rock," Benjamin said, laughing.

"Well, it is true they do sell one," Rebecca said. "Daed, if we have to stay indoors for a while today, can we play some board games?"

"Jah, and we can catch up on our reading," Mary said.

"I don't mind reading in the winter, sitting in front of a fireplace, but this is spring," Joseph said.

"Well, it must be God's will," Mary said, laughing.

They sat around until noon, waiting on the rain to stop. At times it slacked off, but it would come again, twice as hard.

"It would be nice to have a tin roof, we could lay in bed and sleep gut, listening to the rain," Joseph commented.

"Maybe on Sundays anyway," Mary said, smiling.

It was after dinner that Joseph began to get uneasy. "I wonder how long it is going to rain; all of the horses are standing out in the rain."

"Lord have mercy, John's mules are soaked to the skin," Mary looked out the window. "I wish we had a barn."

Joseph stood up. "Boys, get your raincoats on; we're going to build a barn."

"You can't build a barn in this weather," Mary said.

"Where there is a will, there is a way," Joseph said. "I am going to push the buggy out from under the lean-to, and cover it with a tarp. Then we can partition off some walls to hold the animals in until this weather breaks."

"That just might work," Mary said, smiling.

"Jah, it will work. You tend to your biscuits, woman, and I will tend to the horses," Joseph said.

"If you are not careful, your biscuits will be burnt," Mary said.

Joseph grabbed his rain coat quickly. "Boys, I will meet you under the lean-to. At least we will have shelter from the rain while we work."

Chapter Fifteen

Joseph headed out to the utility building. The rain continued to come down hard. In a few minutes, his raincoat and his pants were soaked. He moved very rapidly to the lean-to, trying to find shelter. Once inside, he grabbed a tarp and rolled the buggy out away from the building a few feet. Then he set the brake and covered the buggy with the tarp.

By the time the boys arrived, Joseph was ready to build some temporary stalls for the horses. He would need four stalls altogether, two for John's mules and two for his own horses.

"Hang your raincoats up, boys, and let's get to work," Joseph said.

"Okay, Daed," Caleb said as they hung their coats up.

When Mary came out a little later, they had the stalls framed off, and were putting up the last few boards. The rain, surprisingly, hadn't stopped. The rain would slow down some and then come back harder.

"You shouldn't be out here, Mary," Joseph said.

She was soaked through, despite wearing one of his old raincoats.

"I brought you all some leftover ham sandwiches and something to drink," Mary said.

Joseph grabbed a couple bales of hay out of the outbuilding. "Let's sit on these and have our lunch."

The boys gladly agreed, everybody sitting on a bale of hay.

"I bet John is worried sick about his mules, because we don't have a barn," Mary said.

"I will treat his animals like they are my own," Joseph said. "As soon as we are done, the mules will be in a dry stall. And then we can dry them off with a brush."

"John will be happy to know that," Mary said. "This area has been known to flood on occasion. And it has been known to rain for three or four days, especially in the spring."

"I hope not. It will delay our spring planting for another week." Joseph took his hat off and ran his fingers through his hair. "It is a hard land, Mary. Though whatever happens, we must trust God always—in famine, sickness, and in health."

"I try not to doubt God. He is the only thing that has kept me going," Mary said.

Mary was sitting there on a bale of hay eating with them, a very humble lady.

"I am so blessed to have you, Mary," Joseph said. "A woman that will sit down on a bale of hay and eat with you is worth something."

"Denki, Joseph," Mary said, smiling.

"You all finish eating. I will be back with the mules first," Joseph said, getting up. He came back a few minutes later, leading both mules.

"Open the gate, boys," Mary said.

Joseph led the mules inside the dry stalls and then went back for the horses. He brought the buggy mare in first. Once she was inside, he went back for Lucky. The boys were throwing the mules some hay when he got back.

After the animals were fed and watered, Joseph got a brush to dry them off. He took an old blanket and wiped them down. Mary brushed the mare, while the twins took a mule apiece and Joseph gave Lucky a good working over.

"Now the horses are as dry as they would be in a real barn." Mary ran a brush down the mare's shoulder.

"I appreciate the help," Joseph said. "Now I got to take care of the chickens. Then we will be done out here for the day. There is not much we can do in this rain."

"Well, I'll head on in and finish cooking dinner." Mary grabbed her raincoat.

Joseph finished his chores outside; a raincoat sure was handy in this country. He had heard about it flooding to the point where they had had to shut down the interstate for days. The flooding would send a lot of detour traffic through their neighborhood. It was not a welcome sight for an Amish man to see so much traffic coming through his neighborhood. The fast lane and the Amish slow pace of living do not agree.

Joseph was thinking about getting caught up on some of the inside jobs that needed doing. There were places in the house that the floor gave when you stepped on them. After dinner, Joseph repaired the floor inside the house.

He finished up the wall boards in Sharon's room and then installed a small gas heater. He hoped Sharon would like it. Mary and Rebecca put a flower vase on the table and hung hand-sewn curtains for the room. Rebecca spread a new rug down on the floor; it was now ready to go.

Outside, the rain beat on. It seemed like Mother Nature was mad. The water's fury holds back for nay man. Surprisingly, the rain continued on for days without letting up. The creeks and streams around the house were filling up fast, and they now looked like small rivers.

Joseph and his sons put their raincoats on and went out to take care of the animals on the fourth day of the downpour. And then they returned to work on the house inside. After about an hour of work, they were done for the day; the house had been partially remodeled from the inside.

Joseph was bored; he stepped into the living room where everybody was sitting. "You all get ready. We're going for a ride. I'm going to go hook the buggy up. Then we will go."

"We can't go anywhere in this rain," Mary said, laughing.

"Jah we can. Get ready. It has rained for the last four days. I can't take it anymore." Joseph went out the door without looking back.

Joseph pulled up in front of the house to pick up his riders a few minutes later. He got out to help them inside the buggy.

"The rain is slacking off some, Daed," Rebecca said as he helped her inside.

"Hopefully, it is about over with," Joseph said.

Once they were all set, they were on their way. Fiery was picking her hoofs up high on account of all the mud. It looked like the horse was having trouble going with all the mud. Pilgrim came out chasing the buggy, barking with every breath.

"I think he wants to go with us," Benjamin said, laughing.

Joseph stopped the buggy, and the boys loaded the dog up. "He is part of the family too," Joseph said, noticing Mary frowning.

The muddy dog sat down between the boys, looking out the buggy window.

"Where are we going, Daed?" Rebecca asked.

"To see how high the water is and how much damage it has done," Joseph said.

They followed the road slowly, looking at the swelling creek. The water was backing up everywhere. There were a few places where the water was a foot deep in the road.

"Daed, it has stopped raining now," Caleb said.

"Thank God! I know how Noah must have felt now," Mary said.

"Now we have to wait for the water to go back down," Joseph said. "It will take the sun a few days to dry everything up."

Joseph drove on down to the bridge that was a couple of miles below their house. The mare was traveling along smoothly, splashing mud everywhere. Suddenly she stopped. Joseph saw it at once; the bridge was covered with water.

"We are blocked in, my dear," Mary said. "We might as well, turn around."

"Hold on," Joseph set the buggy brake. "You all stay in here."

Going outside, he grabbed a long stick and made his way over to the edge of the creek. He stuck the stick down a few feet, feeling around, trying to hit something under water. When he returned, he turned the buggy around and traveled a few feet.

"What was it, Joseph?" Mary asked.

"The bridge is washed out; we will have to build another one. We are destroyed, Mother, we won't be able to get the crop planted in time. It is like life itself is fighting against us," Joseph said.

"We are not supposed to worry, Joseph," Mary said, touching his arm.

"I know that, but it is easier said than done," Joseph said. "I wish I hadn't come to this God forsaken country. We would have been better off if we had never moved here."

"Joseph!" Mary said.

They rode the rest of the trip in silence, all deep in thought. Joseph rode over the rest of their property; it was in good shape, mostly.

"Well, let's go home, and I will fix us something to eat," Mary said. "Things will look better in the morning."

Joseph didn't say anything. He just dropped them off in front of the house. Then he went to put the mare up and take care of all the animals. When he got his chores done, he sat in the building by himself. A few hours later, Mary rang the dinner hard, trying to get him to come and eat.

Dawn found them up early; all the chores were done before daylight could set in fully. The flood waters were slowly going back down. It usually didn't take long to crest, though everything right now was extremely muddy.

Joseph came through the door with the boys behind him. Mary was standing there with a broom in her hand.

"Boys, take your shoes off before you enter this house. You've got mud caked all over your shoes," Mary said.

"How many boys do you see?" Joseph asked.

"You act like a boy, so I'll treat you like one," Mary said.

They sat down now to eat their breakfast, hot out of the oven.

"I think I will go down and see if the water is off the bridge. Maybe it can be fixed," Joseph said.

"I see you are in a better mood today." Mary poured them all some milk.

"Jah, a man can get down in spirit sometimes. It is just our nature. The most important thing is to never give up," Joseph said. He truly wanted to be a good example for his children.

When everybody got done eating, Joseph went out and, this time, hitched Lucky to the buggy. The horse was going to have to learn at some point. He just wouldn't be a real fast pacer like a Standardbred horse.

He was driving through the yard when he saw the whole family had followed him out.

"Can I go with you?" Caleb asked.

"We will all go," Mary said. "We don't have anything else to do."

"Alright everybody, please climb in quickly," Joseph said, stopping the buggy.

A few minutes later they were on their way.

The goats came out from their shelter underneath the trees in the back pasture and began running along the fence line, wanting something to eat. The young Billy came close to the fence, making a bleating sound.

"That is a gut sign," Joseph said. "Goats only come out when it is real dry. They don't like to get wet."

"The water has gone down a lot overnight," Mary said.

"It is probably flooding people on down the country now," Rebecca said.

The ride to the bridge was a short one. Lucky pulled his load like he enjoyed it, head held proud and his mane and tail blowing lightly in the wind.

Joseph was surprised to see a car parked beside the main road. It looked like it had a flat tire. "I wonder what they are doing out here in this weather?"

"Probably checking out the damage from the flood," Mary said.

Stopping his buggy beside the car, Joseph saw an elderly woman sitting in the driver's seat. She got out of the car to talk to them.

"Hello," she called. "I've been trying to call my husband, but I can't get a signal out here on my cell phone."

"Who is your husband?" Joseph asked. "Does he live around here close?"

"David Stevens. He runs the bank in town. My name is Janet," she said.

"Do you have a spare tire?" Joseph asked.

"Yes, I am just not able to change it," Janet said.

"I'll change it for you," Joseph said, setting his brake.

He got down out of the buggy, and the twins followed him.

"I didn't know you Amish could change a tire," Janet said. "Where do you all live?"

"We live at the last Amish farm down this way off the main road," Joseph said.

"You are not the ones my husband had an argument with are you? He said he tried to buy some land from some very stubborn people."

"That would be us," Mary said, smiling.

Joseph got the spare tire out of her trunk and started jacking her car up.

"You mean you will still help me after you found out who my husband is?" Janet asked. "I know my husband can be a little difficult sometimes. He doesn't have many friends. When you deal with a lot of bank foreclosures, you make a few enemies."

"It is our way to forgive people," Joseph said. "We do not believe in judging. I would have helped even if it had been your husband with a flat."

He soon had the spare tire put on and was lowering her car back down. "That should take care of you. You can stop by and visit us anytime. You are always welcome."

"Please come by and eat some of mamm's peanut butter cookies," Rebecca said.

"Well, I'll tell you one thing. I am going to tell my husband that he has no reason to treat you as bad as he has. I am going to put a stop to it." Janet started her engine up.

She made it a few feet when the car slid into the ditch.

"Hang on, I'll drive it out for you," Joseph said.

"Alright, let me switch sides," Janet climbed over to the passenger seat.

Joseph got in, putting the car in reverse. He backed up slowly, and then put it down in low gear. He punched the gas, bringing the car out of the ditch fast.

"My you can drive," Janet said, smiling.

"Well, cars pull better, in low gear," Joseph said. "Janet, I forgot to tell you that the bridge is out about a mile up the road. You won't be able to get through."

"Well, you might as well turn me around then," Janet said. "And, Joseph, I do thank you."

Joseph drove up the road, looking for a place to turn. There was a wide spot about fifty feet from where the bridge. He saw an Amish buggy driving up to the bank on the other side of the river. He was surprised when the man didn't stop, just slowed down getting a good look at them. The buggy circled around and went back the way it came. It looked like Deacon James was down this way, but Joseph couldn't be sure.

Joseph turned quickly and then drove back up to where Mary was waiting with the buggy. He parked the car and got out. Janet climbed over in the driver's seat and went on her way.

"Do you think that will make a difference in the way Stevens has been treating us?" Mary asked as Janet left.

"Nay matter if it does or not. We must love them anyway. Only God can make a change in somebody's life," Joseph said.

When Joseph got close to the bridge, he saw that it was completely gone.

"They should have anchored the bridge down," Joseph said. "The next bridge we build we'll have to hook a cable to it and anchor it to the two trees there."

Joseph climbed out of the buggy and was looking at the water when he heard a buggy coming. It was John with a wagon load of small logs. He had Samson's mules pulling them. Behind him was a buggy coming with some of the men from church.

"I came out here the other day and saw the damage," John said. "I figured you might need some help rebuilding the bridge."

Mary got out with the children.

"How are my mules doing?" John asked.

"Joseph built a stall and put them in under the lean-to. They are snug and warm," Mary said.

"I knew I could trust him." John breathed a sigh of relief.

"Mary, take the buggy and go back to the house and fix us all something to eat for dinner in a couple of hours," Joseph said. "It shouldn't take that long to build the bridge with everybody helping."

"Okay," Mary said, walking back to the buggy with the children. Mary turned the buggy around then stopped beside him. "Joseph, I told you not to worry." She brought the reins down quickly and they were off.

"Well let's get to work." John climbed down out of the wagon.

John raised the first log up and dropped it across to Joseph. It was long enough to reach across easily. Soon other logs followed, and were nailed down. Now they would have to put the plank boards on and make sure the bridge was sturdy enough; it would need to be braced on the sides. It was just a small bridge, good enough for one buggy to travel across at a time. The bigger bridges in their community had a roof on them.

"We can't have your family missing church anymore," Nathan said to Joseph.

"Now, he won't have any more excuses," John said, smiling.

"I am not allowed to go to church." Joseph walked halfway across the bridge so John could hear him better.

"Bishop Moses has put Joseph on probation for a while until everyone is sure that he is not a drinking man," Nathan said.

"Joseph, if you are guilty, all you have to do is pray and make a full confession to the church," Timothy said kindly.

"Joseph is a gut man. You will see that soon enough," John said.

They worked hard, all seven of them. When they stopped to take a break three hours later, they were done.

"We had best be getting back," Timothy said.

"Mary is cooking us all a dinner right now. I would be pleased if you all would join me," Joseph said.

The men hesitated for a moment.

"Mary will be upset, if you all don't come," John said.

"Well, you should know your sister," Nathan said, laughing.

"We can all ride in the wagon if you want to," John said.

"You go along, and we will follow you in the buggy," Timothy said.

Joseph got in the wagon with John and rode with him back to the house. "Mary will be surprised to see us all; I sent her back to cook, but she was probably going to bring the food to us."

John pulled in the yard a few minutes later. Mary came out on the porch to see who it was. She seemed surprised to see the two buggies full of men.

"Well, I was fixing to bring the food to you," Mary said.

"That is fine. Shall we set the picnic tables up outside?" John asked.

"Nay, there is not that many of us. All of our brethren can eat inside with us," Joseph said.

"I am looking forward to sampling some of your cooking again," Nathan said, smiling.

Mary's face turned red. "Thank you, Nathan."

Mary walked into the kitchen where Rebecca was finishing up

the meal. A few minutes later, they carried their meal out to the kitchen table.

"Rebecca is as pretty as her Mother," Nathan said, smiling. "I sure miss my wife; a home is just not the same without one."

Nathan shut up when Timothy gave him a stern look. Some people didn't know when to be quiet, and Nate must be one of them.

"Let's all bow our heads for prayer," Joseph said.

The food was hot from the oven. There is nothing like hot cornbread and butter, along with fried chicken, soup beans, and fried potatoes, of course. If a man can't eat that, there is something wrong with him.

"This fried chicken is the best I have ever eaten, Mary." Nathan was really putting the food away.

When the men got done eating, they went out on to the porch. Nate was a little too friendly; it seemed like Mary had to practically run him out of the kitchen.

They all sat on the porch talking for a little while. "Thank you, Mary, for the dinner. Now we must be on our way," Timothy said.

The men walked down to the buggy and loaded up; they took off very rapidly, the mare pacing fast. Nathan looked back and waved once, and then they were gone.

"Joseph I will help you plant for the rest of the day. I really like how you took gut care of my mules." John pointed at the mules with their heads sticking out of their temporary stalls.

Suddenly John had a sparkle in his eyes. "Mary, you would have thought that Nathan would have forgotten you after all these years."

"Do what?" Joseph asked, puzzled.

"Nate used to have a crush on Mary years ago and tried to court her," John said, laughing.

Without a word, Joseph got up and strolled away, going back to the planting.

"John, I would appreciate it if you wouldn't say such rude things in front of Joseph," Mary said. "He is a little sensitive, and it is very dishonorable of you to do such a thing."

"Alright, I was just joking." John got up quickly and went to help Joseph plant.

Rebecca got up early and started on her chores. She was hoping for a letter today from David. The mailman usually ran early, and she wanted to be the first one to get the mail. She was feeding the chickens when she heard the mailman coming. He was driving quiet fast in his little white jeep. As soon as he left, she headed for the mailbox. Suddenly, she heard somebody coming behind her down the driveway. She turned around to see her daed following her.

"Are you going after the mail, Rebecca?" Joseph asked.

"Jah, I couldn't sleep. I've been up for a while," Rebecca said.

"Okay, please mail this letter for me." Joseph handed her the letter he had written to thank Bishop Adam for sending the rifle to him. "Nay sense in both of us going for the mail. Go ahead. I have plenty of work to do anyway. And, Rebecca, please remember what I said. God will work everything out. David may not be the one for you, so you need to trust God on that part."

Rebecca nodded and went on. Her daed meant well, but he didn't know how she felt. She found one letter from David and was surprised that Rachel hadn't written.

Finding a private place in the shed, she sat down to read on the work bench. She could tell that Rachel had written the letter for David.

Dear Rebecca,

We can continue to write each other for now. Though I want to tell you the truth. I have been confused lately. I do not wish to hide anything from you.

And this is not Rachel's fault by any means, but we kissed once by accident. It was when she stumbled out of the buggy and fell into my arms. She has asked me not to ever kiss her again and to figure out who I love. I shouldn't have taken advantage of her friendship. So Rebecca, if you could please forgive me, then we can still be friends.

I hope to see you soon,
David.

Shocked, Rebecca read the letter again, then again. She couldn't believe that her best friend would do this to her, especially after all she and David had been through. It just wasn't fair. She was stuck here, and Rachel was taking her boyfriend from her. Some best friend Rachel turned out to be.

The tears came now, and she cried until she couldn't. Finally, she had enough. She got to her feet with the last of her strength and forced herself to move on.

She wasn't going to worry about David anymore. There would be nay more tears shed on her part, although her heart might ache. Actually, it would be a good test for David. She hadn't even been gone that long, and he was already kissing another girl.

Going to her room, she sat down to write David a letter with a heavy heart.

David,

I know we have been separated for a little while, and it is something that we cannot control. If you had really loved me, I don't think you would be kissing another girl.

I thought you meant what you said about us being together some day. That is what has kept me strong, knowing that we would be married someday. I can see now that it was all a lie, and that you do not love me. I was so naive not to see it before. I never wish to speak to you again as long as I live. You are not the person I thought you were.

Rebecca.

The next letter was to Rachel. However painful, she must finish this now. She felt one tear leak out despite her promise not to cry anymore.

Dear Rachel,

I have known for some time that we both cared for David. I just thought our friendship meant more to you and that you would behave with honor. Some friend you turned out to be. How you could do such a thing is beyond me. I haven't been gone all that long, and you are trying to steal my boyfriend from me.

You have taken advantage of David during our separation. I was hoping that we could have been lifelong friends and attend each other's wedding. Life is sure not going the way I planned, but my biggest disappointment of all is your betrayal. I don't wish to hear from you again.

Rebecca.

Rebecca filled out the envelopes, addressing them. Hopefully, nay one would miss her while she slipped out on chore time. It would be tomorrow before the mailman ran again, but she went down quietly, put the letter in the mailbox with the one from her father.

"That is odd," Joseph said to Mary. "Rebecca has been to the mailbox twice today."

"She is going through a rough time." Mary handed Joseph an egg, bacon, and cheese sandwich before he went back to work. "We must pray for her."

"That we will." Joseph planted a quick kiss on her cheek. The back door shut quietly behind him, and he was gone.

Chapter Sixteen

Joseph got up early Saturday morning and went to feed the animals. He was surprised to see some strange cows in their yard, eating the tall grass. Somebody must have torn the fence back down; he was getting tired of this. It made the second time the fence had been torn down, and it was wearing on his mind. There is just so much a man can take. Every man has a breaking point, and he was nearing his.

I will have to pray about this. Every decision he made in his life he prayed about and waited until the answer came. God does not just want to be involved in the big decisions we make in our life, but the smaller ones as well. It teaches us to trust Him.

Now he had to tend to the fence. He was herding the cows when Benjamin and Caleb came out followed by Pilgrim. Mary was standing on the porch watching the cows chew her flowers in their front yard.

"Joseph, get these cows out of here. They're destroying my flowers!" Mary grabbed a broom off the porch and waded in on one cow, giving it a swat in the rear end. The cow let out a loud moo and quickly left the yard.

"You boys are just in time; we're going to drive these cows back," Joseph said.

Pilgrim barked at Joseph like he understood, then went to work herding the cows.

"What are you going to do today?" Mary asked.

"Honey, I've got a fence to repair. I don't know how long it will take," Joseph said.

"Are you going to talk to Ron Harmony and see how the fence keeps getting torn down?" Mary asked.

"Nay woman, I have been praying about the issue," Joseph said.

"Well, this makes twice the fence was torn down. What did God say?" Mary asked, her face red.

"He said to fix the fence, woman. Now if you will excuse me, I have more work to do," Joseph said, walking away.

The boys, laughing hard, followed him. Mary didn't understand that talking about fixing the fence just wasn't getting the job done.

Joseph and his sons were working hard on the fence when they saw a man riding a horse coming their way fast. The horse was trying to run all out, though the rider was holding him back.

"What a horse," Caleb said, pointing.

"He is a thoroughbred," David Stevens said as he stopped beside them. "I have high hopes for him, but he is a gelding. He is just a little wild."

"He is a beauty." Joseph patted the horse on the neck. The horse stomped its hoof impatiently.

"Joseph, I rode over here to thank you for helping my wife. That was nice of you." Stevens shifted in his English saddle.

"It is our way." Joseph stepped back from the horse.

"By the way, Joseph, how does your boundary line run here?" Stevens stood up in his stirrups to look.

"It borders your farm and runs in a straight line with this fence, to that big pine tree down there," Joseph said, pointing.

"I tell you these old deeds can get confusing sometimes," Stevens said.

"I suppose so. Some go back for hundreds of years," Joseph said.

"I guess this rain has about wiped your farm out." Stevens pointed at the muddy fields.

"It will make it a lot harder on us," Joseph said.

"Joseph, just to be a good neighbor, I'll offer you one hundred and twenty-five thousand dollars for your farm," Stevens said, turning his horse around.

The offer was mighty tempting, especially with all of the trouble they had been having. They could easily afford to move somewhere else, maybe even back to Pennsylvania.

"We'll pray about it," Joseph said.

Stevens rode off quickly shaking his head.

That evening, when the fencing was done and the chores were complete for the day, Joseph sat on the porch with his family, sharing a late night snack. It was slightly dark out, but the light was falling fast.

"Mary, David Stevens was over here today," Joseph said. "And he offered a large amount of money for this farm—one hundred and twenty-five thousand dollars to be exact."

"That is a lot of money," Mary said slowly. "Do you think we should take it?"

"I told him we would pray about it," Joseph said. "It seems like everything is such a struggle here to survive."

"Mister Stevens has the meanest eyes I have ever seen. Not one time did he smile," Benjamin said, waving his hand.

"You would think he is a cowboy, the way he rode that horse," Caleb said.

"You mean we might be moving again?" Benjamin asked.

"It is too early to tell just yet," Joseph said. "We will keep his offer in mind; there is a lot to think about."

Looking out in the yard, Rebecca suddenly screamed. Joseph looked out by the corral and saw Mary's grandpa carrying a lantern.

"It's a ghost!" Rebecca yelled, pointing at the man.

"Go check it out, Joseph!" Mary said.

"Nay, I will not, Mary. I have done been hit on the head once. Anyway, I have been thinking about it. Whoever is playing pranks on us is dressed like your grandpa, so nobody will get suspicious seeing an Amish man out this way. They are trying to scare us away, and make us sell this property by believing this place is haunted."

"We have a mystery to solve now," Caleb said to Benjamin.

"Nay, I don't want you boys going near these people. You might get hurt," Joseph said.

"How do you know that the ghost isn't real?" Rebecca asked.

"Well, I will tell you," Joseph said. "A real ghost leaves nay footprints behind. If you go out there right now, as muddy as it is, there should be footprints on the ground."

"Daed please grab us a lantern and we will go see," Rebecca said. "It will give the boys a chance to play detective. They like reading mystery books anyway."

"Alright, give me a minute to grab a lantern," Joseph said. "You all are not going to be satisfied until I prove this to you."

They made their way cautiously, the children following behind Joseph. Pilgrim came running up behind them to see what was going on. They got to where the ghost had been in front of the corral. Joseph held the lantern up so that they could see. Only there were nay footprints on the ground except for their own.

"I can't believe it," Joseph said. "There should be footprints here on the ground."

"I told you that grandpa's ghost was real. He must be trying to tell us something," Rebecca said.

"I think grandpa is trying to scare us away," Benjamin said.

"We will try to find a clue tomorrow in the daylight," Caleb said.

"What do you think it is now, Joseph?" Mary asked.

They were walking back towards the house now.

"I just don't know. I am going to bed. You all can sit up and watch ghosts as long as you want to," Joseph said, going inside the house.

They got all of their planting done, in the next few days. All of their families pitched in to help, even the children. Joseph had been surprisingly quiet the last few days and had hardly spoken a word to Mary. She didn't know why he was acting so strange.

She was standing on the porch, dusting a rug, when she saw a buggy coming down their driveway. Joseph was coming in from the field, so she walked off the porch to greet their guest where Joseph joined her. Mary looked closer and saw the bishop driving his buggy. Moses rode right up to them and stopped the horse, pulling back on the reins.

"I just came from John's house; our church members have got his field replanted, and it looks gut," Moses said. "Different people in our church donated some extra seed for John to plant with."

"John will be grateful," Mary said. "He was worried when he lost a planted field due to the flooding."

"It is gut to see our brethren come together in their time of need," Moses said. "John said that you are in need of a barn. We will start on one here in a few days."

"I don't have enough money to build a barn with right now," Joseph said.

"We will all give a little. That way nay one will have to give a lot," Moses said, shaking Joseph's hand. He didn't even get out of the buggy.

"You all are still going to help me, even though I am on probation?" Joseph asked. "I don't understand why you would do this."

"You are still one of us, Joseph. You are a baptized member, and that hasn't changed," Moses said. "We will get through this eventually."

"Denki," Joseph said. "I will have to clean the mess up, where the old barn burnt. So we can build the new barn there."

"That's a gut idea," Moses nodded. "I will see you in church this Sunday, Mary?"

"We will be there," Mary said quickly.

"One other thing, Joseph," Moses said. "Were you driving an automobile recently? One of our church deacons reported that they saw you driving one."

"Jah, my neighbor Janet Stevens had a flat tire. I changed the tire and then turned the car around for her…nothing more," Joseph said, lowering his head. "These people must not trust me at all."

"Is that what happened, Mary?" Moses asked, looking her in the eyes.

"Jah, it was. He didn't even drive the car that far," Mary said.

"I will keep investigating the allegations. Maybe I will see Janet in town." Moses tipped his hat. "Gut day to you."

When Moses left, Joseph went out and spent the rest of the evening cleaning up where the old barn had burnt. The old foundation for the barn was made out of rock brick and was still in good shape.

Joseph got up the next day at dawn; he was shaving when Mary came into the bathroom. He hard Pilgrim barking outside and thought he heard voices.

"Are we expecting anyone?" Mary asked, handing him a towel to dry off with.

"I don't think so. Let me get my shirt on, and we'll see what is going on." Joseph put his shirt on quickly.

Suddenly, there was a very loud knock on the door.

"Are you up, Joseph?" It sounded like Bishop Moses talking.

"I hope nothing is wrong," Mary said, standing by him.

Joseph opened the door to see the whole church congregation. The whole yard was full of buggies and some wagons loaded down with wood. Pilgrim charged the wagons, barking up a storm.

"Joseph, we meant to tell you, but we are going to build your barn today," Moses said. "When I mentioned it to everyone, they all wanted to do it today, since school is starting back up on Monday now that the spring planting is over."

"That will be fine. I appreciate it," Joseph said. "We can build it back right where the old barn was that burned, that way we can use the old foundation."

"Well, come on out when you get ready," Moses said, walking away.

"Did you know they were coming today?" Mary asked.

"Nay, I did not know," Joseph said. "It looks like all of your family is here as well."

He saw Samson, John, Elizabeth, Lewis, Noey, Malena and Carlonia. Then he saw Hannah and Jeremiah. They were helping an elderly lady down out of a buggy.

"Oh, my mother is back." Mary raced down the steps to greet her.

Sharon met Mary halfway and gave her a hug. Joseph was soon surrounded by his family, and a lot of his brothers and sisters in the Lord.

"Before we start working, come with me, Mother." John took Sharon's hand. "We must show you something first."

Sharon followed them back, along with the rest of the family. "What is it?"

"Close your eyes, Grandma," Rebecca said, leading her.

Sharon gladly obeyed. "Can I open them now?" she asked as they stopped.

"Go ahead," Mary said, standing beside her.

Sharon opened her eyes up to see the two room apartment built on the back of the house.

"Sharon come inside, and let us show you around," Joseph said.

Sharon walked in looking at the two rooms. The rooms were now filled up with family. "It is real nice. Mary, are you going to have another baby?"

"Nay, Mother, these rooms are for you," Mary said, laughing.

Sharon gasped for a minute. "These rooms are for me, really

Mary? Thank you! I can't believe you all went to all this trouble." Sharon hugged Mary, kissing her on the cheek.

"It was actually Joseph's idea," Mary said. "He wanted you to live near me."

"Why thank you, Joseph." Sharon grabbed Joseph, giving him a hug.

"Bring your bags, Mother. This place is yours now," Joseph said.

John cleared his throat. "If we are all done here, we have a barn to build now."

"Be off with you then," Sharon said, smiling. "I am going to sit here and rest for a few minutes."

"There should be enough women to cook for us all. Many have brought something with them as well," Bishop Moses said.

"That is gut, for we were not prepared," Joseph said.

"I have truly enjoyed welcoming your family into our community, even though we still have to sort a few things out," Moses said, shaking Joseph's hand.

"We are proud to be part of this community," Joseph said.

"Well, we had better tell Arnold where you want the barn built. He is the best carpenter in the community and knows his trade very well." Moses motioned for Arnold to come over to them.

"How do you want the barn built, Joseph?" Arnold asked.

Arnold was very slim and tall with a long grey beard. His arm bulged with muscles. He looked close to being seventy years old.

"We will put it where my wife's grandpa had his barn. I would like to build it the same size as the original," Joseph said.

"I can remember how it was laid out and how many stalls they were," John said.

"Denki, that will make Mary happy," Joseph said.

"The barn will be a little smaller then what we usually build, but it should be big enough for your family," Arnold said.

It took the rest of the morning to get the barn framed off. Arnold pointed everyone in the right direction rather quickly.

Joseph had never seen so many people come together so quickly and get the job done right. All the people were working together toward one goal; they looked as busy as little ants running around. Arnold wandered here and there, followed by his sons and all giving orders.

Mary and a few other women brought out refreshments and checked to see if any of the men needed anything. As she brought Joseph some lemonade, he climbed down from the first rafter to the ground. Nathan was there, and he had been paying a lot of attention to her.

"Jah, Joseph, what is it?" Mary asked, giving him some lemonade in a plastic cup.

"Mary, don't be alone with any of the men. It just wouldn't look right," Joseph said, not looking at her.

"Why, Joseph?" Mary asked puzzled. *What in the world is Joseph talking about?* Mary thought.

Joseph didn't answer; he climbed back up and went to work, turning his back to her. Joseph was acting weird; kind of like he did when they were still courting. Joseph had been acting strange ever since John had mentioned that Nathan used to like her. *Why, Joseph is jealous. After all these years of marriage, he's still acting like a school boy.* Though, in a way, it made her feel good.

I will save Joseph an extra piece of pie tonight, she thought to herself. *Maybe that will cheer him up.* Going back inside, she started helping the women make a very big dinner. If everybody hadn't pitched in, there would be nay way that she could have fed this big crowd alone.

The men worked hard for six hours, stopping only to grab a drink or snack as it was brought out. Finally, the women finished dinner; they had fixed many different varieties of food. Some people had brought ham, chicken, and pork. One man had killed five turkeys. That wasn't even counting all of the side dishes that everyone had brought.

The Bible Scripture came to her mind, where Jesus fed many people with a few fish. God always made a way. You might not have everything that you want, but you would have what you needed.

Mary went over to ring the dinner bell when the dinner was ready, but the pull rope was broken. They would eat outside on the picnic tables. And when all the chairs were filled, the rest would have to sit on the ground.

"Moses, tell everybody that dinner is ready, nay one should leave here hungry today," Mary said.

"Denki, Mary." Bishop Moses walked out to the barn, and got everyone's attention. "Come on, brothers and sisters, our meal is prepared."

They all walked over quickly and got a plate. Moses waited until everyone sat down before he stood up. "All heads bowed for a silent prayer of grace. We have so much to be thankful for. What I see here today is the real treasure that we have; and it is each other."

Soon the prayer was done, and the dining began. The men ate fast. This was not a meal where everyone would sit around and talk for hours. They still had about six more hours of work to do today, and then most of the barn should be done. Anything else that was unfinished, Joseph would have to do.

Amos sat down beside Joseph. They had become good friends.

"When are you all coming out my way?" Amos asked. "I have a young mare that I traded for, a yearling. She is a half-sister to Lucky, and looks like him; they would make a gut team together. You just can't breed them together, because they are related."

"If she looks as gut as Lucky, then I will buy her. I am going to show everyone that a Haflinger can work as gut as any mule." Joseph chewed on a chicken leg.

Mary's family was seated all around them, and Hannah and Sharon were sitting at the table with them.

"I will be over in a few days to get the mare," Joseph said. "Since everyone has helped us with the barn, I will have some money left over. The mare and a jersey cow for our family will just about break me."

"Are you going to stay here, Mother?" Hannah asked.

"Jah, I am," Sharon said. "I do need a small place of my own; everybody needs a little bit of privacy. I will probably travel back and forth, visiting my children."

"It is about time for dessert," Samson said, standing up.

"Wait for me," Jeremiah said, following him.

"Those two eat more than anyone I have ever seen," Mary said, laughing. "Joseph, I'll be right back, I'll get us a lemon pie."

Joseph nodded as she was walking off. The line was backing up like you wouldn't believe; everyone wanting dessert.

"How are you doing, Mary?" Nathan came up suddenly behind her in the long line. For some reason Nathan's eyes looked blood shot, and he smelled odd.

"I'm just getting my family some dessert," Mary said, smiling.

"You look very happy," Nathan said.

Mary saw Joseph looking at her now. "I am happy. Joseph is a wonderful man."

"I can see that," Nathan said. "I need to find me another wife. I am going to starve myself to death, eating my own cooking."

"I am sure that God has somebody special for you, Nathan," Mary said softly.

"Why thank you, Mary, that means a lot to me," Nathan said.

She was at the front of the line now, and there were plenty of desserts to choose from. Mary made her way back to the table, carrying two pies. Joseph got the first piece of pie. She leaned over and kissed him on the cheek.

"Thank you, Mary," Joseph said.

The children made short work of the pies; soon everyone was done eating. The men all got up and went back to work. A barn does not build itself. The men might take one break later, but that would be all. Some stopped only to eat and drink, never leaving the jobsite or sitting down, and by nightfall, the barn was complete. The children moved about harnessing the horses to the buggies, and soon, most of the families began heading home.

"I will be back Sunday after church. I have to get all of my clothes." Sharon hugged Mary.

"Your home will be here when you are ready," Mary said as she held her mother's hands.

Her family stood on the porch, watching all the people leave.

"We are so blessed, Mary," Joseph said, taking her arm.

"I told you that all along," Mary said, smiling.

"Well, children, bring a lantern. Let's get these two horses in their new barn," Joseph said. He took off, leading the way, followed soon by Mary and the children. "Boys, throw both horses some hay while I get the horses. I am going to put them a stall apart. That way the stud horse won't be aggravating the mare."

Joseph went and brought Fiery in first, then went back for the stud, Lucky. The boys fed them some hay and corn.

"I will bring them some water." Joseph grabbed two buckets. When he finished, he held a lantern up, looking at the horses.

"They look so happy to be in their new home," Rebecca said.

Joseph grabbed all of his family, giving them a group hug. "This is a big day for all of us, and I couldn't ask for a better family."

"Well, let's go in the house and see if there is any leftover food," Mary said.

"And lemon pie." Caleb rubbed his stomach.

Chapter Seventeen

Joseph woke up to the sound of cows mooing loudly. He opened his bedroom curtain and looked out the window. The cows were grazing around the house; a couple were in the garden he had just planted. *Oh nay, not again.* Jumping out of bed, he grabbed for his clothes, waking Mary up in the process.

"What is wrong, Joseph?" Mary asked.

"Those blasted cows are back," Joseph said angrily.

He had prayed about this, and had he felt that God was going to take care of the problem. The good Lord had all kinds of people asking Him for things, so sometimes it took a while for Him to get back to a man.

"Mary, send the boys out to help me. It is about time for them to get up. I think somebody has cut the fence again. We are lucky our garden hasn't sprouted yet. We just planted it. Though, it won't help it any with them blasted cows walking on it!"

Joseph went outside followed soon by the boys. They drove a few cows back, when a brown pickup truck pulled up into their yard. A man jumped out followed by his two sons that were as big as he was. The truck was old and dirty, but so was the man.

"Who is that?" Caleb asked.

"Let's go see." Joseph walked down to meet him. The man met him halfway; he didn't look friendly at all.

"I'm Ron Harmony, your neighbor over there. I see my cows are in your pasture and garden."

"Jah, somebody has cut my fence three times already," Joseph said.

"Really," Ron said. "Why didn't you say anything to me?"

"It is our way to forgive. I have just been driving the cattle back and repairing my fence," Joseph said.

"Boys, do you know anything about this fence being cut down?" Ron asked loudly.

The boys lowered their heads and didn't say anything.

"I see," Ron said. "I can assure you, mister, it was not me, and it will not happen again. My boys will see to that, and they will also repair your fence by themselves. I do not want you to help them; they need to learn a lesson."

"Alright, that sounds fair. There are nay hard feelings on my part. All is forgiven," Joseph said, shaking his hand.

"Did you hear that, boys? All is forgiven. These people are depending on their crops and farm for a living. It takes a sorry man to mess with that! I have done some bad things in my day, but I have never destroyed another man's crop. Now get them cattle out of here!"

"Yes sir," the boys said, moving quickly.

"Mr. Harmony, would you like something to drink?" Mary offered him a plastic red cup of ice cold lemonade while trying not to spill the pitcher in her other hand.

"Just call me Ron, and yes, I would like something to drink." Ron took the cup of lemonade Mary handed him and drank it quickly. "I think this is partly my fault. The boys knew I resented having Amish neighbors, but I wouldn't have done anything like this. We just came back from town when I saw my cows in your pasture."

The boys were moving the cattle hastily. They moved them so quick that a small heifer stepped in a hole in the ground and fell down. The heifer lay there thrashing around, trying her best to get up.

Joseph and Ron ran over to where the cow lay. Her leg was

twisted badly. Ron took his cowboy hat off and hit it against his leg. "Blasted thing has broken its leg!" He pulled his pistol out and shot the cow between the eyes.

"I'm glad you were here to see how it happened," Joseph said.

"Yes, we have just butchered two heifers; we have more beef than we know what to do with," Ron said.

"I am sorry for your loss," Joseph said honestly.

"Joseph, how are you on meat? Could you use this cow for beef? I truly hate to see anything go to waste. It disturbs me badly," Ron said.

"I don't think we can afford it right now," Joseph said. "I will help you load it up, though."

"Thanks, Joseph, but you can have this cow, just don't let it go to waste," Ron said. "And Joseph, I am sorry for any trouble that we have caused you."

"Denki, Ron," Joseph said, shaking his hand. "I have my work cut out for me now, butchering this cow. We will invite you over to dinner when we are done."

"I just might accept. Now I have to check on my boys. They are going to work out the value of the cow and pay it back. It is their fault. I will have to swing back by and pick them up later. We have so much going on at the ranch today, rounding up some cattle and branding. Come and visit us anytime you want, and bring your family with you. Now I have got to get moving."

"Gut day to you, sir," Joseph said.

Ron went over and talked to his boys before he left. His hands waved wildly as he spoke. Finally, he left, spinning gravel; the man must have been in a hurry.

"Mary, I am going to harness Lucky up and pull this heifer into our new barn. We will have to butcher the cow there. Ron said for us to eat her."

"Oh really, Joseph, that was so nice of him. We can use the meat. I have been praying for a gut steak."

Joseph picked Mary up and turned her around. "The Lord does bless, Mary. We just have to wait on His answer."

"You silly goose," Mary said, smiling when he put her down.

"Mary, see that our young friends out there are fed well today. They may need some refreshments as well," Joseph said.

"I will do that," Mary said, smiling. "I don't think we have to worry about the fence being torn down anymore."

Mary met her mother after church on Sunday. Joseph went to get the horse and buggy ready while they talked. He stopped to load them up a few minutes later. Sharon came his way with Mary, their arms loaded down with luggage. He quickly got out. "Here, let me help you ladies with that."

"Denki, Joseph. I am moving in with you." Sharon handed him her luggage.

"I told you that you were welcome," Joseph said, loading the luggage.

The children welcomed Sharon with open arms.

"Hang on a minute, Joseph," Jeremiah said, coming his way with a feed sack.

Joseph waited until he got up to him. Something in the sack squealed loudly and moved, trying to get out. "What in the world have you got in there?"

"I brought you two small pigs," Jeremiah handed him the sack. "They have just been weaned. If you take gut care of the pigs, they will be some gut eating this fall."

"What do I owe you for the pigs?" Joseph asked.

"Nothing. They are a gift," Jeremiah said.

"Danke, we will have you over for dinner when that time comes." Joseph shook his hand. "Now me and the boys will have to build a hog pen."

"How many buildings are we going to need?" Rebecca asked, smiling.

"Not many more. Our farm is just about complete," Joseph said.

"It has always been complete with just our family there," Mary said.

"Hold on to the pigs, Caleb." Joseph handed him the sack.

"Just keep them nasty things away from me," Rebecca said, laughing.

"Well, we had better be going, Jeremiah." Joseph tied their luggage down on top of the buggy.

"Alright, I don't think you can get anything else in that buggy." Jeremiah smiled as he was walking away.

Joseph climbed in the crowded buggy. It wasn't meant to hold a lot of people.

"If today wasn't Sunday, I would go get that work mare," Joseph said, getting the reins.

"I don't think that mare is in the ditch, son," Sharon said, smiling.

With a flick of the wrist, reins falling lightly on the back of Fiery, they were off.

Rachel sat in her room, reading the letter Rebecca had sent her. She read it in shock at how hard Rebecca was taking everything. Especially the parts were Rebecca had written that she never wished to see Rachel again. A lump came in her throat; she had never meant to hurt Rebecca. They had always been best friends. When she got to the part about betraying Rebecca, she began to cry. Rebecca knew her so well. What must she think of her now?

She couldn't deny that she had deep feelings for David, but she would control herself with honor. David must decide who he wanted. She would not push. He wasn't going to play with two hearts, not on her part. She didn't think David cared about her anyway; he had said that their kiss had just been an accident. The kiss might have been an accident, but she could feel the passion coming from him.

She must write Rebecca back while she had these thoughts fresh in her mind. She got a pen out of her desk drawer, and she sat down to write. The tiny desk was in front of a window upstairs. Sitting there, she could see for miles.

Dear Rebecca,

I hope this letter does not find your heart full of sorrow. And I pray that you don't think that I have betrayed you. I did fall into David's arms when I was getting out of his buggy, and we kissed. I am sorry; I shouldn't have allowed this while he is still your boyfriend. I promise you that the kiss will not happen again. I won't deny that I have deep feelings for David, but as long as you two are courting, I will not interfere.

You can still come and visit me when you want. Maybe someday you can find it in your heart to forgive me. And I pray that we will always be gut friends.

Sincerely,
Rachel

She had barely finished the letter, when her mamm called upstairs, "Rachel, David is here."

Going to the stairs, she looked down. David stood there with an odd look on his face.

"Can David come up for a few minutes, mamm?" Rachel asked. "I need to show him Rebecca's letter."

Rachel's saw her daed's eyebrow go up for a second, but he didn't say anything. He sat there reading a book in his favorite chair.

"Alright go ahead, but keep the door open," Ruth said, smiling.

"Jah, mother." Rachel waved for David to come on up.

David followed her inside the room and sat down in her desk chair. "What's going on?"

"We both got a letter from Rebecca. I will read you both letters," Rachel said softly.

David sat there with his head down while she read, but she could tell he was listening to every word. When she was done reading, David raised his head, and looked her in the eyes. He had a very sad look on his face.

David cleared his throat. "Please tell Rebecca that I don't want to write her anymore until I figure out who I love."

"Alright, now are you ready for today's lesson?" Rachel asked. "I will fill out the letter later for you. Are you sure that is what you want?"

"Jah, and Rachel, there will not be any more lessons or fishing trips until I find some answers," David said. "I must pray and search my heart for the right thing to do."

"Dinner is ready, if you want to eat with us, David," Ruth said, from the stairs.

"David, will you please stay and eat dinner with us?" Rachel asked.

David picked his hat up and put it on. He stood up quickly. "Have a gut day, ma'am."

By the time Rachel came down for dinner and had finished wiping her tears, he was gone.

Chapter Eighteen

The children seemed excited as they got ready for school Monday for the first time in their new district. Mary got up early to see them off to school.

"It will be so exciting starting in a new school." Benjamin grabbed his lunch bucket.

"I can't wait to meet everyone," Caleb said.

"You boys behave today for your new teacher," Mary said, giving them a hug.

"We will," Benjamin said, smiling.

Rebecca walked the boys down to the end of the drive way and caught a buggy ride with their teacher, Miss Miriam. The house seemed quiet with the children gone.

"Mary, get ready," Joseph said. "I got all of the chores done early. We will go on a small date while the children are at school."

"Where are we going?" Mary asked.

"I am going to take you into town for dinner at the steak house there, and on the way back, we will pick the work mare up to match Lucky."

"You are just taking me out to dinner so you can buy that mare," Mary said, laughing. "Let me grab a few things, and I'll be ready to go."

"I'll hitch the mare up right quick." Joseph went out, shutting the door.

Within a few minutes, Mary walked outside with her purse

ready to go. Joseph stopped the buggy in front of the house to pick her up. Getting out, he opened the buggy door for her.

"Why thank you, Joseph." Mary took his hand as he helped her inside.

"A man has to start a date off right," Joseph said. "Five minutes after a date is started the mood is set, and it cannot be undone."

"Well, you're off to a gut start then," Mary said, laughing.

The mare came awake with a bound and was off. It wasn't a long way to town, though it was not like traveling in a car were you could rush everywhere. It took one hour of driving one way just to get there. A man had to allow time for this and leave as early as possible. Joseph pulled Mary closer to him. He really appreciated his wife.

"Nay other man is going to get you, Mary."

"Why, Joseph, what are you talking about? You know you are the only man I will ever love," Mary said, hugging him.

"That is gut, because I don't intend to ever give you up," Joseph said.

"And I have nay intention of going anywhere. You can't pay any attention to John. He just likes to tease," Mary said.

Mary laid her hand on his arm and left it there. For a moment, his heart skipped a beat.

The land looked sleepy. Nothing moved except for a buck eating in a meadow. They passed John's farm. He was already working out in the fields. Joseph waved as they passed, but they did not stop.

"We will have to get back before the children get home from school," Joseph said.

"We can talk to John later," Mary agreed, smiling.

Finally, the road became wider as they pulled out onto the two lane highway. Cars were coming from everywhere. Joseph got over on the right-hand side of the road, trying to stay out of the way as much as possible. A few cars blew their horn at them as they sped by.

"Joseph, be careful! The cars might scare the horse," Mary said.

Up ahead, three more Amish buggies traveled in a single file row. It looked like some Amish people from their district were traveling into town, but they were too far ahead to talk to. The buggy horses paced for all they were worth.

"A pacing horse that can step out and really move is worth something," Joseph said.

"Jah, horse miles are slower than car miles by a long shot," Mary said, laughing.

The small town seemed crowed. Cars and buggies were parked everywhere. Many of the Amish traded in town, selling their goods at the farmer's market.

Joseph traveled slowly to the steakhouse. He knew the prices were a bit steep there, but a man should take his wife out every now and then and not worry about such things. He liked to save his money and use it wisely, but there was no sense in saving every penny.

Pulling up in front of the hitch rail, Joseph tied the mare up. Then he went back and helped Mary down out of the buggy. It was lunchtime now, and he was very hungry.

"John said this was a gut place to eat," Joseph said. "There is nothing I like better than a steak buffet."

Going inside, Joseph got in line; Mary followed close behind him. He placed their order a few minutes later.

"Do you want steak with your buffet?" the waiter asked, smiling.

"Jah, and that is for two," Joseph said.

When he paid, Mary grimaced slightly. Maybe she thought that the price was too high. Joseph picked up the two trays that held the plates.

Another waitress stepped up. "Follow me, and I will get your order." She led them to a table and seated them.

"What can I get you to drink?" the waiter asked.

"Pepsi for two, please," Joseph said.

"It will be a few minutes before your steak is done. Please help yourself to the buffet," the waitress said.

"Mary, grab your plate and let's go. I'm going to see how much I can eat before the steak arrives."

"There is just so much to choose from," Mary said.

The place was packed with English people and Amish. They were big long counters full of every kind of food imaginable. Joseph loaded his plate down with chicken, mashed potatoes, and gravy, throwing some macaroni and cheese on the side for good measure. That would be enough food to get him started. There were a few Amish from another church district that he had never seen before.

"We will see you at church on Sunday?" one elderly Amish woman asked, coming by.

Mary sat down with Joseph at their table. "We will be there, Mrs. Egger," Mary said.

"I used to be Mary's school teacher," Mrs. Egger said.

"It is gut to meet you," Joseph said, shaking her hand.

"Well, I had better be going. My group is getting ready to leave." Mrs. Egger walked away slowly on a cane.

"She is still cheerful after all these years," Mary commented.

Their steak soon arrived, and Joseph tackled his with an appetite, but Mary didn't eat as much as him. The waitress came and filled their glasses with more soda.

"The food is delicious," Mary said. "I haven't eaten this gut in a long time."

"You are worth, it my dear," Joseph said softly.

They sat there for a little over an hour. Joseph took another bite of apple pie. Finally, he had eaten enough.

Mary had quit eating long before him, and was sitting across from him watching him.

"Are you about ready to go, Mary?"

"Whenever you are ready," Mary said.

"I'll leave the waitress a tip for taking care of us." Joseph put a five-dollar bill under their plate. "I think that if we have compassion on others, God will have compassion on us."

He was getting ready to leave when some loud music came on over the speakers. He watched as a few young couples went out on the floor to dance to a slow country love song that filled the room. He didn't know who the singer was.

"Mary, would you like to join me in a dance?" Joseph asked.

"Why Joseph, we haven't danced in forever. Are you sure it's alright?" Mary asked, smiling.

"I don't see why not," Joseph said, getting to his feet.

Joseph led the way, feeling a little silly as Mary laughed at him. He held her close, thinking back on his courting days when their love was young.

"Let's go, Joseph, the dance is over." Mary hit him lightly in the chest.

"Lead the way, my fair lady." Joseph gave her a slight bow.

He almost ran over an Amish man on the way out. They locked eyes, but the man didn't speak. It was Deacon Nathan, followed by Timothy, and a few other men from church.

"You all come again, and I do hope that you have enjoyed your visit," the waitress said as they were leaving.

"Thank you, we will," Mary said, smiling.

"Do you need to buy anything in town?" Joseph asked Mary when they got outside.

"Nay, I don't really need anything. We can look at the hardware store if we have time," Mary said.

"This day is yours, my lady. We just have to be back when the children get home from school. And I need time to pick up my mare," Joseph said. "I bet she is a beauty."

"Joseph, I've got a feeling that you only took me out on a date so you could buy that mare," Mary said.

"Nay, but I figured we might as well buy the mare while we are out this way," Joseph said, smiling.

They spent a little while looking at the stores in town. Mary wanted some sewing material, so he bought some, but that was all. A man should stay away from stores if he can't afford to buy anything. Otherwise, he'll end up buying something every time.

Sitting on the outside of the hardware store was a pop machine. Mary stepped closer, taking a look. Joseph noticed the sign on the pop machine. It was green with ALE8 written in big letters across it.

"I haven't had an ALE8 soda in years," Mary said, smiling. "Joseph have you ever drank one of these pops?"

"Nay, it is the first time I have ever seen one." Joseph pulled a few bills out of his pocket and handed them to Mary.

Mary got them both a pop, and opened them on the side of the machine.

"I didn't know they still made bottled pop." Joseph took a drink. "It seems like pop tastes better in a bottle for some reason."

Finally, they got in the buggy and started home.

"It feels like we're dating again. We need a date night," Mary said, drinking her pop.

"That we do," Joseph said. "A man should spend more private time with his wife to build a better relationship. I know we do have a lot of responsibilities, but we should take the time."

"I will hold you to that," Mary said.

"Now, let's go get my mare," Joseph said.

They journeyed on out of town, away from all the traffic and the fast lane, to just a good old dirt road, where life went a little slower, especially if you were in a buggy.

Joseph saw Amos standing out near his barn when they pulled up in their buggy. He came walking out to meet them with a big smile on his face.

"I knew you would come to look at the mare, but be warned, she is still a little young," Amos said. "Next year the mare will make a gut work horse."

"I'd rather buy a young horse and train it anyway." Joseph got out and helped Mary down.

"Do you want to come in for a while to visit?" Amos asked. He seemed so lonely.

"We would be glad to," Joseph said.

They made their way to the house, and sat down on the rough porch furniture there. Amos plopped himself down in his rocking chair, atop a worn cushion. Amos's wife came out to see them. "How are you doing, Mary?"

"Fine. Joseph took me out to dinner and to buy a horse at the same time," Mary said, smiling.

"Men are always thinking about making a trade."

"Bring us something to snack on, please," Amos said to his wife.

Joseph started to say he was full, but Mary shook her head slightly at him.

"When we have a guest at our home, we must make them feel like they are welcome," Amos said softly.

"I do feel welcome. Thank you, Amos," Joseph said.

"We will give account to God on how we have treated others." Amos rocked slowly, rubbing his beard. "If Christ was standing at your door, how would you treat Him? As you have done it unto the least of my brethren, you have done it unto me."

His wife came out a few minutes later with some peanut butter cookies and milk. The cookies had steam coming off them.

"Thank you." Joseph grabbed a few cookies.

They sat there a little while, visiting with Amos and his wife. It actually felt good to get out of the house for a while. Every now and then a man needs to get away.

"Joseph, let's go take a look at that mare and see if you might be interested in buying her," Amos said. "I may breed a few of my mares to Lucky later on."

"Just come and get Lucky anytime you need to, or I'll bring him here to you," Joseph said.

Amos led the way to the barn and brought the mare out. The mare favored Lucky a lot, but had a little more white on her legs.

"She will be as big as Lucky, and she is very gentle," Amos said.

"A man could start by getting her used to a harness while she is still young. They make better horses that way, jah sir."

"How much do you want for the mare?" Joseph asked. He had paid Amos off a few weeks ago on what he had owed him for Lucky.

Amos named his price, and Joseph hesitated for a minute.

"Joseph, just take the mare with you, and pay me when you can," Amos said. "I know you're in a tight spot financially with moving and everything. There is nobody else that I want to have her anyway. I'm a little picky about who I sell my horses to."

"A man should be." Joseph shook his hand. "I'll take her with me as I go. There is nay sense in making two trips."

Joseph got the lead rope and led the mare to the back of the buggy, tying her there. Fiery looked back and nickered to the mare.

Mary came out to meet him. He saw a twinkle in her eyes. "Joseph, do you have enough horses now?"

"I have about everything I need, woman, except for a gut milk cow." Joseph helped Mary in the buggy, and then he climbed in after her, grabbing the reins.

"A milk cow. Now they don't come cheap." Amos shut the buggy door.

"We will be back to visit soon," Mary said.

"It is a shame really. We are old, and our children don't come around to visit much," Amos said. "Most of our children live in another Amish district."

"Well, we must be on our way. Our children will be getting out of school soon," Joseph said. "Thank you for your hospitality, Amos."

"You're welcome. Please come back and visit anytime," Amos said.

Joseph pulled out slow, giving the colt time to follow. The scenery was pretty with spring grass everywhere and the trees were in full bloom. The birds were chirping loudly, singing praises to God above. He felt thankful to see all of God's beautiful creation, made for all of us.

John was still working on his farm when they came in. He met them at the road. "I see you've bought another one of them ponies?"

"Jah, and by this time next year, my horses will be out-pulling your mules," Joseph said. "And if you get stuck in the ditch with your mules, give me a holler, and I'll pull you out."

John snorted. "I would have to give you a holler, because you don't have a telephone. Mary, do you know how a woman got her name?"

"Nay," Mary said, smiling.

"Well, when God first made Eve, he woke Adam up to see her. Adam took a long look. Because she was so beautiful that she took his breath, he said, 'Whoa Man!' God looked at Adam and smiled. 'That is a gut name for her, son.'"

Mary and Joseph laughed until they had tears in their eyes.

"It is gut to see you two smiling again," John said.

Elizabeth came out to meet them. "Are you coming in for supper? It's just about ready."

"Nay, I must get back and put this mare in her stall," Joseph said. "I've got a few things to do before the children get home."

"Thank you for inviting us, Elizabeth," Mary said.

"We will go camping sometime with all the children," Joseph said. "They would love the pond out back on the farm. It has quite a few catfish in it."

"We'll go camping next Saturday, if nothing comes up," John said.

"Gut deal. We'll see you then," Joseph said, taking up the reins.

Joseph rode home, just enjoying the day and God's gentle sunshine. It seemed like it warmed the soul. It was through the stillness that you see nature as God intended.

"Mary, so often, the modern world will rush by in a fast car and cannot see what is right in front of them," Joseph said. "God's love is all around. It's in the air, like a gentle song of a bird as it sings praise to the Creator. It is only through our own selfishness that we bring ugliness into the world."

"Jah, you are right," Mary said. "Our time here on earth will soon be up. What are we doing with our time?"

They were soon home. Mary looked tired. Sharon came out on the porch to meet them.

"Mary, I am so sorry, but there have been county surveyors here all morning surveying our fields." Sharon straightened her apron.

"What in the world is going on?" Joseph asked, helping Mary out of the buggy.

"The surveyors said there is a property dispute, and they have a court order to survey the property." Sharon handed the paperwork to Joseph.

"Who is claiming our land?" Mary asked, stepping closer.

"Let me guess…Mr. Stevens. He has gone too far this time!" Joseph slammed the court order down on the porch rails, sending papers flying everywhere.

"We will have to get a lawyer, maybe even hire a surveyor," Sharon said. "The property dispute will have to be handled in court."

"I don't know what to do. We don't have any money to fight this," Joseph said. "We will just have to let the judge decide."

"Nay, we will let God decide. All we can do is pray about it," Sharon said.

"I'll go inside and start our supper," Mary said sadly.

"Well, I have to take care of these horses." Joseph drove away quickly to put the buggy up.

He turned the work mare out to graze in the field with Fiery. When Lucky saw the new mare, he exploded around the corral, bucking and running for all he was worth.

"Did you finally figure out that you are a stud horse?" Joseph asked.

In the summer months he didn't keep the animals in the barn a whole lot unless it rained. Horses love to graze on grass and needs it for its diet. If you leave a barn or shelter open, a horse will seldom come inside the barn. Sometimes flies will bother the horses bad enough on hot summer days that they may seek a cooler place. He had seen fly bites bad enough to draw blood before. People could buy a spray that would help keep the flies off the horses.

It was about time for the children to get home from school, so Joseph went onto the porch. Mary moved on the swing beside Sharon. It was getting close to suppertime.

"Joseph, when you get time, could you put me a cooking stove in my room," Sharon said. "That way when I am feeling gut, I can do my own cooking."

"There is an old stove in the shed your daed had," Joseph said. "I think it is in pretty gut shape. The next time John comes over, I will get him to help me put the stove in."

"We are waiting on the children to get home from school." Mary shifted on the porch swing.

"There they come now." Sharon pointed down the road.

Joseph saw the children's teacher, Miriam, pulling away in her buggy. She had already let the children out. Miriam waved once, and then she was gone.

The children soon reached the porch. "Have you got any treats, Grandma?" Benjamin asked, walking up the steps.

"How did you ever guess?" Sharon smiled as she opened a small picnic basket that she had sitting beside her on the porch floor. "I made a few rice crispy treats."

"At least the rice crispy treats are warm. They won't last long anyway." Rebecca passed them out.

"I'll have to fix the stove quick, if Sharon keeps cooking like this," Joseph said, smiling.

Chapter Nineteen

Joseph felt tired. It was time to take a break. All work and no play made him feel low in the spirit. He needed time for some relaxation, like fishing or camping. He had promised the boys that he would take them camping once the planting was done. The Lord said to shut down on the Sabbath so that man could have time to rest and to praise God.

Joseph took his time out in the barn harnessing up the two horses, Lucky and Lacy. When he worked with a new horse, he moved very slowly so as not to startle the animal. Lacy was too young to work right now, but he wanted her to get used to the harness. They were going camping today with John's family. John should arrive soon. Mary had risen before dawn and had already fixed their breakfast.

He was grateful that Sharon had come to live with them. Mary seemed happier when she was around. The children too loved their grandma's company, and often the boys would go back to her rooms to visit with her.

He started loading the camping equipment on Lucky and Lacy. It would do the mare good to pack a small load and start her training as young as possible. They were going on a small hike through the woods to the pond out back of the farm house. There they would spend the day fishing and cooking out and stay the night sleeping in a tent.

He finished loading up the horses when John arrived in his

wagon loaded down with supplies. The mules were pulling it this time. Elizabeth sat close beside John on the wagon seat, their children moving around in the back of the wagon.

"John, it is about time you got here," Joseph said.

"The children woke me up before dawn, wanting to go camping," John said, laughing.

"We brought enough food to feed the whole community," Elizabeth said, smiling.

"You will need it," Joseph said. "I had better hitch the buggy up right quick for Mary and the children to ride in."

Joseph came back a few minutes later to load his family up. The pack horses he let trail along behind the buggy. They weren't going all that far, but the horses needed the training.

"Can we take Pilgrim?" Benjamin asked as they all were loading up.

"Just turn Pilgrim loose. He should follow along behind us," Joseph said.

John moved out slowly, leading the way with the mule team. Joseph followed him in the buggy. Pilgrim came running along behind. The dog had grown a whole lot, and was about halfway grown.

"John sure looks funny with the mules pulling a wagon," Mary said, laughing.

It was about a mile to where they were going camping, a good adventure for the children. They never got the horses out of a walk the whole way, just enjoying the day.

"It has been a while since we have done anything this fun," Rebecca said. She was sitting beside her mother, looking at the scenery.

"We are just about there," Joseph said. They had come to a little hill, and the pond was down below.

Going down slowly, they pulled into the campsite, and Joseph stopped the horse and set the buggy brake.

"You children help your mother with whatever she needs. I'm going to stake these horses out to graze in the grass."

"That is a gut idea," Mary said.

Joseph unhitched the buggy mare and led her out first. He had brought some ropes along to tie the horses out with. As long as he kept Lucky tied away from the mares, he should be alright. Lucky had never acted up, but a stallion can't be trusted around mares. It would be hard on the horses to stand tied up all night, so he would let them graze until dark and then bring them in closer to the camp for the night. Suddenly he heard someone coming up behind him.

"You got any more of them ropes?" John asked.

"Jah, I have a few more. Come on, follow me, and I'll let you use them." Joseph tied the mare up quickly.

They tied all the horses out, even the mules, though Lucky they kept closer to the camp.

"That is one thing I didn't think about…rope," John said.

"A man should take gut care of his animals," Joseph said. "I think God requires it of us. He has put the animals in our care."

"Jah, you are right," John said. "If a man can't take gut care of his animals, then he doesn't need them."

"Well, we had better get back and put the tents up," Joseph said. "I expect that the women will have plenty for us to do."

Joseph and John walked back quickly and started setting the tents up for the night.

"You boys build us a place for a campfire with rocks around it. We don't want to catch the woods on fire," John said.

John's three boys and the twins quickly obeyed.

"Can we have a tent to ourselves tonight?" Caleb asked. "We don't want to sleep near any girls."

"That will be fine, and the girls can have their own tent," John said.

Four tents were quickly put up and staked down for the night.

"I brought along some firewood. It might do us for the night." Joseph pointed out his small bundle of wood.

"That will probably be enough wood. We will let the fire go out when the children fall asleep," John said.

It took a little while for the women to put everything where they wanted it for the night. They were camping close to the pond, though back enough from it to be in the shade. Thick gigantic pine trees were all around them. They looked like they could touch the sky.

"There is nothing better than camping out under some thick pine trees," Elizabeth said. "The needles and pinecones smell so refreshing."

"We had better tie our food up high where nay animals can reach it," John said.

"You boys get your fishing poles. We are ready to go fishing," Joseph said.

The boys left quickly, coming back with their fishing poles. Rebecca and Sarah got their fishing poles, though Sarah brought a book with her.

"Just in case I get bored," Sarah said to Mary.

"I see you're reading love stories," Mary noted, smiling.

"Well, they are interesting," Sarah said, smiling.

"Are we riding or walking to the pond?" Caleb asked.

"You boys are getting lazy," John said, laughing. "Of course we're walking. Now let's go."

The boys rushed on ahead eagerly. Sarah and Rebecca walked along behind them, talking. Sarah and Rebecca were about the same age, and they were in the same grade at school. Joseph walked behind the girls with Mary, holding hands, followed by John and Elizabeth.

"The boys are sure excited about this camping trip," Elizabeth said.

Going on down to the pond, they spent the rest of the morning fishing. The boys caught quite a few fish, though most of them they threw back. They only wanted to catch enough for their dinner.

"I think I caught one," Sarah said as her pole bent over. She reeled it in slowly, "I have never seen a fish fight so much."

"What a fish!" Rebecca said as Sarah held up a catfish.

"That is definitely a keeper. It will probably weigh ten pounds." John grabbed the fish, putting it on a stringer.

"You will have to bait my hook again, Daed," Sarah said, smiling.

"Can you believe it? The girls will fish, but they won't bait their own hooks," John said.

"It is about like a girl," Mark said.

"It is just so gross," Sarah said as she waited for John to bait her hook.

Elizabeth suddenly looked at her pocket watch. "Mary, we had better get back and start fixing dinner for everyone."

"I think we have had enough fishing," Sarah said.

"Daed, we don't have to quit fishing now, do we?" Mark asked.

"Boys, tell you what," John said. "You all carry the fish we have caught here back for your mothers, and then you can fish here until dark if you want to."

"We'll be back in a few minutes then," Caleb said, getting up.

"I'll sit with the boys a little longer, Joseph, if you want to go ahead and build us a campfire," John said.

"You boys behave then and listen to your uncle John," Joseph said.

"They won't be any problem," John said.

Joseph went ahead and carried over the firewood he had brought, getting everything ready for the night. The campfire was mostly just for looks, though they would roast a few hotdogs and marshmallows over it.

"Joseph, are we cooking over a fire?" Elizabeth asked.

"Nay, I brought my small grill and some charcoal for you ladies to use. There is nay use making it hard on you women. After all, we are just camping," Joseph said, smiling.

"Denki, Joseph, you are appreciated," Elizabeth said.

"I will get the grill out of the buggy," Mary said, walking towards the buggy.

The smell of cooking soon filled the camp. Catfish never smelled any better. By the time John came back with the boys, dinner was ready.

"Something sure smells gut," John said.

"Where's the fish?" Elizabeth asked looking at him.

"Sorry, honey, we didn't catch any more fish," John said. "I think I like fishing as much as the boys do. Fishing just seems to relax me for some reason, makes me feel at peace. It doesn't really matter how many fish you catch, just the time spent doing what you enjoy with your family."

"John, I know what you mean," Joseph said. "I always spend more time in the woods when I go hunting than I intend to. The gentle peace of the forest is hard to get away from."

"Let's spread a table cloth on the ground and eat right here," Mary said.

And so they did. It was so peaceful just to be able to relax and to sit around a campfire.

"Why did so many people move here in the old days?" Rebecca asked.

"I would say our ancestors had a rough life. Just camping out like this makes you feel like a pilgrim," Sarah said, laughing.

"I think it was the call for something greater—was the reason so many settlers poured into this country. A chance for a home with freedom of religion and for personal rights," John said. "It was not the weak-kneed people that settled this wild land, but men of character, integrity, and honor. Men who held a firm belief that all men were created equal."

"The greatest man that ever walked this earth did it with humility. He wore sandals on His feet instead of enjoying the spoils with kings," Joseph said. "Humble thyself in the sight of the Lord, and I will lift you up."

"Joseph, you have just about turned into a preacher," John said, laughing.

"Don't get him started," Mary said.

They sat around and talked the rest of the evening around a campfire. Joseph brought his horses in and tied them closer so that they wouldn't get tangled up in the ropes at night. John brought the mules in as well, feeding them all out of a feed bag.

Pilgrim followed the boys' every move, barking at everything that moved.

"I truly enjoy spending time with everyone," Mary said as they were getting ready for bed. "Thank you for coming with us, John."

"It has truly been my pleasure," John said, smiling.

"We have had more fun today than we have had in a long time," Rebecca said, smiling. "Thank you, Daed."

"You are welcome, Daughter. Time with family is always well spent," Joseph said.

When Joseph looked around again, everything was just about completely dark.

"I think it is time for us to turn in," John said. "Me and Joseph will keep the fire going for a little while longer, if you women want to go to bed."

"Gut idea. I was about to fall asleep," Elizabeth said.

The girls were excited to be spending the night together. The boys talked and carried on awhile in their tent before they finally went to sleep.

About an hour later, Joseph went to bed. Mary was asleep when he lay down beside her. He left the tent door half open let in fresh air. All was still except for the collie dog that made his rounds, checking out the surroundings for intruders. The fire burned down low until it was just a glow, and then it went out.

The home place seemed quiet the next morning when the weary bunch of campers returned.

"Hold up, John," Joseph said, stopping the buggy horse. "Let's let the women fix us all some breakfast while we put a cook stove in Sharon's room."

"All right, women, get to cooking," John said, smiling. "And cook us something gut now; we will probably work up quite an appetite."

"I have already installed the pipes. I just have trouble trying to lift the big stove," Joseph said.

They backed the wagon up and loaded the cook stove in it. John held the stove in the wagon while Joseph drove over to Sharon's room.

"She is probably asleep." John climbed down from the wagon and knocked on her door.

"I'm over here. I've already started cooking breakfast," Sharon said from the house porch.

"That is what you call a smart woman," John said, smiling.

They carried the stove inside, and by the time the women had breakfast ready, the stove was hooked up.

"Why did she want a cooking stove for?" John asked.

"I think she wants to do a little cooking for herself," Joseph said.

"Well mamm always was an independent person," John said, smiling. "Now let's go eat."

Joseph thought that things around the farm were getting back to normal until he went out to get the mare the next morning at five in the morning, and she wasn't there. Somebody must have sneaked in the barn last night and turned his horses loose. He grabbed his flashlight to see with and took off walking up through the fields. He spent close to two hours rounding up the horses. The children were at school today, so he had no help. He was very tired as a result of walking several miles in pursuit of the horses.

Mary was going to town today for a few supplies she needed, so he had risen early. Maybe he would have to put a lock on the barn door, but then again, they might just cut the lock. He had thought that when Ron Harmony had made friends with him that his troubles would be over.

He didn't tell Mary, but now he thought that there was more than one family trying to drive them off. David Stevens, for one, didn't want them living out there. It wasn't like they were bad neighbors that stayed drunk and rowdy all the time. Folks should appreciate a good neighbor who was an honest hard working man and who bothered no one.

Finally, he had the buggy mare hitched up, and they were on the way into town. All was quiet and still; the earth not yet awake. The darkness still lay upon the land. The gentle call of a few wild birds was the only sign of the life that would be resurrected at the first break of daylight.

"It is weird how the earth lives on forever," Joseph said, breaking the silence. "Each older generation of people must leave and make room for the ones that are to come. I wonder how many generations of people have traveled this same road. Nay doubt they had to carve out a living with their bare hands."

"Joseph, do you think about things like this all the time?" Mary asked, looking at him.

"Maybe it is God who puts the thoughts in my mind," Joseph said. "I often wonder about the Indians who roamed this land never to be seen again. Maybe they buried their dead here in unmarked shallow graves."

"We probably walk on graves all the time, and don't know it." Mary said, shaking slightly.

"Well, a man's life is like a vapor upon the water. It appears for a little while then it is gone. That is all we are, a bubble that will bust never to be seen again. We must give back to the dust from which we came; only the earth remains."

Joseph suddenly saw a long dark car coming their way.

"Slow down, Joseph. There is a car coming," Mary said.

Joseph got over to the right side of the road as far as he could. It wasn't a two lane road, but one wide lane that both directions shared. The car came on. Its lights were on so bright that Joseph could barely see the road. At the last second, the driver swerved, barely missing them. Joseph got a quick look at David Steven's face for a second as his buggy light shined on him. It looked like the man was deliberately trying to hit them.

Joseph pulled the buggy over a little more to the right. Suddenly he heard a loud clang as the buggy went down, and leaned over sideways. The wheel of the buggy had hit hard in a hole in the ditch, and broke in two.

"Get out, Mary, before the buggy tilts over!" Joseph said, setting the brake.

Mary climbed out quickly and waited on Joseph to get out. The driver of the car had gone on and hadn't stopped.

"What was the matter with that driver? He didn't even stop!" Mary cried.

"I think he did that on purpose, Mary," Joseph said.

Joseph looked the buggy over. They were about a mile from John's house. "Mary, it'll take a team of mules to pull the buggy out onto the road. Do you want to stay here or walk with me to John's house?"

"We will have to walk I suppose."

"Fine. Let me tie the mare up here off the road. You could ride her, but I don't have a saddle and your clothes will get dirty."

Joseph tied the mare up off the road, and then they started walking. John was doing his chores when they came walking up to his barn. He came out to meet them, sitting his feed bucket down.

"Mary, what is going on?" John asked.

"We need a pull from those famous mules of yours. I ran off the road in the dark and broke the buggy wheel," Joseph said. He wasn't going to tell John that somebody had run him off the road.

"Sure thing. Let me get my buggy hitched up with the mules," John said. "We will drive the buggy out there; there is nay sense in walking."

John soon had the mules hitched up and they were on their way.

The mules twitching their long ears some as they pulled the buggy. When they got there, John unhitched the mules and backed them up in front of Joseph's buggy. The mules pulled the buggy on to the road like it weighed nothing.

"I will help you change your buggy wheel," John said.

"Denki, John, this has set me back a lot financially," Joseph said as they were changing the buggy wheel.

"Things will work out; they always do with God's help. Where were you all going anyway?" John asked as Joseph hitched his buggy mare back up.

"Mary needs a few things in town. I guess we might as well go on and get them," Joseph said. "Denki again, John, for your help, but we had better be on our way."

Joseph helped Mary into the buggy and then climbed in quickly behind her. They were on their way to town once again.

Sheriff Clemons found them later in the hardware store. "I am sorry, Joseph, but here is your court summons. Mr. Stevens is taking you to court over the property dispute. He said he owns half of your land, and he was just trying to be nice. You need to hire a lawyer. I never thought he would actually go this far to get your land."

"Denki anyway, Sheriff," Joseph said. "We had better be getting home."

Chapter Twenty

It was time for a homecoming a few weeks later. Joseph had everything ready, and their home was just about complete. He just about had the farm the way he wanted it. He had been shoeing horses for everyone in his spare time. Folks came for miles around to have their horses shod, and even people that weren't Amish gave him a lot of business.

Sadly, most people didn't pay him with money; everyone was always broke, though they did have an animal or something else to trade for the labor. Joseph never turned anyone away in need; he didn't figure God would want him to. Whoever has mercy on the poor, God will have mercy on him as well.

The only thing Joseph needed badly was a milk cow. John and Herman had been supplying his family with fresh cow milk. It would be nice to have a cow; a man could make some fresh butter and cheese. Fresh milk was better for you anyway, and a lot richer. A man could have plenty of cream for his coffee.

Mary had wanted to have a homecoming and a big dinner now that they had their farm work complete. Joseph had risen early and started on the chores. All of Mary's family would be here today. They would also be staying on through the night with them. It would be a very busy day.

He looked forward to spending the day with them. Today felt like a holiday. The farm had been worked over and put in working order. It is weird how well a woman will clean a house when she knows that she has company coming. If you drop in on her unexpectedly, the house might not be as clean.

Joseph walked back towards the house as the first buggy approached. It looked like John and his family. Jeremiah and Hannah followed close behind them in their buggy. The whole yard soon filled with family. The kinfolk had arrived.

Herman and Linda were the last ones to arrive. Tied behind Herman's buggy was a milk cow that followed along slowly.

"We all pitched in, Joseph, and bought this cow for you," Herman said, stopping his buggy near Mary. Herman's two girls, Cynthia and Lexi, jumped down followed by the boys, Michel, Austin, and Stephan. "We recently pulled a calf off her, so she should give plenty of milk for a while."

"We don't have much money," Mary said, slowly.

"It is not a loan, Mary. The cow is a gift from all of your brothers," John said.

"Don't forget me! We helped too," Hannah said.

"I will pay you back when I can," Joseph said.

"There will be nay more talk of payment," Sharon said. "Please honor the gift my children have given you and Mary."

"Oh, I didn't mean to sound ungrateful," Joseph said. "I just wanted to pay for what we have, though a gift is gut too. Thank you all, and may God bless you."

"Well, you had better put Daisy in the barn then," Samson said, smiling.

Joseph got Daisy's leash and led her to the barn. Caleb and Benjamin followed close behind him. Daisy seemed very calm and friendly. After making sure she was fed and watered, he went back to the others.

"We will have to milk Daisy tonight." Joseph messed Caleb's hair up. "She will have to be milked twice daily, seven days a week."

"Oh man, more chores, Daed?" Caleb asked.

It was close to dinnertime now, and everyone had brought something for the meal. Joseph was grateful to have such good family members. Sharon looked happy today, visiting with all her children. The women soon had the dinner served on the picnic tables, all the food a man could eat. There seemed to be peace in the air. The birds chirped softly.

God must love to see families coming together in a homecoming. Someday soon, all the Christians will be going to a homecoming and a land without sorrow. There will be no more pain, and it will be a time to spend with families forever. We will never have to say goodbye again.

Joseph missed his mother and father badly. He felt like he was all alone in the world. It felt sad not to have any real family of your own. Yet as he looked around at all of Mary's family, they all felt like family to him now. With God's help, he would be able to endure, whatever life would deal out to him.

He that endures to the end shall be saved. Though if you look at the definition of the word endure, it means you will have to go through some things here on this earth. Sometimes, a man has to be like Job in the Bible. Whatever happens, to God be the praise. The Lord gives and He takes away, though blessed be the name of the Lord.

Joseph had looked around when they were burying his father, and he didn't want to go on with life. He saw a lot of people there that he loved as well, especially his mother. Each person has their own special place in your life. He knew he must go on with life for all of them, even though he felt he could never be happy again.

He remembered a song his dad used to sing on his guitar. His dad was of the Mennonite faith, where the Amish don't believe in musical instruments. Joseph missed the music; he could play the guitar a little himself. He hummed the song softly as he walked. "Coming home, coming home, never more to roam. Open wide God's arms of love, Lord I'm coming home."

Dinner was on the table when he got back, and all the dishes everyone had brought were warmed up. Nothing tastes better than soup beans, fried potatoes, chicken, and fried cornbread. Everyone had brought some kind of meat. Jeremiah had even brought some fresh deer meat. Every chair was filled up around the tables as all the children sat down.

"Let's bow our heads for a silent prayer," Joseph said.

All heads were bowed for a few minutes as everyone prayed, and then it was time to eat.

"I have never seen so many family members together at one time," Joseph said.

"Jah, sometimes a man is blessed and he doesn't even know it," John said, smiling.

"I think they gave our neighbor Abraham up to die," Herman said. "His children are coming in from out of state to see him."

"His own children haven't visited him in years," John said, shaking his head.

"It is weird how people rush to somebody's death bed and say things we should have said a long time ago," Sharon said. "Sometimes we all fail miserably as human beings, though as long as we are in a flesh, we will continue to do so."

Food was passed around quickly as everybody helped themselves. Joseph ate until he couldn't. That wouldn't hurt a man every now and then. Besides, there were so many desserts that he didn't want to insult anyone by not trying at least a little. It was kind of like at the holidays of Christmas and Thanksgiving. A man usually eats more than he should.

"You all don't forget my lemon pies. I brought several," Hannah said.

"You might have brought several pies, but there are not several left," Samson said, grinning.

They all sat around eating and talking, just taking their time. Sharon smiled, sitting by Mary and Hannah and looking like she was enjoying herself. Rebecca sat beside Sarah and a few of her cousins that were close to her age.

The boys had already eaten and had run off to play in the barn loft with John's boys and a few others. Finally, everyone had enough to eat, though they would continue eating on the feast throughout the day.

"Well, let's go play some horseshoes," Lewis said. "I think me and Noey will beat you all this time."

"Jah, we have been practicing," Noey said. "We will take the first game of horseshoes, though it might be a long day if we beat everyone."

"You're not supposed to brag until after you are done playing," Samson said, laughing.

"When you are as gut as we are, you don't have to wait to brag," Lewis said.

They played horseshoes, and most of the men played until late in the evening. Some of the women were inside the house, and a few others were sitting on the porch. Sharon sat on the porch in a rocking chair, with some of her grandkids sitting around her. Joseph finally went to milk the cow, followed by Herman and the boys.

"Daisy is pretty gentle. The people I got Daisy from said that she never caused any trouble when they milked her," Herman said.

Joseph tied Daisy up in the stall so that she could eat, keeping her mind off the milking. Daisy chewed her feed quietly while Joseph and Herman milked her; she didn't even twitch—a good milkier indeed. Finally, they were done. The milk they poured in pails so they could take it to the house. The milk would have to be strained before it could be used.

"It will be nice to have some homemade cow butter," Joseph said.

"Well, you should have plenty of it," Herman said, laughing.

Herman carried the milk to the kitchen door and gave it to Mary.

"You would think we have a cow on the place," Mary said, taking the milk to the kitchen sink.

"The milk will be gut with some peanut butter cookies later," Joseph said.

"Is that a request?" Mary asked, smiling.

"It is a demand," Herman said loudly.

"Hear now, you won't get any cookies acting like that." Mary came over and shut the kitchen door.

John and a few others wandered off to fish in the pond. Right before darkness fell, the men put their horses up for the night. Every stall in Joseph's barn was full, so they tied two of the extra horses up in the barn's central aisle. After all the animals were fed and watered, the men began to relax.

Soon they all went inside for the night. Amish go to bed early, usually when God shuts the lights off. Mary fixed Herman's snack, peanut butter cookies and fresh milk. They had been eating all day the food that the guests had brought, so there hadn't been much cooking. Sharon sat at the side of the table with all of her family around her, and the house looked very crowded.

"Thank you, Joseph," Sharon said. "You have made me happy."

"I try," Joseph said with a grin.

"We had better light some lanterns. It will be dark soon," Mary said.

"I will get us some blankets and mattress to sleep on," Joseph said. "A few of the children can use the couch cushions as a mattress and sleep on the floor."

Joseph, Mary, Hannah, and Jeremiah soon had everyone a place to sleep for the night.

"Mary, we can sleep in the living room, with our guests," Joseph said.

"They are our family, not guests," Mary said quietly.

"You're right, Mother," Joseph said, smiling.

"Make a small fire please. I love the light it gives off." Hannah shifted on a mattress on the floor.

"It is too hot for a fire," Herman said quickly.

They sat up a time, the men and women playing a few board games. The coffee kept coming freely until long into the night. Eventually, just about everyone had dozed off. Mary went around and shut down all the lanterns, and then made her way back to Joseph.

It had been a wonderful day for everybody, a homecoming like no other. The women would all have to rise up early the next morning and cook breakfast for everyone. And then the men would be off on their separate ways, back home to their own families and their busy lives.

The smell of fried bacon and eggs filled the house when Joseph woke up. Mary and Elizabeth stood in front of the stove, frying eggs. Rebecca and Sarah rolled out biscuits on the table; their aprons were still white with flour.

Joseph grabbed his hat, heading outside to do his morning chores even as most of the men were waking up.

When he came back inside an hour later, the house had been put back in order. Every mattress, couch cushion, and blanket had been put up. It looked like the entire house had been cleaned and the floors swept and mopped.

There were not enough chairs for everyone to sit at the table, so some of the men sat on the floor. Joseph gave Sharon his chair. He would sit with the men and children on the floor and put the women first.

"We should have borrowed some benches from the church." John sat down beside Joseph on the floor.

"Now you think of it," Joseph said, smiling.

The women fixed everyone a plate and brought it to them. They all took their time eating, simply enjoying each other's company.

"My cows are probably wondering what has happened to me," Lewis said.

"Jah, we had all better go," Herman said. "Linda, I'll get the buggy and pick you up out front."

The other men followed Herman out, and they soon had their horses hitched up to the buggies. It was time to leave. The men all had farms of their own to run. Mary went around and hugged all of her brothers and Hannah before they left.

"Mary, we will see you at church on Sunday." Jeremiah helped Hannah into the buggy.

"Lord willing, we will be there," Mary said.

The buggies left slowly out of the yard, one following the other in single file. Mary stood on the porch and watched the buggies driving away until they were nay longer in sight.

Joseph drove the buggy in slowly for the church service. The service was being held at John's house, and folks had come from miles around. The children were all dressed in their Sunday church clothes and looked their best. Even Sharon and Mary looked pretty with their hair pulled back and head bonnets on.

"Daed, are you going to church with us today?" Benjamin asked.

"Nay, I am still on probation," Joseph said.

"I don't think it's right, the deacons treating you this way," Rebecca said. "I will sit outside with you."

"Nay, we must honor the bishop and the church wishes," Joseph said, turning into John's yard. "You all go in and enjoy yourself. I will sit here in the buggy and read my Bible after I put the mare up."

"Joseph is right. We can't fight evil with evil. It takes love to overcome," Sharon said as they stopped in front of the house.

"We will see you in a little while." Mary planted a kiss on his cheek.

After he took care of the horse, Joseph read for a while. He would never tell Mary how it made him feel, being isolated from his family was a terrible feeling. The deacons were treating him like he was an animal. A small tear rolled silently down his face and hit the Bible he was reading.

A few hours later, the service was over and people came out for the dinner. He had already hitched the mare back up and was ready to go.

Bishop Moses waved at him to stop as he came his way. "What are you doing, Joseph?"

"I was catching up on some Bible reading." Joseph set his Bible down.

"That is gut." Moses cleared his throat. "Joseph, did you know that dancing is frowned upon, especially dancing to worldly music?"

"Nay I did not. Why did you ask?"

"I got another complaint on you. Somebody said they saw you and Mary dancing to worldly music in a public place," Moses said.

"I didn't know it was wrong, and it will not happen again," Joseph said.

"Each time you get in trouble, it adds more time on to your probation. Now are you going to eat with us today? You are more than welcome." Moses looked him in the eye.

"Nay, I brought some boloney sandwiches with me. I am not worthy to eat with you until my name has been cleared," Joseph said.

"Alright, Joseph, I respect that," Moses said, walking away.

He saw Mary and Sharon coming his way along with the children. They were all carrying plates in their hands.

"What is going on?" Joseph asked curiously.

"I told everybody to fix a plate to take with us," Mary said. "That way you wouldn't feel left out."

"Moses sent you a plate, Daed. I heaped it high with dessert." Rebecca handed it to him.

"I wasn't going to eat," Joseph said, getting the buggy moving, but he stopped seeing the hurt look on Rebecca's face. "Just as soon as we can find a wide spot beside the road, we will pull over and eat."

"Denki, Daed," Rebecca said, smiling.

"You are the only one that can do anything with Joseph," Sharon said, laughing.

One week later, Rebecca got a letter. She had almost forgotten about Rachel and David. *I wonder what the love birds wrote this time,* she thought to herself.

"I'll be back, in a minute," Rebecca said to her mamm. "I am going to sneak to my room and read their letters right quick."

"Okay dear, just don't stay too long," Mary said, smiling.

"Rebecca, take your time," Sharon said. "I'll help finish up supper."

"Denki, Grandma," Rebecca said as she went down the hallway.

Sitting down at her desk, she tore open the envelope. There was only one letter inside. How odd.

Dear Rebecca,

I do hope that you have truly forgiven me. I read your letter to David, and I am sorry to inform you that David doesn't want to write you anymore until he can make a decision. I was tying to help him learn to read and write so that you all could write to each other. I feel like I have pushed him away.

He also said he wasn't going to spend any more time with me, and he has quit studying. I fear we both may have lost him as a friend. I didn't mean to make a mess out of things.

Your friend,
Rachel.

Rebecca read the letter twice before ripping it up and pitching it in the trash basket. The only thing she had left to remind her of David was a small flower vase that he had bought her. Picking the vase up with a cry, she threw it hard against the wall. She watched in shock as small pieces of the vase shattered everywhere.

If David wasn't sure, then she wasn't going to worry about

him anymore. Maybe her daed was right, and they were still too young. She decided that she would trust God in this matter. When God picks your mate, then you would be blessed for seeking His guidance.

"Rebecca, are you alright?" Mary came running down the hallway, opening the door.

"Nay, Mother," Rebecca said as her mamm pulled her into a hug. "Rachel has stolen my boyfriend from me. Rachel just wrote to tell me that David won't be writing me anymore until he can figure out who he wants."

"It will be okay, dear," Mary said, rubbing her hair.

Her mother held her until the crying finally stopped. "Tell you what, Rebecca. You clean this mess up, and I will bring your supper to you. There is nay sense in you facing everyone when you're so upset."

"Denki, Mamm," Rebecca said, wiping the tears from her eyes.

CHAPTER TWENTY-ONE

Joseph was finishing up the feeding in the barn when he saw a car pull in with its headlights on. He walked forward to see who it was. He saw a strange man get out of the car, wearing a suit and tie. He carried a black leather briefcase in his hands. Every hair on his head was slicked back.

"Are you Joseph?" the man asked.

"That will be me," Joseph said.

"I need to talk to you and your wife." He stuck his hand out for Joseph to shake. "I am Toby Miller, an attorney for Davis Stevens. Is there any place where we can talk in private?"

"Toby, have a seat on the porch, and I'll get Mary." Joseph walked up on the porch. "Would you like something to drink?"

"Yes. Whatever you got will be fine," Toby said, opening his briefcase.

A few minutes later they were seated outside, enjoying their lemonade.

"As you know Stevens has filed a property dispute case against you," Toby said.

"Jah, the sheriff has already served the court summons," Mary said.

"What I am here for is to try to settle this case before we go to court." Toby downed his last sip of lemonade.

"What do you mean?" Joseph asked.

"Well, if you go to court, it will cost you both thousands of dollars," Toby said. "So I am here to offer you two hundred and fifty thousand dollars for your land. If you need time to think the offer over, we have until the court day which will be few months from now. I am sure we can win the case in court. The judge is a good friend of mine, and Stevens has a lot of political power."

"I appreciate you coming out." Joseph stood up. He felt his face getting warm. "I have made my mind up; you can tell Stevens we will see him in court."

"I hope you don't hold the case against me personally," Toby said, standing up. He grabbed his briefcase. "I'm just doing my job."

"It's not your fault, but if God is truly for me, then who can be against me?" Joseph said.

Toby just smiled, shaking his head, and then he was gone.

Joseph was still shoeing horses, having risen before dawn. It would take a while for him to get caught up on his work; folks were bringing horses from miles around for him to shoe, which was a blessing. He worked slowly, heating up the metal; he wore a leather apron in the front. He spread out a horseshoe with a hammer to make it wider when a horse came trotting into the yard without a rider.

He had seen David Stevens ride by earlier on this horse, alone. Joseph had waved at Stevens, trying to be neighborly, though the man hadn't waved back. Stevens had just given him a mean look and thrown an empty beer bottle down in the yard. Since then, it had been raining hard for several hours, and the horse was soaking wet. He was probably breaking the young horse to ride. The horse must have thrown him off somewhere on down the trail.

Joseph grabbed his raincoat, caught the horse, and put him in the corral so that the horse wouldn't wander off. He hitched up his two work horses to the wagon. He was getting ready to ride out when Mary and the children came out.

"Where are you going, Daed?" Caleb asked.

"I think Stevens' horse threw him. The horse came back here

without him," Joseph said. "I'm going to ride down the trail and see if I can find out what is going on."

"We will all go," Mary said.

"Well, climb in and we will be off," Joseph said. "Though you had better put a raincoat on. I'll put a tarp over the wagon right quick."

Mary and Rebecca got in the wagon, and Caleb and Benjamin helped Pilgrim in, who came running out at the last minute, wanting to go.

"It looks like the whole family is going now," Joseph said, smiling.

The horse trail was muddy, barely wide enough for a wagon. After about a mile, they came to a creek. David Stevens lay in the creek, hanging on to some tree roots on the bank. The water had been rising. It was up to his chest and rising fast. Steven's face had turned white. It looked like he was barely hanging on.

"Hurry, I can't hold on much longer," Stevens said.

"We'll get you out," Joseph said.

He drove the team up real close to the water and jumped out. He grabbed his rope and jumped in the water, wading over to where Stevens clung to the roots. He made a lasso and quickly slid it over Steven's shoulders. He pulled it tight. The water was very cold, and he saw Stevens shiver. The man smelled of alcohol, and his eyes looked bloodshot.

"Caleb, tie the other end of the rope to the wagon. Mary can use the team to pull him out," Joseph said, holding on to Stevens. "I will stay here and guide him out."

The boys tied the rope to the back of the wagon. Mary jumped in the driver's seat and, with a loud crack of the reins, drove the team forward.

Joseph started guiding Stevens out slowly, when suddenly he slipped. Joseph fought for his balance as he went down in the cold water. *Oh, my God, let Stevens be alright,* he prayed as he went under water, knowing he had dropped the rope.

He came up fighting for air, trying to get the water out of his eyes so he could see. The water was only about four feet deep. He didn't see Stevens anywhere as he watched Mary still driving the team forward. Mary went on about twenty feet or so when Joseph heard one of the boys holler at Mary.

Joseph ran to the bank as fast as he could go in the water. The rope reached the edge of the back when suddenly Stevens appeared still tied up with the rope around his shoulders. Stevens hit the bank and lay there on dry land now, but very wet. Joseph doubted if he was even alive, for he had been dragged underwater for about thirty feet.

"Stop, Mary!" Joseph screamed as he ran to Stevens, when he reached him he was laying on his stomach. And he wasn't moving or making any sound at all. *Lord have mercy*, Joseph thought, *I have killed a man.*

He had done some CPR training once, but it had been years ago. It had been part of a job requirement as he had worked on a logging crew. A tree didn't always fall where you thought it would every time. He tried to remember the right thing to do as he knelt beside him. Steven's chest wasn't moving at all and Joseph was sure he had drowned.

Mary and the children came running up behind him. "What can we do to help?"

"Just keep the children back for now, Mary." Joseph said. "I am going to try to do CPR on him."

"I'll take the boys back to the wagon." Rebecca grabbed the boy's hands. "And keep them there. Mamm you can help daed."

"Thanks, Rebecca." Mary knelt beside him, looking at Stevens.

"Mary, help me get him on his side," Joseph gasped, grabbing a hold of Stevens. *Help me, God, to remember what to do*, he thought. They rolled him over on his side, trying to see if any water would come out of his mouth. Joseph checked Steven's pulse at his wrist and couldn't find one.

"Now let's roll him over on his back," Joseph cried, trying not to panic. Joseph and Mary rolled him over quickly, knowing that time was very crucial. It was possible that Stevens' time on earth was finished.

All he could remember from CPR about drowning was chest compressions and blowing in their mouth. It would have to work; he didn't know anything else to do. If the man died, then at least he had tried to save his life.

He straddled Steven's legs in the front, and did thirty chest compressions in the center of his chest. When he was done, he raised the man's comatose head and pinched his nose shut. Taking a deep breath, he knelt over Stevens and gave him two quick breaths. *It is kind of weird,* Joseph thought, *this man hates me and I am trying to give him back his life.* A small tear rolled down Joseph's face on the man's chest; he hadn't even realized that he was crying silently.

"Please pray for him, Mary," Joseph cried, starting the chest compressions again.

When he finished with the compressions this time, he was getting tired. If help didn't come soon, he didn't know what he was going to do.

On the second breath, he thought about how God in the Bible breathed life into man. *Please, God, spare his life, I know You can if You want to.*

Suddenly, Stevens gasped and moved. Joseph had barely time to move as the man threw up everywhere. It was a awful mess, but at least the man was alive, maybe.

He didn't know if Stevens was going to live or not. The rancher sat there gasping for breath. Joseph moved closer to help get him out. The man still hadn't spoken, but he seemed to be breathing again. *Maybe now, he will be a better man,* Joseph thought.

"Let me help you up." Joseph knelt offering Stevens his arm.

"Get your hands off me! This is your fault!" Stevens shouted, his face turning red. Suddenly, without warning, the man moved quickly. Joseph saw the fist coming his way too late. It caught him squarely on the jaw and knocked him down across Steven's legs.

Joseph felt the pain across his head, but the shock hurt more. This crazy man had hit him—even after all he had done for him. Not counting saving his worthless hide, this was one time he was going to pay.

With a cry like an angry bull, Joseph jumped on top of Steven's legs. The man looked up and smiled like he was enjoying it. Joseph grabbed him by the throat with his left hand, and drew his right fist back. This was going to feel good, showing this man that he couldn't run over every body.

"Joseph, what are you doing?" Mary cried in shock coming toward him.

Joseph's fist was in the air and he swung with every thing in him. He could feel years of hard work behind it, and he knew he still had a powerful blow. At the last second, he looked down at the man whose life he had just saved. The fist stopped just inches from Mister Stevens' nose, and he was not amused.

"Why don't you hit me?" Stevens shouted. "You know I deserve it! Go ahead, you coward!"

"Nay, I am not afraid of any man." Joseph still held him firmly by the throat. And Stevens wasn't moving, even though he was trying to. Finally, he quit squirming when he realized that Joseph was stronger than he.

"How can I hit a man whose life I just saved?" Joseph asked, looking him in the eye.

"What are you talking about?" Stevens snapped. "All I can remember is going under the water. You never saved my life!"

"Jah, he did," Mary said, crying. "Joseph performed CPR on you while we prayed to God for your life!"

Stevens still didn't look convinced as he glanced back at Joseph. Joseph got off him and walked away a few feet, trying to calm down. His arm was shaking slightly, and he felt like he couldn't breathe.

"Give me a few minutes to get my breath," Stevens gasped. "Then get me out of here!"

"Are you okay?" Joseph asked Stevens when he had settled down a few minutes later. "Your horse came to our house without you, and I figured we had better check on you."

"I do not understand. Why would you check on me after the way I have treated you?"

"It is all about forgiveness," Joseph said. "We must learn to forgive others as God has forgiven us."

"I would find that hard to do," David Stevens said.

"Once you start forgiving people, it will get easier each time," Joseph said.

"What if you can't learn to forgive?" Stevens asked. "A lot of people have actually done me wrong over the years."

"Then it is simple. God will not forgive us either. It is in the Bible." Mary climbed out of the wagon and was looking at Steven's leg.

"What happened to you anyway?" Joseph asked.

"I was riding my horse across the stream and a wild pheasant flew up. Anyway, the pheasant spooked the horse, and he reared up and fell, and landed on my leg. He caught me right above the ankle. What sacred me the most was the rising water. I don't know how much longer I could have hung on. You all saved my life, and for that, I thank you."

"That is what a gut neighbor is for," Mary said.

Joseph checked his leg. "Jah, your leg is broken. I can set it, but I don't know if you want me to. Anyway we must get you into the wagon first."

Getting a hold of his shoulders, Mary and Joseph helped Stevens up into the wagon. There they laid him down on his back. "Do you want me to set your leg?" Joseph asked. "It looks like you lost one of your silver spurs."

"Yes, I must have dropped my spur when the horse threw me. I will wait and let the hospital set my leg. If you touch me again, I will have you thrown in jail!"

"We will drive slowly." Joseph climbed in the wagon seat

ignoring Stevens and turned the wagon around. "Rebecca, you and the boys hold on to Stevens, and don't let him fall out."

Finally, Joseph had Stevens back on their farm.

"I almost forgot. I have a cell phone. Hopefully it will still work," Stevens said. The ambulance was soon informed and on its way.

"Mary, go inside and bring Stevens something to drink," Joseph said.

"I don't want anything to drink," Stevens snapped, his face red.

When they were all inside the house, Stevens turned to Joseph as they were waiting on the ambulance. He still had a mean look on his face. "Joseph, what if I forget this and keep acting the way I have been? Are you still going to keep forgiving me?"

"It does not matter. I forgave you a long time ago."

"I don't understand what you're taking about," Stevens said.

Joseph handed Stevens back his silver riding spur that he had recently found.

"Where did you find my spur?" Stevens asked suspiciously.

"The night our barn burned down, this spur was lying beside it. I picked the spur up before the sheriff saw it, and I have been waiting for the right time to give it back to you. Now the barn was old, and I figured somebody was just trying to scare us away. If they had meant any real harm, they would have tried to burn the house."

"You mean you suspected me all along?" Stevens looked at him.

"Jah, all is forgiven. Nay matter if you never speak to me again," Joseph said.

Joseph heard the ambulance coming. Stevens turned his head away and wouldn't look at him anymore. He was strangely quiet.

They soon had him loaded up in the ambulance and the medics left with Stevens. Joseph turned to Mary. "Let's load the children up and deliver Steven's horse back to his farm. His wife might not know what has happened to him."

"You want to deliver a horse in the rain? You've got to be kidding me!" Mary said, smiling.

"It will be fun," Caleb said, smiling.

CHAPTER TWENTY-TWO

It was harvest time a few months later, and everyone was excited. Five months had passed since they had first planted their own crop, along with enough hay and corn to feed their animals all winter. Joseph had spent many a day, using a single plow with Lucky to keep the weeds down between the rows. What he couldn't get in their garden with a plow, the boys had weeded with a garden hoe.

Joseph bounced around as he cut hay with a horse drawn hay cutter. The hay turned over as it lay down. The hay cutter had a seat on it for the driver and threw the cut hay off to the right hand side. All of their equipment was horse drawn—the hay cuter and the rake they used to flip the hay. The work was very slow.

In a couple of days, the hay would have to be flipped a few more times with a rake to let the hay dry out in the sun. Then the hay would be baled and stored in the barn loft for the winter. Joseph could walk overhead in the barn loft and throw the hay down to a manger in each stall. The corn also would have to be harvested and stored in the two corn cribs that he had built.

Joseph turned Lucky around slowly and started another row. When he was out working all alone, he felt close to God. Even Jesus went into the wilderness to pray, time spent alone just talking to God. It was good for the soul. He was thinking about David in the Bible, how he would pray and ask God for advice before he made any decisions or entered a battlefield.

They still had a lot of work left to do. They had to get all of the hay baled and put it in the barn. And they still needed to finish harvesting their corn crop and all their garden produce for the winter. It would probably take another week or two of work to get everything done, working from daylight to dark.

Joseph worked on. Lucky pulled hard, giving Joseph a jerk. The sweat ran freely down the animal's sides. Lucky looked so stocky and well-built that it seemed like he was enjoying the hay cutting. Whatever Joseph asked Lucky to do, he put his whole heart into it. He couldn't wait until Lacy was big enough to use with Lucky as a team so that he wouldn't have to borrow John's mules anymore.

A man felt a little better when he could stand on his own two feet, with God's help, of course. His favorite Bible verse came to mind. "I can do all things through Christ which strengthens me."

Four hours later, he saw Mary and Rebecca bringing him out something to snack on.

"Denki, Mary." Joseph took the lemonade. "A gut woman never has to be told to check on her man. It is in her character. Actually, one of the most beautiful verses in the Bible is about a woman's character and is found in the book of Proverbs."

"I'll try to remember that," Rebecca said, smiling.

"Denki, dear God, for the lemonade," Joseph said as Caleb and Benjamin came up to them.

"Daed prays about everything," Caleb said, smiling.

"Children, please don't let a cup or bread touch your lips without giving God denki for it first," Joseph said.

"I think we are about out of birdseed," Mary said. "Caleb please run down to the shed and get some more seed."

"Mother, why do you like the wild birds so much?" Benjamin asked.

"There is a Bible verse about birds and how God feeds them and even knows where they fall," Mary said. "He compares us, His children, to the birds. This is my small way of helping God feed them."

"Mamm, that is a beautiful story. I never thought of it like that," Rebecca said.

Joseph got the feeder down from where it hung in a tree. Mary had got him to make a bird feeder for her when they had first moved onto the farm. Caleb came quickly with a small bag of bird seed, and Joseph waited while he filled it up.

Soon, Caleb had it filled, and Joseph hung the feeder back up.

"Denki, Caleb," Mary said.

"Nay problem, Mother," Caleb said, smiling.

"I had better finish cutting the hay." Joseph placed a kiss on Mary's cheek.

"Don't forget me," Rebecca said, smiling.

Joseph gave Rebecca a kiss on the cheek. "I could never forget you. Just yell at me when dinner is ready."

"Men, all they think about is food," Rebecca said, laughing.

Joseph went back to work. An hour later, he saw Mary waving at him. Rebecca rang the dinner bell loudly. It was time for dinner. Daisy, the milk cow, rang her bell as she walked over to him in the pasture to see what was going on. He kept a small bell on her to help find her quickly. Daisy was a gentle cow and pretty. She was light brown in color with dark brown spots all over her.

Daisy came closer, wanting Joseph to pet her. He rubbed her between the eyes. "Not now, girl. I don't have any sugar cubes."

Joseph stopped Lucky in the shade and unhitched him before turning him loose. Another day of work and he would have the hay cut. He hoped it would not rain. He had nay way of checking the weather. An English man, who he'd shoed a horse for, had told him the weather report. It was supposed to be dry all week.

If the hay got rained on much at all, it would be ruined. Some people would try to use the ruined hay anyway, maybe for cattle or goats, but it would be dirty hay and could possibly harm an animal.

Going inside the house, he saw that everyone was already at the table waiting on him, except for Sharon. She ate with them most of the time. He was very dirty, but a working man usually is. Going to the utility washroom, he used the sink there to scrub himself down good with a bar of lye soap.

The children already had their food on their plates by the time he went back to the table. "Let's bow our heads for a silent prayer," Joseph said as he sat down. He was beginning to appreciate this way of praying.

"I think I am getting an ear ache," Benjamin said.

"Benjamin, pour a little groundhog grease in your ear and you'll be alright." Sharon came into the kitchen and sat down at the table.

"Groundhog grease? You've got to be kidding me," Benjamin said.

"When I was growing up, a gut home remedy that we used was groundhog grease. We used the grease for many things, including an earache. A few warm drops in each ear works well," Sharon said.

"So you had to make do with what you had instead of running to the store for every thing?" Joseph asked.

"Jah," Sharon said. "A lot of the Amish still make lye soap like the early settlers did with ashes from a fireplace. The soap works well and smells a lot better than you might think. It would probably surprise most people the things that we make stuff out of. The early settlers in this country, our ancestors, had to make about every thing that they used. In fact, a lot of them used spices, herbs and different things to help cure a sickness. The teas they made were used for medical purposes, and they ate certain plant roots."

"Mamm made me drink a nasty tasting tea for a sore throat when I was little," Mary said, laughing.

"Sassafras tea cures many things," Sharon said, laughing.

"Denki, Sharon," Joseph said. "I have always enjoyed history for some reason. It is our heritage."

After dinner, Joseph and Mary went out and sat on the porch. The boys went outside to play. They had already done their chores, and Rebecca was inside reading. Joseph sat there and watched the goats eating the weeds. A few goats would stand up and knock a small tree over, and then they would all eat the leaves off it. Goats rarely eat grass. They love weeds, trees, and sometimes even flowers. They are better suited on a hillside than in a pasture.

"How many goats have you got now?" Mary asked.

"Seventy-five nannies and five billy goats, plus twenty-five sheep," Joseph said. "I don't need any more goats. If we got anymore, we are going to have to do something with them. Maybe take the extra goats to the livestock sale or butcher them."

"Joseph, if you would quit letting people pay you with animals for shoeing their horses, we would be better off," Mary said.

"It makes me feel bad to turn a man down," Joseph said. "People are hurting right now financially, but they can still pay in other ways. We have so much to be thankful for."

"The most important thing we have is our family," Mary said.

"I guess I will finish up the hay cutting tomorrow," Joseph said. "I don't know if John will need my help with anything or not."

"I'm glad you and John get along so well," Mary said, smiling.

It wasn't long until the darkness set in, and it was time to go to bed. Work would come quickly in the morning, and they had a lot of it.

Joseph got up early and ate his breakfast. He had to finish cutting the hay today. When he had a job to do, he couldn't rest until it was done. Going outside, he harnessed Lucky up quickly to the sickle and began.

He cut row after row, refusing to let up. He would reach the end of a row, guide Lucky around with the plow lines, and start down another one. He was halfway done, and it was getting close to dinnertime. He saw Mary come outside with a pitcher of lemonade. He was very thirsty.

Mary stepped out on the porch and started down the steps towards him. When Mary's feet hit the third step, it seemed like her legs flew out from underneath her. Down she went, throwing the glass pitcher in the air. The pitcher shattered on the bottom step, sending lemonade splashing everywhere. It looked like her head might have hit the side of the step.

Joseph heard Rebecca scream. He ran fast to Mary, leaving Lucky still hitched up to the hay cutter. He made it to Mary as fast as he could. *God, please let her be alright.* The boys reached their mother first, helping her to sit up. Joseph knelt beside Mary. She had a knot on her head about the size of a hen egg.

"Mary, are you okay?" Joseph asked.

It took Mary a few minutes to answer him. "I feel so weak; I think I must have fainted."

"Did you trip on the steps?" Rebecca asked.

"Nay, I just felt a little dizzy." Mary's head was bleeding a little, though not bad.

"Mary, I am going to take you to the doctor," Joseph said. "You may need stitches."

Sharon had come out by then.

"I don't want to go," Mary said.

"You had better go with him, just to be on the safe side," Sharon said.

"Go inside, Rebecca, and get me something to clean up with right quick," Mary said.

Rebecca went inside and came back with a wash pan. She helped Mary clean up as best she could.

"I will hitch the buggy mare up and put Lucky up. You children look after your mother. Sharon, you can come with us if you want," Joseph said.

"Thank you. I will be ready," Sharon said.

Joseph rode Lucky back into the barn and unharnessed him there. He would have to feed the horses later when he got back. Leading the mare out, he harnessed her up in the barn hallway between the stalls. He had the buggy in the back of the hallway now, so he backed the mare up to it and hitched her up to the buggy.

He climbed in quickly. "Get up, Fiery." The mare took off,

pulling the buggy. She snorted as Lucky stuck his head out over the stall door, trying to bite her.

Riding up in front of the house, Joseph stopped the mare and set the brake. He got out and helped Mary, Rebecca, and Sharon inside, Mary still looked pale. The twins jumped in with a bound; they were ready to go.

"Mary, just lay back and rest. I'll get you there shortly," Joseph said.

Rebecca sat beside her mamm holding a wet cloth to her head. Joseph rode out of the yard in the buggy at a steady pace. He would get Mary there as soon as possible. The road seemed to take forever, though the mare really ate the miles up. She could move when she wanted to. In a little while, they passed John's farm and went onward into town. He was trying to catch the doctor before his office closed for the day. Joseph didn't stop anywhere until they made it to the doctor's office at the edge of town. Finally, they arrived. Mary was asleep now.

Joseph shook her gently. "Wake up, Mary. We are here."

Mary came awake with a jerk. "Where are we?"

"You are at the doctor's office," Sharon said. "The fall must have addled her some when she hit her head. She can't remember anything."

"Alright, children, let's get your mother in to see the doctor," Joseph said.

He helped Mary down and walked with her, holding her arm in case she started to fall. There were a lot of Amish people inside the doctor's office. They all seemed to be from another district, so he didn't know them.

"Can I help you?" the secretary asked behind the desk.

"My daughter has cut her head. We need to get her in as soon as possible," Sharon said.

"Just fill these papers out." The secretary handed the papers to Joseph.

After Mary was signed in, they walked to the back seats. The big office was built very plain, with no decorations at all. Mary sat down beside her mother Sharon and the children sat down beside her. After about thirty minutes of waiting, the boys became restless. Joseph stepped outside with the twins for a few minutes to get some air. When they came back inside, Mary was gone.

"It probably won't be long now, boys," Joseph said.

"We should have brought our dinner with us," Caleb said.

"We'll get something to eat when we get out of here," Joseph said. "It's too late for your mamm to cook today anyway. She will need her rest."

"Can we go to McDonalds?" Benjamin asked.

"I don't know exactly where one is or if they have a hitch rail for the Amish," Joseph said.

After about another hour of waiting, the nurse came to the door and motioned for Joseph to come in.

"Mary wants to see you." She smiled very big.

Joseph tried not to worry, but his stomach felt odd. Something must be wrong. He made his way back to the room. Mary sat on the bed in a white gown, where they had examined her. Sharon was sitting in the chair, and Rebecca was standing beside her Mother, holding her hand.

Joseph made his way quickly to her side. "What is wrong Mary?" He took her hand. "Is everything okay?"

The doctor came in. A short man, who was as wide one way as he was another and partly bald on top.

"I am Doctor Goodwill." He shook Joseph's hand firmly. "Have you told him the news yet, Mary?"

"Told me what?" Joseph asked.

"You are going to be a father again," Mary said, smiling.

"Do what? It can't be!" Joseph said stunned.

"Yes, that is the reason she fainted. Mary will have to eat healthier and get certain vitamins to take." The doctor hit Joseph lightly on the shoulder.

"Are you happy?" Mary watched his face closely.

"Jah, I thought something bad was wrong with you. It is hard to believe that the Lord is giving us another child after all these years."

"The Lord works in mysterious ways," Sharon said, laughing.

"Mary, you are free to go. Just follow my instructions carefully and come back when you need to," the doctor said.

"Thank you, doctor, for all your help." Joseph shook his hand.

"Yes, I guess you can pass out the cigars now," the doctor said, smiling. "Now I had better get back to work." The doctor went out quietly, shutting the door behind him.

"Mary, please don't tell the boys. We will tell them while we're eating dinner," Joseph said. "I want to surprise them."

"Alright," Mary said, smiling. She slipped out of her gown, and dressed quickly.

Joseph went out and paid on his doctor bill. The doctor was pretty good about letting people make payments on their bills.

Going outside, he helped the women get inside the buggy. There was an older Amish man standing nearby. Joseph went up to him and spoke to him for a few minutes. The man smiled as he answered and looked towards the buggy where the boys waited.

"What was that all about?" Rebecca asked as he got in the buggy.

Joseph didn't answer. He just backed the mare up a little and took off. The horse's hoofs sounded like music as it made a clicking sound in the road. A half mile down the road, Joseph pulled into a parking place for the Amish. There were some buggies already parked there. The parking place was straight across the road from a McDonald's restaurant. He parked there beside the other buggies, and then helped Mary down and across the road. Rebecca was walking with Sharon, holding her hand.

"Joseph treats me like I'm an old woman," Mary said.

"You had better enjoy it while you can." Sharon smiled.

They made their way inside, and Joseph found them a table. He then went with Rebecca to get their food.

"I'll get our drinks." Rebecca got a tray. She fixed them all a coke. They carried their food to the table, and after a silent prayer, they all tore into their food.

Joseph waited until everyone got settled before clearing his throat. "Boys, besides falling, there was something else wrong with your mother. She is going to have a baby."

"A baby? Are you sure?" Caleb asked.

"Jah," Mary said.

"Gut, I want a brother," Benjamin said.

"Well, we don't know what your mother is going to have right now," Joseph said.

"We will have to let God surprise us," Mary said. "That was the way He intended it. Actually, before they came out with all this modern technology, nobody knew if they were having a boy or a girl baby."

"It will either be a girl or a boy," Rebecca said, laughing.

"It could be both. Twins do run in this family," Sharon said, laughing.

"Mother, don't even think something like that," Mary warned.

They sat there a while, eating. Joseph kept trying to get Mary to eat more.

"You are eating for two now," Joseph said.

"I'm just about stuffed," Mary said.

Joseph went and got them all an apple pie desert. After they all had eaten their dessert, Joseph stood up and threw their trash away.

"Mary, we had better be on our way. We need to get back before dark," Joseph said. "My buggy has got a few lights on it, though some of the bulbs need to be replaced."

Joseph held Mary's hand and walked her back across the road to their buggy. A few minutes later, they were all loaded up and ready to go.

"I think I'll lay back and rest," Mary said. "I am very tired; thank you, Joseph, for the dinner."

"You are welcome, my dear," Joseph said. "Mary you are going to have to quit working so hard and take better care of this baby."

The town finally disappeared behind them as the buggy rolled on into the sunset. Joseph stopped to talk to John and Elizabeth for a few minutes. They stood out in their yard, planting flowers. John held a shovel in his hands and he looked a little embarrassed.

"I am going to have another baby!" Mary sat up in the buggy.

"A baby? That is always gut news," Elizabeth said, smiling.

"We do have to keep the Amish population going," John said, smiling. "The bishop will be pleased to get another church member."

"I will cook you something to eat tomorrow so that you can rest. I'll have John bring it out," Elizabeth said.

"If you all need anything, please let us know," John said, smiling.

"Rebecca and me will start cooking breakfast until Mary gets over her morning sickness," Sharon said. "I was a very gut cook in my younger years."

"You still are a gut cook, grandma," Caleb said. "She makes the best rice crispy treats."

"Well, we had best be on our way," Joseph said, bringing the reins down lightly. They were off.

They made their way on home. Joseph let Mary off at front of the door. Joseph walked Mary into her room and helped her get comfortable on the bed. He went back outside with the boys to put the mare up and to feed all the animals. It had been a very long day, but a good one nonetheless.

CHAPTER TWENTY-THREE

Rachel sat at home quietly on the couch, trying to read a book by her favorite author. Over the last few weeks, Rachel hadn't been able to talk much to David. Every time she had looked up at school, she always found his eyes on her, but he hadn't even spoken to her. It seemed like David was going out of his way to avoid her.

Rachel laid her book down and headed out of the living room a few minutes later when her mamm spoke suddenly. "Rachel, is there any reason that David hasn't been coming over?" Ruth asked. "You two haven't had a fight have you?"

"Nay, Mamm." Rachel avoided her mother's eyes.

"I have got some catfish laid out that you all caught," Ruth said. "You can invite him over to dinner Friday evening, if you like."

"Okay, Mamm, but I don't know if he will come," Rachel said softly, holding back a tear.

"Well, it doesn't hurt to try any way," her daed spoke up.

"I think I'll go to bed early," Rachel said. "I'm worn out."

David lay on his bed, staring up at the ceiling. He had been praying hard about the girls and searching his heart. Both girls were pretty; there was nay doubt about that. He could never see Rachel before because he had only eyes for Rebecca. Rachel had stayed back in the shadows, even though it was clear that she liked him.

He thought about what Rachel had said, about not coming between him and Rebecca. He thought about how she had taught him to read and write. He still needed to improve, but he was getting better slowly. Nobody else had ever taken the time to teach him to read, not even Rebecca. It is odd, David thought, but Rachel seemed very humble. She had always put others before herself.

The last time he had kissed Rebecca, he had felt attraction, but with Rachel, it felt like he had a hold of a passionate young woman. He could feel Rachel's heart next to his, beating loudly.

He got out a pen and paper and wrote Rebecca a letter—this time in his own handwriting.

Dear Rebecca,

I have searched my heart, and it saddens me to have to tell you that I care deeply for Rachel. You both are pretty, and you will make some man proud someday. It is the gentle way Rachel has about her that I have come to love.

Remember when we were younger and we found a stray dog by the road that had been hurt? We were all in a hurry that day, but Rachel wouldn't leave until we carried the dog to a neighbor's house and bandaged its leg. I am sorry that it has taken me so long to make my decision, and we can always be friends. It is just that Rachel has my heart, and I cannot deny my love for her.

Your friend,
David.

He put the letter in his shirt pocket, and then it suddenly hit him that he must tell Rachel tonight. He would get Rachel to mail the letter to Rebecca for him. He hadn't spoken to Rachel in a while. He slipped out of his room and went quietly down the stairs.

A few minutes later, he had his horse saddled and ready to go.

It wasn't that far away. He just hoped that Rachel was not already in bed. His daed would never know that he was gone. Flint chased him out of the yard and down the road, barking wildly. He hoped the crazy dog wouldn't wake his father up.

When he rode into Ruth's yard, the dogs there charged him making a noise like you wouldn't believe. He tied his horse up on the steps' rails. He tapped lightly for a few minutes, and then banged hard on Ruth's door.

"David, what are you doing out here at this time of night?" Ruth asked, opening the door. "Did you smell the catfish that I have laid out of the freezer?"

"Catfish? Nay, I have come to talk to Rachel," David said. "It is very important."

"Sit on the porch then." Ruth pointed outside. "I'll get Rachel up and give you all a few minutes of privacy."

"Denki, ma'am," David said as Flint came running up on the porch. David held Flint there, afraid the other dogs would eat him.

A few minutes later, Rachel came out in her bathrobe. She looked a little sleepy.

"What is going on?" Rachel sat down beside him on the swing.

"I've written Rebecca a letter, and I want you to mail it for me," David said.

"David, couldn't this wait until in the morning?" Rachel yawned.

"Nay, it cannot." David pulled the letter out of his pocket and gave it to Rachel. "Please read it," David said.

All was quiet as Rachel read the letter. Halfway through, she paused and read again, and then she looked at David puzzled.

"What does this mean?" Rachel asked.

"Keep reading," David said.

Finally, Rachel spoke, "You mean I am the one you love?"

"It took you a while," David said, smiling.

"David, are you sure?" Rachel asked.

"Jah," David said. "It is your heart I'm trying to win."

"You already won my heart long ago," Rachel said honestly.

"Gut, it is settled then," David said, smiling.

"David, would you like to come to dinner Friday? My mother is cooking catfish," Rachel said.

"I wondered what she was talking about." David leaned forward and gave Rachel a quick kiss on the lips. "You had better believe it; I will be here from now on."

"Well now, let's not rush things." Rachel smiled.

"I don't believe in losing a woman for courting too slow," David said.

"I think you have listened to the song 'Old Smoky' one time too many." Rachel laughed.

Ruth came to the door. "We had better go to bed," she said with a smile. "We have got a lot of work to do tomorrow. David, are you coming over for dinner Friday?"

"I will be there, Mother." David climbed on his horse.

"Mother, that has a nice sound to it." Ruth said, smiling.

"It sure does." Rachel smiled as she shut the door.

A large church congregation was gathered at Deacon James's house when Joseph drove their buggy into the yard with his family. There were buggies parked everywhere as far as the eye could see. Joseph dropped his family off in front of the house, and then led the buggy mare into the barn. It took him a little while to feed and water her.

He still wasn't allowed to attend the church services, but now it didn't bother him as bad. He figured when God got ready, He would move on his situation. It would do him nay good to worry. He treated all the church members with respect, nay matter how they acted toward him.

He walked back to the buggy and was surprised to see someone leaving with their back to him. There were quite a few buggies parked real close to his. Joseph turned the page in his Bible when he noticed Bishop Moses, Timothy, and Nathan coming his way.

"What are you doing, Joseph?" Moses stopped beside him.

"I am just catching up on reading the gut book." Joseph smiled, holding up his Bible.

"Joseph, I've got a report that you have been drinking beer out here." Moses shook his head. "Somebody said that you have beer in your buggy right now."

"That is a lie," Joseph said.

"You don't mind if we check your buggy then?" Nathan asked.

"Go ahead, and if you find any beer in my buggy, I will leave and never come back," Joseph said.

Nathan walked over and looked in the back of the buggy. There was an old blanket in the buggy. When Nathan moved it, Joseph saw a small pack of beer. It was the same kind of beer that Joseph had found in his shed.

"Joseph, this looks mighty bad," Timothy said. "I honestly thought you were innocent this whole time. I'm afraid that you can nay longer be a church member. There have just been too many incidents against you."

"Moses, what do you think?" Nathan asked.

"I think you're right. Somebody is hurting awful bad. To be sneaking around drinking like they have, maybe they are doing it because they are grieving," Moses said slowly. "I agree with Timothy that they can nay longer be one of us—as a church deacon that is."

"What do you mean as a deacon?" Timothy stepped closer to Moses.

"I stepped out on the porch for some fresh air while Deacon James was preaching, and I saw Nathan put the beer in Joseph's buggy," Moses said. "I know that Nathan used to like Mary when she was younger. I just can't believe that he would let it go this far."

Nathan's face turned white. "I'm sorry, Joseph, please forgive me. To be honest, I was hurting so bad when my wife died that I wanted somebody else to suffer besides me. It just didn't seem fair that Joseph should be blessed with such a gut family...and you all were giving him a warm welcome into the church. I blamed God for taking my wife from me. Once I started drinking, it just became easier to lash out at someone."

"You are forgiven." Joseph held his hand out for Nathan to shake. "I figure it was the grief that made you act this way."

Nathan shook Joseph's hand without looking him in the eye.

"Jah, you just can't be a deacon anymore, Nathan; I also expect a full confession to the church," Moses said. "And, Joseph, you are one of us now."

"Moses, please let's not bring anything else in front of the church for Mary's sake," Joseph said. "All I want is to be a full church member."

"I will give it some thought." Moses nodded his head. "Now follow me, please."

Joseph felt odd at all the eyes upon them as he followed the bishop to the front of the church congregation. He looked back and saw Mary staring hard at him.

"May I have your attention, everyone." Moses waved his hand. "We have heard many complaints about Joseph. One was that he has a drinking problem. It has now come to my attention that somebody has been telling lies about him. Joseph has been cleared from all charges and is now a church member in gut standing," Moses said, looking around the room.

"Who lied about him?" Deacon James asked loudly.

"Joseph has requested that I not reveal this information to anyone. At this time, I will honor Joseph's request while I pray about what to do," Moses said.

"One thing we can learn from this incident is not to judge a man too quickly," James said loudly.

"That is right. Joseph has preached to us in deeds not in words," Moses said. "Church is dismissed, by the way."

Joseph walked down slowly and shook a few people's hands; John hugged him. "I appreciate you, John."

Rebecca reached him next and gave him a hug, "I love you, Daed."

"Rebecca, you always had faith in me." Joseph squeezed her a little hard.

Mary reached him then, and she was crying slightly. She gave him a quick hug. "Who was it, Joseph, that caused all this trouble?"

He saw Nathan tense up for just a second. He could easily put Nathan through the same pain he had felt. "I will never tell you. Now let's go home. I am very tired."

Joseph was eating his morning breakfast when Caleb came running back inside the house. "Daed, come quickly!"

"What is wrong?" Joseph asked rushing outside.

"Somebody left that out here." Caleb pointed towards the house.

Joseph stared hard. Leaning against the wall was a new buggy wheel. His old wheel had been broken when someone had forced him off the road. There was nay note on it, just a yellow ribbon tied around the wheel.

"Well, I wonder who left that wheel," Mary said puzzled.

"The Lord works in mysterious ways." Joseph smiled.

"What are you keeping from me, Joseph?" Mary stepped closer to him.

"Nothing woman." Joseph put the wheel up. "I have got work to do now."

He went to do his morning chores. The twins followed close behind him.

It was along about dinner time when the yard began filling up with automobiles. There were cars and trucks coming from everywhere. Even a sheriff's car was there.

"What in the world is going on?" Joseph asked the twins as they threw hay down from the barn loft.

The barn had a very good view from the loft. He could see

for miles around. Somebody blew a car horn loudly. Several more horns joined in and things were getting pretty loud.

Mary and Rebecca came outside on the porch and stood there staring.

"We had better go see what is going on." Joseph laid his hay rake down. He made his way down the barn loft ladder and then went quickly to Mary.

A long black car pulled up and stopped. Out stepped David Stevens and his wife Janet. Stevens pulled out a pair of crutches to lean on. Next he saw Ron Harmony and his sons, and a few people that he did not know. They were all carrying something in their hands.

"Joseph, where can we eat at?" Stevens smiled at Caleb. "We have brought dinner for everyone. We want to welcome you into the neighborhood. I even brought a cake."

"Now we can't cook as well as you Amish, so we brought some Kentucky Fried Chicken. It is the next best thing," Janet said carrying a bucket of chicken.

"Don't forget the pies," Ron said. "Every thing came from KFC of course."

Joseph couldn't speak for a minute.

"Well, where do you want to eat?" Janet asked loudly.

"Over there on the picnic tables will be fine," Joseph said. "Mary, come on out and let's eat with our neighbors."

They all sat down at the picnic tables. The sheriff sat across from Joseph.

Mary passed out paper plates for every one to eat on. "Joseph, don't forget to say grace."

Joseph nodded. "All heads bowed for grace." Every head bowed as he prayed. "Dear Heavenly Father, thank You for Your many blessings. And denki for bringing all of our neighbors together for a meal on this beautiful day. I do pray that they all will come to know You as a Father. In the Lord's holy name, I pray, amen."

"David told me that you and him have worked out your

differences." Sheriff John Clemons shook Joseph's hand. "Is there something you two are not telling me?"

"Nay, everything is as it should be," Joseph said.

"Fine then. I'll take your word on it. Joseph, who do you think burned your barn?"

"Lighting could have hit it, Sheriff," Joseph said softly.

"Well, lighting can hit in the most unusual places," Sheriff Clemons said, smiling.

"I don't think that lighting will strike in the same place twice," David Stevens said, smiling.

"Well, it had better not, or I will have to put it in jail," Sheriff Clemons said, laughing.

"You can't put lighting in jail, can you?" Caleb asked.

"Son, I am the sheriff. I can do anything that I want to. Anyway, I am not trying to spoil a party. Let's eat. I will not bring it up again."

"By the way, Joseph, the property dispute with your neighbor has been dropped." Clemons handed him the paperwork. "You do not have to appear in court. I think it was all just a misunderstanding."

"When God fights for a man, you cannot lose." Joseph took the papers without looking at them and put them in his pocket.

"You've got that right," Stevens said. "The more I fought against Joseph, the more he tried to befriend me. I haven't been to church in years, but I think I will go back now."

"I'm so proud of you." Janet laid her hand on Steven's arm.

They were all busy eating when Bishop Moses pulled up in his buggy, along with John and Timothy.

"Pull you up a chair, men. We are having a welcome party for Joseph," the sheriff said.

The men sat down on the benches.

"Joseph, we just came over to check on you," Moses said. "John had some suspicions about the way your neighbors were treating you. He said you broke a buggy wheel when somebody ran you off the road."

"It was just an accident," Joseph said. "Anyway somebody brought me a new buggy wheel this morning. It was leaning against the house with a ribbon tied on it."

"John must be misinformed, for we all love Joseph and his family," Stevens said, smiling. "This dinner was my idea in fact."

"You mean you all get along with each other?" Moses asked, looking at John.

"Never better," Joseph said, which was the truth.

"Well, we might as well eat since John has got us all the way out here for nothing." Moses smiled.

"Jah," Mary said, smiling. "John worries too much."

"Bishop, we have been seeing ghosts out here!" Benjamin said.

"Ghosts? I don't believe in such things." Bishop Moses laughed.

"I don't think you have to worry about the ghosts anymore." Ron Harmony leaned in closer. "Ghosts are usually just trying to scare you away."

"We saw a ghost," Caleb said. "Daed checked for its tracks and it didn't leave any. It had to be a ghost."

"Well, I don't know," Ron said. "I saw a man on a western movie that tied rags around the horse's hooves, so it wouldn't leave any tracks. A man could tie rags to his shoes, and not leave any tracks."

"That explains it," Joseph said, smiling.

After everyone had eaten, they sat around talking. Some of the men played a few games of horseshoes, the sheriff included. Finally, they all began to leave. The day had brought about a beautiful and unexpected end, and it had all started with forgiveness. Love will take over your heart once planted, and it just requires care.

"Don't think you are getting away from us so easy, Joseph. We will be back many times. You are my neighbor now and a friend," Stevens said, shaking Joseph's hand. "Joseph, I do feel bad about the lighting accidentally hitting your barn. I have more money than I know what to do with. Can I pay you for your loss?"

"Nay, to be honest, the barn was about ready to fall, and we were not going to use it anyway. I was going to tear the barn down," Joseph said.

"Are you sure?" Stevens asked.

"Jah, to have us all become friends is enough payment and is more than I expected."

"Well, you are a good man, Joseph." David Stevens hobbled over to his car and then left with Janet driving.

"Daed, you are the most forgiving man I have ever seen," Rebecca said. "How do you do it?"

"It just takes practice, Rebecca." Joseph patted her arm.

"Rebecca if you don't learn to forgive, it just leaves an empty place in your heart," the bishop said, smiling. "And the Bible says that we can't go to Heaven with un-forgiveness in our hearts."

"Bishop Moses, I need to speak to you a minute in private," Joseph said. As briefly as possible Joseph told him what had been going on with the neighbors and their recent treatment.

"Why did you keep this a secret, Joseph? We would have helped you if we could," Moses said.

"I didn't wish to worry anyone. I prayed about it, and I felt the best thing to do was to put the problem in God's hands and to just show forgiveness."

"You were right, Joseph," Moses said. "I will have to alter my text for church Sunday. You have inspired me more then you know. Now I guess we had better go. I will have to give John a lecture. He did figure out something was wrong."

Chapter Twenty-Four

Rebecca sat alone in her room, burning a night lamp. It gave off just enough light to read and write with. Her heart still ached from losing her true love, but now she realized that it wasn't meant to be. If it had been true love, it would have endured the test of separation.

What really had inspired her was the way her father had shown forgiveness to their neighbors. She would have had trouble doing so. Rachel and David hadn't done half the stuff to her that had happened to her father, and she had trouble forgiving them. She had watched her father stand tall and refuse to tell the bishop of their troubles. She had been so proud of him.

Now she saw un-forgiveness as being ugly, and she didn't want to be that way any more. It was such a beautiful thing to forgive someone. She wanted her heart to be full of forgiveness and open for love.

She took out some paper and began.

Dear Rachel,

I am writing to let you know that I have forgiven you and David. I thought you took my boyfriend from me, but God must have other plans. I do believe that God has someone special for each of us. I just honestly thought that David was the one for me. I do pray that you both will be happy together.

It was nice of you to teach David to read. You have always had a special way about you. Please never forget who you are. I am your friend if you still want me.

Rebecca.

She would mail the letter tomorrow, but for now it had brought a sweet peace to her heart.

Joseph got up early and hitched Lucky up to a single plow and started uncovering the potatoes. The boys followed along behind him with a wheelbarrow. Once they got as many potatoes in it as they could handle, they would push it over to the cellar and store them there. It wasn't that hard of a job. It just took a long time, because the plowing was slow.

Mary, Sharon, and Rebecca were going to can some garden produce for the winter today. They had grown enough potatoes to last all winter. He had a cellar that he kept his potatoes in. Mary's grandpa had built it years ago.

He saw Mary coming out to check on them.

"Benjamin, save me a few of the smaller potatoes for dinner today," Mary said.

"We will bring a feed sack full of potatoes in the house for you to use." Joseph stopped beside her with the plow. "I can't have you carrying anything real heavy, honey."

Mary laughed. "Joseph, if you are going to treat me this well, I think I will just stay pregnant."

Joseph rolled his eyes. "Mary, it was a special feeling when I found out that I'm going to be a father again. When you look into those little eyes and take a hold of a baby's finger, there is nothing else like it."

"The most precious gift that God gave us was life," Mary said, smiling. "Let's sit down and take a break for a few minutes."

"Well, a little dirt won't hurt anybody." Joseph sat down between the garden rows.

"If it did, we would have died a long time ago," Mary said, laughing.

They were sitting there taking a break when he saw John walking up the road.

"What's wrong with him?" Mary asked. "John rarely walks anywhere."

"I don't know." Joseph shrugged.

John saw them out in the field and made his way over to them. "I need help, Joseph. I was bringing Mary something to eat that Elizabeth fixed when I ran off the road with my mules. The buggy is stuck."

"How far away is it?" Joseph asked.

"It is about two miles or more," John said. "The buggy must be stuck pretty gut, because the mules couldn't even pull me out."

Joseph nodded, trying to keep from smiling. "Mary, get the children ready. We will take John back there as soon as I can hitch up the team."

"We'll be ready," Mary said.

Joseph strolled off, though he didn't harness up their buggy mare. Lacy, the other Haflinger, had grown a lot and was about as big as Lucky. He hitched Lucky and Lacy up to their work wagon instead of the buggy. He drove on up to the house and picked the rest of his family up, including John.

"I got over too far to the right," John said. "I ran into the ditch, a pure mud hole at that."

It took a little time to reach the stuck buggy. John and Mary were catching up on old times. He could see the mules up ahead still hitched to the buggy. The wheel was covered in mud and the buggy was leaning sideways.

"All this rain we've had made a mess of things." John shifted beside him on the wagon seat.

"John, are you sure your mules can't pull your buggy out?" Joseph asked, smiling.

"Jah, I am sure," John said. "The mules have tried several times already."

"John, unhitch your mules then, and I will pull the buggy out with my team of horses," Joseph said.

John laughed. "You'd be better off hitching them in front of the mules. Maybe all of them can pull it out together."

"I can get your buggy out. Just get the mules out of the way," Joseph said. "And then I will help you."

"Mary, you have married a very stubborn man," John said. He unhitched the mules. "You are wasting your time."

Joseph parked the wagon then hitched the team up to the buggy. The horses backed into it willingly enough. They looked small compared to John's big mules.

"Please stand back everyone," Joseph said to Mary and the boys. They got out of the way quickly.

Joseph got off to the side of the buggy where he could guide them from. With a flick of the reins, he said, "Get up, Lucky. Show them what you can do."

The team came together quickly, pulling against the buggy gently at first. The horses were knee deep in mud, but they gave it all they had. Still, the buggy never moved, though Joseph saw it shift some to the side.

"I told you. It was a waste of time." John stood in the road, holding the reins to his big mules. He didn't look too happy.

Joseph didn't answer; he went and got a few chains out of the wagon. He moved the horses up a few feet so they wouldn't be pulling in the mud. This time, he felt a little better. He knew what his little work horses could do.

The horses hit it this time with full force and started digging their hoofs in. Mud went flying everywhere. Joseph heard a slight noise, and then the buggy came free. The horses pulled the buggy back up on the road.

Joseph felt satisfied now. He saw Mary standing there, watching him. A woman tries to see how her man measures up in front of other people like her daed and her brothers, though a man should be himself first and never try to impress anyone.

Joseph was having fun now with John. He unhitched the horses and brought them back to his wagon.

"You can hitch your mules back up now, John. I think you will be alright now," Joseph said, smiling.

John just grunted. "Thank you, Joseph."

"His mules have won a ribbon in the county fair for the last three years," Mary said. "They have a county fair to see which team of mules can pull the most."

John hung his head and didn't say anything.

"I am not interested in a county fair. I just wanted to show John that these little horses can pull as gut as any mule."

"That they can. Hey, I almost forgot your food." John handed Mary some food in a picnic basket.

As they were getting ready to pull out. John waved for them to stop. "Joseph, I won't be teasing you about them little Haflingers anymore."

"We had better head back. These little horses have done enough today," Joseph said, smiling.

"Denki for the food, John," Mary said.

John just nodded.

The team pulled on, passing John and his mules and onward toward home.

"Mary, did you see him? There isn't a horse in this country that can pull like ole Lucky."

"Don't forget Lacy. She pulled too," Mary said, smiling.

They rode back in silence, simply looking all the beautiful land God had given them.

"A man brings nothing with him into this world, and he will

not take anything with him when he goes back out," Joseph said softly.

"We are so blessed." Mary rubbed her stomach.

"That we are." Joseph pulled Mary to him. He gave her a hug on the wagon seat. "In more ways than one."

As they went on the short journey home, Mary spoke, "I have come home to stay."

ACKNOWLEDGEMENTS

I feel a need to write books of a more gentle nature. God's gentle ways are in my heart, and I can not get them out.

I had a reading assessment done by Dave King, editor. *Self Editing for Fiction Writers* was written by Dave King and Renni Browne. The first three chapters of my novel was edited by Kathy Ide, and Greg Baker from Affordable Christian Editing is finishing up my book. I take my writing seriously, and I'm trying to learn all I can.

It is my dream to be able to write successfully one of these days. I am currently writing my second Amish novel. I would just like the chance to be able to reach some people for God if I can.

About the Author

Jason H. Campbell lives in Kentucky with his wife Cheryl and their two children, Jaron and Joshua. Jason was one of eight children born to Hobert and Sharon Campbell. Jason writes weekly for a local newspaper and has been published in hunting magazines. Writing is a dream he has wanted to pursue since childhood.

His first book, *Tex's Bloody Ground*, has been published through Publish America. The book is on the internet and Barnes & Noble. He had a short story called *Riding Lonesome* published in *Outlaws and Lawmen* by La Frontera Publishing. His education includes high school and a couple of years of college.

He grew up in a very strict Christian Pentecostal home, kind of similar to the Amish, though they did have electricity. Television wasn't allowed in his home and a radio was used only sparingly. Often, he'd visit his grandmother to watch TV when he could get away.

He developed a passion for reading mostly because he had little else to do. Most of the time, he would read a book in just one night. He'd check out another the next day at the school library. The Principal would laugh at him for going to the library so much. He read all the popular books of his day, and as he grew older, his passion for reading only increased. He truly enjoys to write as well.

Even today, he only has a VCR and a DVD player in his home; He has no satellite or cable TV. His family only watches a couple of movies a week, usually checked out from the local library. His family spends a lot of time reading in the evenings.

Printed in the United States
By Bookmasters